Revenge Honeymoon

K. J. Gillenwater

Suraya,
thank you for friending
me on Twitter! I've
enjoyed getting to know you.

♡ KJG

Revenge Honeymoon

Copyright© 2022 K. J. Gillenwater

ISBN Print: 978-1-7357207-5-3

ISBN eBook: 978-1-7357207-4-6

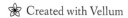 Created with Vellum

Dedication

Thank you to my friend, Suraya M., for the inspiration to write this story. You never know where your next best idea will come from.

Chapter 1
The Idea is Born

Emily Small grimaced as she listened to the person on the other end of the bride's cell phone. She'd been assigned to manage it while her best friend in the whole world, Ruby Madison Evers, prepared to marry the love of her life, Tyler James Hardy.

The perfect couple.

The most beautiful couple.

Better looking than Brad and Angelina.

They were going to have the most gorgeous brown-eyed, curly-haired babies ever, ever, ever.

So how was Emily going to tell Ruby the truth?

As she set down the phone, her hand shook.

Across the choir room converted into a bride's dressing room, Ruby lifted the skirts of her Monique Lhuillier knockoff gown, rested one dainty foot on a chair, and slid a lacy garter up her thigh.

"What is it, Em?" Ruby asked, her cheeks pink with excitement and professionally-applied blush. "You look like you've seen a ghost."

Those words hit her like a punch to the gut—exactly like Emily's older brother, Hunter, used to do when they were kids. Sock-o, blam-o. Punch. She wished with all her might she could be at her childhood home in Roanoke, Virginia plucking a lime popsicle out of the freezer to soothe her pain and her wounded psyche.

"Em?" The bride waved off her two bridesmaids, cousins on her father's side and eager to be part of the Ruby Wedding Spectacular, and swished over to her maid-of-honor. "You're worrying me. Is it the caterer? Or maybe the DJ? I forgot to check in with them this morning, and I really should have double-checked they knew the address."

Ruby's gleaming auburn hair had been twisted into the perfect Rapunzel braid, which lay artfully across one shoulder. The stylist had secured her Bruges lace veil with a diamond-encrusted comb supplied by her mother and worn by several generations of Madison women before her. She fluttered her thick-yet-false eyelashes, maybe not used to their weight and view-obscuring tendencies.

Emily's only positive thought before she broke the worst news of Ruby's life: at least she won't have mascara running down her face.

"That was Tyler," she gulped. Her mouth so dry she wished she had a bucketful of water to drink. "He's not coming." Her voice dropped to a bare whisper.

The cousins gasped and clutched one another in horror.

The make-up artist, who had been waiting to do final touch-ups, packed up her case in a flash and squeaked out of the room without a word.

Ruby's eyes widened, her mouth formed an 'o,' and her body vibrated a fine tremor. "Oh no, was he in an accident? I told him not to drive himself. I've read so many stories about

2

brides and grooms getting in accidents on the way to the church. Nerves, they said. Should I go to him? Where is he? Was he driving his father's car or the rental? I hope he wasn't driving the rental. We have to make it to our suite at the Hilton tonight, and I really don't want to take an Uber. Or have my father drive. Oh, that would be so embarrassing."

"Ruby." Emily grasped her friend's arm, the fine Mikado silk cool under her fingers. A long-sleeved dress for a late fall wedding maybe was too warm for the Tampa location, but it had been so gorgeous on her friend's slender body there had been no other choice at the bridal boutique. "He's calling off the wedding."

Nausea soured Emily's stomach.

Why did she have to be the one who picked up the phone?

One of the cousins burst into tears.

Ruby stood stock still in the middle of the bride's dressing room. "But—"

Rhonda Madison Evers entered wearing a royal blue mother-of-the-bride dress covered in sequins. "My darling. The make-up artist told me the news. How could that man be so cruel?" She curved her arms around her only daughter.

"Mom, I don't understand. How could he not be coming?" Ruby crumpled to the floor.

"You'll crush your dress!" Mrs. Evers gasped and knelt beside her. She yanked at her daughter's arm as if her will alone would lift up the one-hundred-twenty-five-pound woman and her ten pounds of underskirts and heavy fabric. "We can still return it."

"No, we can't. It's been altered." The bride spoke in a monotone.

"Well," said Mrs. Evers, "there's always eBay or Craigslist, I suppose."

"Facebook Marketplace is better," mumbled a cousin.

Mrs. Evers shot daggers in the woman's direction.

"I need to talk to him." The bride snapped her fingers at Emily. "Get Tyler on the phone. I will just demand that he come."

Emily gulped and bit at her lower lip, then got up the courage to tell her best friend since grade school the worst thing a best friend could say. "Tyler doesn't want to get married. Do you really want to force a man to marry you, Rubes?"

"But he promised me. He gave me this ring." Ruby held out her hand for the cousins, her mother, Emily, and now the florist who'd arrived with her wedding bouquet. A gorgeous pear-shaped 2 ½ carat diamond decorated her left ring finger. "Would he have given me this ring if he didn't want to marry me?"

"He doesn't want to marry you, Rubes." Emily knelt and put an arm around her friend. The bride sagged against her.

The florist quietly set the bridal bouquet on a chair and scrambled for the door.

Emily led Ruby to an empty chair and her mother sat beside her. "He's an awful man. A terrible, mean, awful man. Who would do that to my little girl?" Mrs. Evers took her daughter by the hand and gripped it tightly.

"Ow, mother, that hurts." Ruby pulled her hand out of her mother's grasp and began to nibble on her freshly manicured nails. "What do we do about the guests?"

"Your father is telling them now," Mrs. Evers reassured her.

"What will we do about the reception?" Ruby pulled the veil out of her hair.

"We're inviting everyone to meet us over there," her mother answered. "We've already paid for the hall, the food, the entertainment. We might as well have a party, don't you think, darling?"

"What will we do about the honeymoon?" Ruby kicked off her satin heels and rubbed her toes.

"Well, I guess you'll have to cancel," sighed Mrs. Evers. "Maybe they'll give you credit."

"No, wait, I have a better idea," said Emily.

And that's when the revenge honeymoon took shape. That very moment. And Emily Small's life would never be the same.

As the taxi pulled up to the cruise terminal in Tampa, Emily smiled. She'd always wanted to try out a cruise. It had sounded so exotic, so luxurious. But she'd never had someone who wanted to go with her. And who takes a cruise alone?

"I can't do this." Ruby cringed in the back seat. Her perfect, but caked, bride makeup had been washed away last night in the Hilton honeymoon suite the two had shared and had been replaced this morning with a simple black mascara, nude lipstick, and a pinch of blush. She wore a blue sundress with a flared skirt, and a wide-brimmed straw hat sat in her lap. "I'll look like a fool. Everyone will be wondering."

"Wondering what?" Emily had her mind on the miracle of FedEx who'd shipped her passport overnight. Thank goodness her mother knew exactly where she kept it: bottom drawer of her old dresser next to her tax returns. She'd never complain again about what a nosy mother she had. Ever. Okay, maybe she would. But not today. Today, she was her best friend's rock. The solid thing she could rely on after her terrible, awful, no-good—but very attractive—fiancé left her at the altar. Emily was dependable. Emily was loyal. Emily was beginning to sound like Ruby's pet dog.

"This is a honeymoon cruise. For couples only," Ruby said with as much sympathetic whining as she could muster. "You know, just married type of couples."

"I seem to recall you mentioned that when you booked it last spring." Emily checked her appearance in a compact she kept in her purse. At least on a honeymoon cruise full of couples in love, no one would be fawning all over Ruby and ignoring her plain Jane best friend. Years ago, Emily had learned her limitations when sitting next to her model-like bestie. When Ruby had gotten engaged to Tyler on Valentine's Day nine months ago, Emily secretly hoped it would be her time to shine.

Ruby was sweet and kind and truly didn't realize how naturally gorgeous she was, so it was hard to be mad at her. Hard to be jealous of her. Hard to be anything but appreciative of what a wonderful friend she could be.

"There will be all of these newlyweds in love all around us." Ruby leaned forward to talk to the taxi driver. "How much to take us to the airport?"

Emily pulled on her friend's arm, "No, you don't want to do that, Rubes. This is about you getting over Tyler and what he did to you."

"I did that last night at the reception when I ate half our wedding cake. The lemon layer only, though. I wanted all lemon cake, and Tyler had insisted on alternating layers of strawberry, lemon, strawberry, lemon. He didn't even seem to care I was allergic to strawberries."

"Well, real strawberries, right? Not strawberry flavoring?"

Ruby sighed a big exaggerated sigh. "It was the principal of it. He didn't seem to care at all that I couldn't eat strawberries. That I loathe them."

"True. That wasn't very considerate of him."

The taxi driver rolled down his window and lit a cigarette. He must've sensed his two female passengers weren't going anywhere anytime soon. A cool November breeze blew into the car and carried the smoke inside.

Emily sneezed.

Ruby shivered. "It's going to be warm in Cozumel, right?"

Emily smiled brightly. "See? We are going to have the time of our lives. Caribbean here we come!"

The former bride shook out her cinnamon locks and stepped onto the pavement in her four-inch espadrille wedges.

The driver stubbed out his cigarette in the ashtray sitting on the front passenger's seat and leapt into action. Before Emily could join her friend, the burly driver had set their luggage on the sidewalk.

"Thanks so much." Ruby paid the driver with cash from her reception's money tree. "I'm spending every dime of this on you and me this trip, Em." She flashed an envelope full of fifties and hundreds. Even Tyler's family, at least the ones who hadn't slunk away in shame after the wedding had been called off, had given Ruby cash. A consolation prize of sorts.

"You don't have to do that." Emily collected her single bag, packed only for a few days in Tampa, and headed toward the terminal entrance. A line of couples had gathered to be screened before moving further into the building where they'd drop their luggage and have their documents scrutinized.

Ruby whipped out the handle of her large roller bag – three times the size of what Emily had – and caught up to her friend. "I want to do it. Don't say another word about it."

The two women joined the long line of newlywed couples and filed inside.

A young couple in matching bright yellow T-shirts with 'bride' and 'groom' printed in blue lettering smiled as Emily and Ruby queued up behind them and waited for screening.

"Oh, hello there," gushed the woman in the 'bride' T-shirt. "I love that this cruise is open to *all* newlyweds." She elbowed her new husband in the ribs. "Isn't that right, Tim? Love is love."

Tim gawked at Ruby and Emily. He seemed particularly flabbergasted at the sight of beautiful Ruby. Most men were, but in this case he had an added level of surprise.

Emily blushed at the misinterpretation. "Oh, no, we're not...I mean...she and me we're just—"

Ruby butted in, "Oh, thank you so much. We're super excited, aren't we, honey?" She hugged her best friend tightly to her side. Too tightly.

Emily didn't know how to respond. Her mouth gaped open, and no words came out.

"We've always wanted to go to Cozumel, and when we saw the advertisement for the 'newlyweds only cruise,' well, we couldn't pass it up. And, it was such a great deal."

Emily couldn't believe Ruby would want to create such a deception. Was this how they were going to act for the next ten days?

Tim replied, "Yes, a really great deal. Nice to meet you both." He seemed relieved when the cruise employee called him and his wife forward.

"Toodles!" The bride wiggled her fingers at them in a supremely feminine wave and plopped her oversized bag on the table before she walked through the metal detectors.

Emily took the opportunity to hiss at her friend, "What do you think you are doing?"

Ruby made a moue. "I really didn't want to tell them about my day yesterday. I couldn't bear the thought of it. Everyone's so happy." She gestured to the crowd of honeymooners, including a few other gay couples in line. "Who wants to hear a story about a jilted bride? It would make everyone feel sorry for me. And nobody feels sorry for Ruby Evers. Nobody." She spoke the last few words with fervent conviction.

As the screeners beckoned them forward, Emily mulled over her friend's words. Although she didn't like to deceive people, she also didn't want her friend to be emotionally tortured for a second time. If she'd confessed to Tim and his bride that Ruby's fiancé had left her at the altar, the news would probably spread around the ship in no time. The sympathetic looks and sad whisperings would take away from the fun of the trip they wanted to have.

"I understand that, Rubes." She squeezed her friend's hand. "I guess I don't mind letting people think what they want."

Ruby smiled and sashayed through the metal detectors.

When Emily joined her on the other side she added, "But I'm not going to be doing any fake kissing or whatever to keep up appearances. Let's agree that we will keep our reasons to ourselves why we're on this cruise. We don't need to announce anything. Agreed?"

Ruby grabbed her bag from the table. "Agreed."

A smartly-dressed cruise employee, wearing navy blue slacks and a crisp white shirt with a name tag that read 'Stan,' approached them with a tablet, "Names, please?"

"Ruby Evers and Emily Small." Ruby gave the man a thousand-watt smile.

Stan downscrolled. "I don't have either of you on the list." He looked up from his tablet with a frown. "Tickets please?"

Ruby showed him a QR code on her phone.

A couple who had passed through the same security line squeezed by them to engage with another cruise employee who waved them forward to prevent a backup of passengers.

Ruby looked over her shoulder at the growing line of cruisers. Their problem was causing a delay and attracting undue attention. Worry lines marred her perfectly smooth, perfectly spray-tanned brow.

Stan took a quick snapshot of the QR code with his tablet. "Oh, Ruby Hardy and Tyler—?" He stared hard at Emily.

Ruby leaned in and whispered to the man, "Tyler won't be coming on the cruise. I called late yesterday. I had a substitution. The cruise line said it would be okay. They promised it wouldn't be a problem."

Emily could hear the tears coming on.

"Please, sir, do we have to do this here?" People were starting to stare as Ruby sniffed and rubbed her nose.

More couples walked around them. Cruise employees stepped further away from the security line to give passengers room to pass.

"I'm sorry, miss, I don't see your name on the list." Stan didn't seem to enjoy the problem the two women were causing him either. "You'll have to go talk to my manager." He pointed at a tall, thin black woman in a navy suit jacket wearing a name tag that read 'Sylvia.'

Ruby sniffed once more and then rolled her massive suitcase toward Sylvia. Emily followed behind. Her stomach twisted. Maybe their plan wasn't going to work as easily as they thought. She'd bent over backward to make her revenge honeymoon plan work, and now it was falling apart.

An inner fire grew inside her. She would make this cruise happen for the both of them no matter what. No matter who she had to step on. No matter who she had to swear at. Her best friend was going to have the cruise of a lifetime. She'd make damn sure of it.

Emily ran smack into a man who'd crossed in front of her. A tallish, muscular, oh-so-attractive-it-hurt man. The kind of man women only dreamed of existing in the real world. The kind of man she'd only seen in magazines and Google searches for 'hot man' photos when she was lonely on a Saturday night without a date.

She tripped over his roller bag and crashed to the hard concrete floor.

Fantasy ripped away.

He kept walking toward Sylvia. She'd been so unnoticeable, he'd crashed into her as if she were a post. Or a trash can.

"Excuse you," she muttered under her breath.

Ruby, who'd reached Sylvia before the hottest man in the room, gasped at her friend sprawled out on the floor. "Are you okay?"

The man, who Emily wanted to despise but who made her stomach turn flip-flops by merely taking in the sight of his tight ass in blue plaid, form-fitting shorts, noticed Ruby. The same as every man noticed Ruby. She was absolutely one-hundred percent never not noticeable. Beyonce could walk in the room, and Ruby would still draw all male attention her way.

"Excuse me?" He had a bewildered look on his face. An 'are you talking to me' kind of face that most men had when even a single word came out of Ruby's ruby lips.

Ruby gave him a hard stare, rushed to Emily's side and helped her up. "What happened?"

Within seconds, Mr. Gorgeous was in deep conversation

with Sylvia. He'd bumped them out of line. But what good would it do to put up a fuss? Ruby already was humiliated and embarrassed they hadn't been able to sail onto the ship like everyone else.

"Oh, nothing. It was an accident." Emily brushed her mussed hair out of her eyes and checked her knees and elbows for scrapes. No blood, That was good. But her backside sure ached from making contact with the concrete.

"You poor thing." Ruby gave her shoulders a squeeze. "Let's hope our luck improves. I don't know if I could handle one more bad thing happening."

Emily glanced at Mr. Gorgeous. Everything about him was perfect. Perfect hair. Longish, but not too long. Dark and slightly wavy. Eyes of an indiscernible color, but mysterious and sexy. A well-defined jawline with a scruff of beard. A purposeful scruff that looked as if it never was shaved and never grew longer. A fit physique, wide shoulders, bulked up arms, sculpted chest under a clinging linen shirt.

Some lucky young woman managed to score a prize when she married this fine specimen. Even though his manners left something to be desired, perhaps his wife didn't mind as long as she got to stare across the breakfast table every morning while he drank his coffee and ate his eggs.

Then she thought of Ruby's Tyler. Also a fine specimen. Also physically perfect in almost every way. But his affections for Ruby had been hot one minute, cold the next.

Although Ruby's best friend, she had thought it not her place to speak ill of him. Ruby had been smitten from the very first date. She could have her pick of men, and Tyler had been her choice. So Emily had assumed a lot about the kind of man Ruby had been looking for. When he'd proposed, Emily did have a few stray thoughts that her friendship with Ruby would

12

likely cool before too long. Tyler had made it clear he didn't think much of Ruby's friends and definitely didn't warm up to Emily.

Emily surveyed the packed space. She wanted to see if she could figure out who Mrs. Gorgeous could be. Probably tall. Probably blonde. Probably a model.

"I'm sorry I'm late," Mr. Gorgeous was saying to Sylvia. "I tried to be here at eight, but I couldn't find a taxi, and my plane was delayed last night."

Emily's ears perked up. He said nothing of a wife.

Chapter 2
The Pact

"All of our working passengers are supposed to board before the ticketed passengers," Sylvia scolded. "I thought that was made clear in the documents I emailed you."

Mr. Gorgeous paled.

Emily couldn't believe such a confident, attractive man would grow pale under such circumstances. Shouldn't he be effortlessly cool at all times? Shouldn't he be able to let criticism slide off his back like water?

"Well, yes, I read them, but you see—"

Sylvia waved her hand. "I don't have time to argue with you." She picked up a tablet, tapped on the screen and scrolled. "Maxwell Keeling."

"Max," he corrected.

Sylvia read on without even flinching, "And your guest Penelope Friedman?" She glanced around.

Max the Gorgeous let out a sigh and said quietly, "She's not coming."

"So you're traveling alone?" Sylvia tapped on the screen

several times without even looking at the man standing in front of her. "All right, I'll make note of that." She snapped her fingers, "Raul."

A Hispanic, middle-aged man in uniform made his way from the screening tables to the podium where Sylvia stood.

"Can you please show Maxwell to his room? He's late, and I don't have time to deal with this mess right now." Sylvia glanced over at Ruby and Emily and smiled apologetically. "I have customers who need my attention."

"It's Max," said the most stunning man in all of Florida or quite possibly in the whole of the southeastern United States.

"Come on, Em," said Ruby, as if she didn't even notice Max Keeling.

How could that be?

Max followed Raul and disappeared.

Emily let out the longest of sighs.

Ruby rolled her massive suitcase forward. "There seems to be a problem with a guest switch, Sylvia." She gave her most sincere and toothiest smile. She leaned in to whisper, "My fiancé left me at the altar yesterday." Her eyes instantly shone with tears. "And your very lovely cruise line's customer service told me I could bring my maid-of-honor as my guest instead."

Sylvia's demeanor brightened. "Why, of course, I can help you."

How could anyone's demeanor be anything less than one-hundred percent over-the-top wow after Max Keeling's appearance? Emily wished she could've watched him walk away again in slow motion. One slow, sexy step after another. Left. Right. Left. Right. His bulky arms swinging purposefully at his sides. Because all she'd probably ever be able to do is admire him from afar. Men like Max Keeling did not notice women like Emily Small.

Not ever.

Not once.

No way.

No how.

Ruby snapped her fingers. "Em, hello? We need your passport."

Emily brought her mind back to the current situation. She fiddled in her bag, one of those bright straw numbers with big colorful flowers on the side that could fit a small toddler inside it. "Here you go." She blushed, wondering if Sylvia or Ruby knew why her attention had been elsewhere.

"Thanks." Ruby took it and handed it to Sylvia. "We're hoping even though my situation has changed that we can still have fun. We *can* still have fun on a cruise for honeymooners, right?" Her voice had an anxious note to it.

Emily stared at her best friend. She'd been so confident last night when they were curled up on the heart-shaped bed of the Honeymoon Suite wearing heavy terry cloth robes and painting their toenails the same exact shade: Mexican Coral.

"Of course you can," Sylvia answered brightly. She produced a sunshine yellow sheet of paper. "Here is the schedule for this evening." With a pen she circled the eight o'clock dinner time. "The two of you are already signed up for the second dinner seating. I hope that still suits."

Ruby nodded.

"And before dinner it looks like you have your Honeymoon Photo Shoot at 5 o'clock." Sylvia frowned. "Well, we can cancel that, of course. There are plenty of other activities besides that...trivia at the Coconut Club, um, Daytime Dance Party pool side—"

"We want to do the photo shoot." Ruby crossed her arms.

"We do?" Emily said

"You do?" Sylvia said.

"Of course we do. It's part of the package." She stomped her adorable size seven espadrille on the floor. "And I want everything the package included."

Sylvia's expression changed immediately from confusion to graciousness. "Of course, Ms. Evers. We wouldn't want it any other way." She handed Emily her passport and gave Ruby the day's schedule. "You're all set ladies. Here's your room assignment and key cards. Just follow the signs to the luggage drop off and then head for 'Boarding.'"

Ruby tucked her key card into her bra and readjusted the neckline of her low-cut sundress. "Thank you so much."

"My pleasure." Sylvia gave a wide smile and waved as the two women headed toward a sign that said 'Luggage.'

* * *

Ruby and Emily lay sprawled across the king-sized bed in their balcony stateroom and giggled. They'd both consumed a bottle of champagne that had been waiting for them inside the room when they'd finally found it on Deck Eleven. They'd also managed to eat half the fancy chocolates in the gift basket and a package of crackers.

Although they'd been in a celebratory mood when they saw the size of their suite (Ruby mentioned what a great deal she'd gotten on it), an hour or two of laughter and commenting on the worst features of Ruby's ex-fiance grew tiring.

"What was I thinking, Emily?" Ruby rolled off the bed and took both empty champagne glasses with her.

"That you were in love." The former maid-of-honor rested her hands behind her head and stared up at the ceiling. "That

Tyler was the man you wanted to spend the rest of your life with."

"Why didn't anyone tell me?"

"Tell you what?"

"Tell me to think it through?"

Emily pushed herself up onto her elbows. "You're almost twenty-nine. I guess everyone thought you knew what you were doing. Not as if you haven't had long-term boyfriends before." But in her gut she'd known Tyler had a few negative qualities. And Ruby was right, she'd never said a thing. Why not? They'd always talked about boyfriends before. But not this time. This time Emily had stayed out of it.

Ruby set the glasses on the narrow dresser across from the bed. She caught sight of herself in the mirror hung on the wall above it. "Sometimes I think I'm cursed." She shook out her hair until it covered half of her face. "Maybe this cruise is my chance to forget about all of it."

"Forget about all of what?" Alarm bells rang in Emily's head. This was supposed to a fun cruise to get some revenge on Tyler and enjoy themselves on a luxury trip, not sink into some sort of depression.

"Oh, I don't know, weddings, romance, men." She twirled around, leaned against the dresser, and let out a heavy sigh. "Let's have a pact."

"What kind of pact?" Emily didn't like the sound of this. Last time Ruby asked her to make a pact, they'd ended up deciding to be each other's dates for New Year's Eve until the helicopter pilot swooped in and changed Ruby's mind on December 30th. Emily had been left to nibble canapés alone in a corner at the big party they'd bought tickets to attend and watch all the couples kiss and fondle each other at midnight. Yeah, pacts never turned out well for Emily.

"For the next ten days, we are strictly about fun."

Emily nodded.

Okay, that sounded all right.

"And no talking about men, dating, love lives, all that crap."

For a fleeting moment Emily remembered Max the Gorgeous who'd boarded without his female partner. Sure, he was out of her league and probably would never notice a woman like her, but maybe once they arrived in Cozumel, there'd be other semi-attractive, right-in-her-league men to flirt with. In fact, that had been one of the reasons she'd been happy to change up her plans at the last minute and sail on the cruise. Her romantic life had been practically non-existent in the last year. She'd grabbed a chance to take a break from the stress of her everyday existence and be someone else—relaxed, fun, experimental.

"Em, are you with me?" Ruby bumped her friend's foot with her thigh.

The lost look on her best friend's face jarred her into answering, "Of course. I'm with you." She swung her legs around to the side of the bed. "I will do whatever you want me to do. This is about you, friend. We are here to have the best damned cruise possible." Emily scooped up the daily schedule Sylvia had handed to them. "Photos at five, dinner at eight. What else do we want to do?" She glanced at her watch. "It's only one o'clock. We should be setting sail any minute."

A horn blew loudly.

"See?" Emily approached the sliding glass door that led to their balcony. She pushed the door open, and a gust of wind blew in.

Ruby joined her outside. "Oh, wow. What a view."

They surveyed the port and all the other cruise ships

waiting to depart. Slowly, their ship maneuvered toward the ocean.

Emily leaned over the plexiglass panel that acted as a railing and took in the distance from balcony to dark blue waves. "This is going to be the best damned vacation you ever took, Rubes."

* * *

Ruby and Emily stood in front of the elevator waiting to ride down to Deck Two where the photographer would shoot their honeymoon photos.

The former bride held back a laugh. "I can't believe I talked you into the photo shoot." She wore the outfit she had selected to wear with Tyler for the event: a beautiful floral print dress with cap sleeves, a cinched in waist, and a flared, full skirt.

Emily had been present when her friend had picked it out. They'd gone on a shopping spree with Tyler's credit card. He'd insisted that she buy whatever she wanted since her father had paid for the cruise. They'd purchased shoes, hats, and bags; dresses, shorts, and bathing suits; make-up, scarves, and perfume.

"If your father paid for it, we're doing it," Emily said.

"That's the spirit." Her friend smiled. "We get to keep an eight-by-ten portrait without any extra cost, and I want something frameable."

Emily noticed a tall, scrawny husband paired with a large-bosomed, stocky wife ogle her friend. A not so unusual occurrence, Emily knew. Ruby had the air of a fashion model: perfect posture, tall, slim and a cloud of thick, auburn hair around an angelic face. The dress fit her so well and in all the right places, it was hard not to stare.

Ruby, oblivious as usual, stepped into the open elevator door with a regal bearing that made everyone else feel unimportant. The doors closed. The tall husband managed to stand to the left of Ruby, and it was almost as if he'd died and gone to heaven. His wife finally noticed the distraction two inches from her new husband and linked her arms with his, tugging him closer to her ample side.

Emily yanked at her outfit, something borrowed from Ruby. Although their heights were different by a number of inches—Emily being the shorter of the two—their sizes were almost the same. But Emily's distribution of weight didn't translate well for some of the clothes Ruby had brought along on the cruise. Emily had wider hips and a fuller bust. The dress she'd chosen was a bit tight at the hip and had a straight skirt, so as she walked the hem rode up her thighs.

It was a wild print that clashed horridly with the pretty floral Ruby wore, and the jilted bride thought it would make for an outrageous photo.

"I think I should've worn pants."

"You look great." Ruby addressed the full elevator, "Doesn't my wife look fantastic?"

Emily nudged her. "Please, Ruby." The last thing she needed was an elevator full of newlyweds staring at her in her too-tight dress.

Too late.

A half a dozen pairs of eyes looked her way.

The stocky wife with the tall husband smiled with relief at the discovery the gorgeous model woman was a lesbian, "Oh, yes, honey, you look amazing in that. Just amazing."

"Thanks," Emily mumbled.

"See, babe?" Ruby glowed. "Amazing."

The elevator dinged. The doors opened. The two best

friends masquerading as a honeymooning couple exited into the crowded lobby of the photography studio.

"Number sixty-two? Sixty-two?" called out a young woman dressed in the uniform of the ship's crew. "I'm looking for couple number sixty-two—the Moskowitzes?" She tapped a pen on the clipboard she held.

"Over here." Mrs. Moskowitz, middle-aged and wearing bright pink culottes and a zig-zag print top, stepped forward. "Honey, it's our turn." She practically shoved her husband toward the woman with the clipboard.

She checked them off and ushered them past a velvet rope and toward the photographer's set-up at the other end of the room. "Maxwell will be your photographer tonight. Your photos will be available tomorrow evening. Give him your number." She handed the couple a bright yellow paper square with the number sixty-two printed on it.

Emily's ears perked up at the name "Maxwell." It couldn't be, could it?

Surrounded by a crush of newlyweds, Emily couldn't see much—only the fake tropical backdrop, a cluster of bright lights, and several couples lined up nearby waiting for their turn.

Where was beautiful, perfect, sexy Maxwell?

Emily tingled at the thought of her fantasy man posing her, telling her what a great model she was, and even asking her out on a cruise ship date where they could stare at each other lovingly over shrimp cocktail and champagne. Maybe her dress was sexy tight, rather than embarrassingly tight. So sexy, he wouldn't notice Ruby at all.

"You need to check in with Martina," said a male crew member who corralled the couples like a group of unruly wild mustangs. "The one with the clipboard."

Emily's dream bubble popped.

The two women navigated their way to the front of the line behind the velvet rope to reach Martina of clipboard fame.

"Ruby Evers and Emily Small," Ruby said. "We have a five o'clock appointment."

Martina greeted them with a tired smile. "We're running a little bit behind, so I hope you can bear with us. Our photographer is new and isn't used to how we do things." She checked them off the list and handed them a yellow number slip. "If you could stand at the end of this line, we'll call your number when it's your turn."

"Of course." Ruby followed the line that had formed behind the velvet rope. She giggled. "Look at our number, Em." She waved the slip of paper in front of Emily's nose. "Sixty-nine."

Emily snatched the paper out of her friend's hand. "We don't need to make a big deal out of it. What is this? Seventh grade?"

Ruby raised her perfectly microbladed eyebrows. "I always wondered what it was like to go to public school. Looks like I missed an experience."

The ex-maid-of-honor snorted. "Yeah, it was an *experience* all right."

At this closer vantage point, Emily briefly tilted her body around Martina to get a look at Max the Photographer.

"Shit." A deep male voice carried across the crowded room. "These lights are shit."

Maxwell Keeling stepped into view. His gorgeous features locked into a frown, a sheen of sweat on his perfect brow.

Emily's stomach rolled. He was better looking than she'd allowed herself to remember.

"As I said," Martina intimated, "he's not used to how we do

things." She widened her kohl-rimmed eyes and busied herself with her clipboard.

"Come on, Em." Ruby waved at her from the end of the line, her gorgeous smile lighting up the room. "Over here."

Emily gave up her perfect viewing spot for a place at the back. Her only solace was the fact eventually she would be in the presence of Max, and she could drink him in for as long as their photo session lasted. As she contemplated that thought, she had an idea. She felt guilty for thinking it, but let her mind work on the possibility anyway. Perhaps it was a flaw she'd been born with. A bad connection in her brain, which usually made her expect the best, even though her life as of late had been a series of worsts.

The cruise became a fishbowl from which neither she nor Max the Gorgeous could escape. With happily marrieds surrounding them, Emily could attract Max's full attention and convince him over the ten-day trip that she was the perfect woman for him. She'd be witty and sparkling. She'd outshine Ruby with amazing outfits she bought at the ship store. She'd comfort him over the loss of some woman who'd stood him up and who clearly wasn't worthy of his fantastic, beautiful, sexy self.

"Em, hello?" Ruby snapped her fingers in front of Emily's eyes. "Are you in there?"

Emily blinked. They now stood behind one other couple and had almost reached the velvet rope.

"We need to plan our shots. This is going to be hilarious."

Right. Their plan. Their stupid, idiotic and possibly very juvenile and tacky plan. The plan that would likely mean Emily's dream of wrapping up her cruise in a most romantic sort of fashion would have to wait. Or, actually, never ever ever have a chance of coming to fruition with what they were about to attempt.

Emily half-heartedly smiled. "Yes, our hilarious plan."

Ruby's eyes lit up. "Okay, I will be the girly one and you're going to be the groom." She scanned Emily in her ill-fitting dress. "Hm, maybe you should've worn pants like you said."

Emily's face heated. "It's bad, isn't it?" At that minute, her super supportive, very positive, very lovely friend made her feel as ugly in the dress as she'd suspected. And she knew that wasn't Ruby's intent. Heaven knew her best friend of almost her whole entire life had never put down her looks, her body, her less-than-perfect anything. But it still stung.

"Oh, no, that's not what I meant at all, hon." The jilted bride enveloped the ex-bridesmaid in a tight hug. "That dress is ninety-nine percent gorgeous on you. Really. I wish I had all those curves."

"Uh-huh." Emily knew. 'Curves' was skinny-speak for flab. She tugged the hem self-consciously.

She heard a rip.

She and Ruby exchanged horrified glances.

A draft of cool air drifted up her backside. She turned so her friend could assess the damage. "Oh, God, is it bad?"

"Sixty-nine? Number sixty-nine?" The woman with the clipboard grinned widely. "You're next."

Chapter 3
Jealousy is Not a Good Look

"I t's not that bad," said Ruby as they approached Gorgeous Max who tinkered with the unruly lights.

"It feels pretty bad." Emily tugged on the skirt and had the strange sensation the slit in the skirt had reached half way up her ass.

"It's not that bad," her friend repeated. "Just a few photos. It's only going to be from the front. Nobody will see. I promise."

This was not how Emily imagined her first meeting with Maxwell the Perfect—stuffed into a too-small dress with her very unsexy, very matronly underwear on display.

"I want to go back to the room," she whispered. Her armpits were damp. Her heartbeat sped up to the pace of a racehorse on his last stretch of the Kentucky Derby. She was about to meet the sexiest man alive, and...no, it wasn't going to be like this.

Was it?

"Number, please?" Maxwell said with a masculine rumble that nearly shook her ovaries loose.

He barely looked at them as he attended to the light stands, readjusting them, while mumbling, "It will be only a week, he said. Great money, he said."

"Excuse me?" Beautiful, innocent, vulnerable Ruby asked.

Why did she let Man Magnet Ruby have the first words? The story of her life. Ruby took a single step, and men fell all over her. Emily exposed her ass to the whole room, and it was as if nothing happened.

Maxwell brought his gaze up from his work. His green— yes, they were green!—eyes caught the dazzling lights and glowed as if they were on fire. Green gorgeous fire from the depths of some Irish fairy tale come to life. Were there Irish fairy tales? Was Maxwell even Irish? Did she care?

"Oh," his voice caught in his throat.

His gaze stuck to Ruby like glue.

Yeah, the usual. Emily's fate as cruise third wheel had begun. But maybe it was for the best. She kept her backside facing the wall behind them—the only safe angle. If she moved too much to the right, the rest of the newlyweds waiting in line would figure out that Kim Kardashian's Skims line really did work miracles. If she moved too much to the left, well, Maxwell might have to hold back a laugh...and Emily wanted to avoid that humiliation as much as possible.

"Miss, your dress." Maxwell picked up a suit jacket he'd laid across the back of a chair near his equipment and handed it to Emily. "You might want to put this on."

What? He'd noticed her and handed her a jacket that smelled like manliness and muscles and sandalwood?

She must be dreaming.

"My dress?" Oh, God, did his jacket smell incredible. Was she clutching it too closely to her nose? Was that weird?

"The rip?" He gestured at the wall behind her.

"What?" She looked over her shoulder. A full-length mirror stood leaning against the wall. The giant rip that had created a fault line the length of Florida up the back of her skirt assaulted her eyes. "Crap." She slipped into the jacket smelling of gorgeous man and attempted to laugh off the humiliation. "I had no idea," she said.

Yet she had every idea. And so did Ruby. But Emily wouldn't let on. No, she wasn't about to admit that she'd continued to stroll about the room knowingly in such a state. That any number of Moscowitzes and whoever the hell else stood in line for their oh-so-important free honeymoon portrait got a good look at her unmentionables and that they weren't even newlyweds and this whole idea had been stupid, stupid, stupid from the very beginning.

"That actually looks really good on you," Mr. Beautiful said. "Somehow it works."

Ruby took a step back. "He's right."

"It does?" The sleeves hung down below her wrists, and the shoulders sagged on her narrower frame. But she was willing to believe anything that came out of the sexy mouth of their photographer. Two perfect lips accentuated by the dark bristly shadow of his beard.

"You just need to zhuszh it a little bit." Ruby pushed the sleeves up to her elbows. "See?"

Ruby spun her friend around so she could view the transformation in the evil mirror that had exposed her Skims-encased rear to the perfect Maxwell.

He nodded his approval. "It gives your photo a little more of that 'bride and groom' aspect." He sucked in his breath. "Was that offensive? I mean, there's nothing wrong with two brides."

And everything that Emily had been building up inside her head crumbled at that very moment.

Right. The lesbian newlyweds.

* * *

After fifteen awkward minutes of posing in different lovey-dovey couple-y poses, their time with the hunky photographer was up.

"All right, ladies, it's been a pleasure," Maxwell said with the most heart-stopping beautiful smile. "Unless you wanted to do that kiss photo after all. I think it could be really cute." He closed one eye and splayed his hands out. "I can see it hanging over your fireplace. Walnut frame. Some can lights spotlighting it."

Ruby had a look in her eye. A look Emily had to shut down that very second before she crossed over to the 'other side' like her freshman year college roommate hoped she might. "No, thanks, Maxwell."

"It's Max," he corrected.

"I'm sorry, yes, Max." Didn't he know Maxwell sounded so much more sophisticated...and hot? "You did say we could call you that, right?"

"Yes, you asked me several times." He set his camera on a nearby chair they'd used a few minutes earlier for a pose—lovely Ruby seated with Barbie doll legs crossed perfectly, Emily standing behind her, hands on her friend's shoulders.

They'd only taken a single shot in that arrangement. Must've looked awful. But was it Emily who ruined it or the pose? Or something else? Hard to know.

"Right. Good. Yes." Emily fumbled with the buttons on his jacket. "Oh, I need to give this back."

He gestured at the equipment set up. "These lights are so hot. Not sure why I bothered wearing it."

Yes, exactly. He shouldn't have bothered wearing anything at all. So, so hot.

Emily's gaze roved over the tall, hard body of Maxwell—Max. When she reached his perfect face, their gazes met.

Oh, God.

Emily sneezed. A pretend sneeze, but she didn't know what else to do. He'd caught her staring. He could see right through her. Every attempt she'd made to hide the fact she thought he was simply the most attractive man she'd seen in her life possibly had been ruined with that one glance.

Crap.

"Bless you," Ruby said.

"Thanks," Emily muttered. "Here, let me give it back. Even if it's too hot."

"Oh, that's all right." He waved her off. "You can bring it by another night. I do photo sessions every afternoon until the last dinner seating."

She could see him again? Talk to him again? Even if he thought she wasn't interested in men, she didn't care. He'd been sweet and funny during their whole photo session. He even made Star Wars jokes.

For one pose he had the two friends stand holding hands and staring into each other's eyes with fake adoration. Ruby stood as still as a statue and froze. Emily worked hard to hold back a laugh. The whole set up made her giggle.

He'd quipped, "Why couldn't Luke Skywalker find love?"

"Why?" asked Ruby out of the corner of her mouth so as not to ruin their serious pose.

"He was looking in Alderaan places."

Both women had burst into laughter.

* * *

Martina with her clipboard didn't seem too happy with all the frivolity and chattiness going on at their end of the room. Possibly as punishment, she called out, "Five more minutes, Maxwell. The line's not getting any shorter."

"It's Max," Emily said in her loudest voice.

Max's full and sexy lips pulled into a bemused smile.

"Let's go, babe."

Ruby had started to call her babe.

That better not stick. Cruise Nickname only. She'd make Ruby promise.

"Right. Okay. Yes." Why did her mind say yes, but her feet say no? She couldn't force her feet to take a single step away from her future dream husband.

"Number Seventy!" Martina called out. "Couple number seventy, you are next up for portraits."

"Dinner's at eight," Ruby reminded her. "We get to pig out. Time to ditch this dress and put on something more comfortable."

Ruby had never pigged out a day in her life. Once, if Emily's memory served correctly, she'd gotten two scoops of ice cream on a waffle cone on their disastrous double date with the Hoffman twins—fraternal, not identical—but she'd never actually finished it. The woman had the lightest, bird-like appetite. Naturally thin with little effort and no starvation tactics.

"I think I've got some yoga pants in my bag," Emily said.

"Perfect." Ruby grinned. "I've heard you can order as many desserts as you want to try."

"Really?" Max leaned in. "What about entrees?"

Did his breath smell like chocolate and peppermint? Or was Emily only fantasizing about unlimited desserts?

"I think so," Ruby said. She grabbed for her tiny purse that held maybe a lipstick and a credit card—oh, and the whole day's itinerary. How did she manage that? "See, right here? *Your Cruise Dining Experience?*"

Max leaned over her perfect shoulder to peer at the paper Ruby unfolded.

Emily's stomach burned. She didn't like the emotion surging through her at that very moment. It was not best friendy. Not in even the slightest way. To avoid that emotion growing into something even bigger and uglier, she snatched that paper right out of Ruby's hand much to the shock of the bride and the photographer.

"Yep, right here." Emily's face heated. Why did she do it? Why did she do something so rude and stupid and childish? "Looks like you can—order more than one entrée, more than one appetizer, too. Wow. Great. Fantastic. We can all gorge like starving wildebeests." She shoved the paper into the pocket of Max's jacket.

A poof of Max's manly scent assaulted her nose, and she almost lost herself in it. Like put her face behind the lapel and take a long, weird sniff that would reveal her very ridiculous crush on a man that was so stupidly unsuited for her.

Why, if Emily were honest, she should shout off the highest deck of their cruise ship that Ruby and Maxwell—her best friend and the most gorgeous man she'd ever seen—were perfect for each other. It's as if the gods rained favor upon them and created the ideal couple.

Everyone could see it.

Emily could see it.

And inside her chest, her heart deflated to the size of a molecule.

Chapter 4
Surprise Dining Partner

"I'm never wearing another thing out of your wardrobe," declared Emily as she slipped into her favorite 'office' yoga pants, which she'd paired with a bright pink wrap blouse that tied at her waist. "There, I look fine dining suitable, but with plenty of room for the food I plan to consume." She patted her stomach.

"My dress looked great on you." Ruby stood behind Emily as they shared the one large mirror in their cabin. She'd decided to keep wearing her floral dress—of course, why wouldn't she? She looked like a model in it—but swapped out her heels for a pair of more casual sandals. "It was bad luck about the rip. I wish I had your curves." She eyed her friend's cleavage.

Emily tugged the edges of her blouse together. "Oh, is it too much?"

Ruby batted her hand away. "It was a compliment, not a criticism. Most women would die for those." She gestured at Emily's ample chest. "I still have yet to find the perfect push-up bra."

Emily smiled at her friend and finished putting on her lipstick. "What would I do without you, Rubes?"

"Probably die of boredom. Come on, let's go eat. I'm starving."

Emily grabbed her purse off the bed. Max's jacket lay across the foot of it. She fingered it for a moment. "Sure was nice of the photographer to lend me this."

"Wasn't he so kind?" Ruby fluffed her hair and tossed a Chapstick into her bag. "Hard to find a nice guy like that these days."

For a split second Emily let her fantasy mind wander. She'd head down to the photography studio after dinner, the room would be dark and empty. Nobody around. She'd sneak over to his equipment stash with the jacket, a note tucked into the pocket with her phone number. As she turned to leave, Max would be standing there. His dark hair half-covering his face, almost like the Phantom of the Opera—sexy but a little dangerous. He'd grab her by the elbow without saying a word, reel her into his hard chest, tip her back, and kiss her like Samantha and Jake in the 80s classic, *Sixteen Candles*, except without the birthday cake and the candles burning...and, well, okay, maybe Max reminded her of Jake a little bit.

"Are you feeling sick?" Ruby asked.

Emily snapped back to the cruise ship, her best friend, their fake marriage, and the next week of pretending. Max would be a distant memory and maybe, if she was lucky, a good dream tonight. "No, I'm fine. Maybe a little tired."

"You probably are calorie deprived." She grabbed her friend by the hand and pulled her out into the hall. "Let's go get you some food, bestie."

A young Asian couple reared back from being trampled by the former bride and maid-of-honor.

"Oh, sorry, sorry," Ruby said as she stumbled and caught herself. "Did you know they let you eat as many appetizers as you want?" She touched the arm of the Asian woman whose rounded eyes matched the circular frames of her glasses.

"Uh," stammered the shocked woman. She slid her gaze to her brand new husband, possibly hoping for some help.

"Well, they do." Ruby linked arms with red-faced Emily who wished she was anywhere else but in the hallway at that moment. "Appetizers, entrees, desserts. Whatever you want. It's amazing, really."

Ruby could get away with silly behavior. Easily forgiven. All she had to do was pour on the charm and smile. People wanted to like Ruby. People wanted to love Ruby. People always ended up loving Ruby.

"Okay, thank you," said the husband with a faint smile. He'd fallen for the Ruby charm already. It hadn't taken long. "I thought that's what the brochure said," he intimated to his wife.

Ruby pointed forward. "We are off to the dining room!"

Emily gave the wife an apologetic smile. Not so sure the woman had absorbed the Ruby Charm as quickly as her spouse.

* * *

The maître d' at the fine dining restaurant stared at the two women. "I do not seem to have your reservation here." He scrolled through his iPad—up and down and then up and down some more. He may have even scrolled to Sunday night's dinner reservations to make sure they didn't have the wrong date.

They didn't.

The Asian couple they'd left open mouthed in the hallway,

who stood in line right behind them, pretended they'd never met. The wife examined her bright red nail polish, and the husband busied himself with the large oil painting of a ballerina dancing with a bear that hung on the wall.

Ruby smiled a winning smile—she had several of them, and this one was at half-power. "Robbie," she began.

"It's Robert," the man corrected.

"Robbie, my wife and I were told our dinner reservation was at eight o'clock. We're hungry. Very hungry, aren't we, babe?" Ruby nodded at Emily. "And we want our seven appetizers."

"Seven?" the maître d' scratched his jaw.

She waved her folded itinerary in the air. "Three, seven, what difference does it make?" She faced the line growing behind them. "Don't let them cheat you out of your appetizers. You can have as many as you like. The paper says so."

The guests behind them began to murmur quietly.

"Ruby, dial it down a little," Emily hissed. Although Ruby ate small meals, when she didn't eat regularly, she could turn hangry. Poor Robert.

"I'm sure it was a mistake," the man said. "Evers and Small?"

"Yes, Ruby Evers and Emily Small." Then she whispered, "It might be under Hardy—Tyler and Ruby Hardy. My fiancé left me at the altar."

"Oh my. I see." Robert tapped on his iPad again. "I have you under cancellations. They forgot to rebook the table with the new names. I apologize."

"So we won't get our appetizers?" Ruby frowned.

"Don't worry, Ms. Evers, I will find you and your—uh—" The maître d' eyed Emily.

"Emily," Ruby filled in.

"Yes, Emily. I'll find you a table. Give me a moment." He zoomed in on tables with possible empty seats, looked on both levels, and tapped on a table. "If you don't mind, we have a table for four with two seats available. It's not the best table, and I could try to move you for tomorrow night...maybe if you switched to an earlier dining time?"

"We'll take those seats."

"Are you sure? The table is right by the kitchen. It's usually reserved for staff."

"It'll be fine." Ruby's stomach growled audibly.

The man's eyes widened. "Come this way, ladies. Right this way."

Ruby and Emily entered the dining room. It was in a circular design at the prow of the ship. In the center was an open space with a staircase winding down to the next level of dining. The maître d' handed them over to a server who led them to the steps, unhooked a velvet rope, and ushered them past. As they descended the stairs, a grand piano on a raised stage became visible. A woman in a long black dress and a string of pearls pounded out a concerto. Tuxedoed servers rolled carts throughout the room covered with heaping plates of food. Another server filled wine glasses and water goblets.

"Wow, this is amazing," Emily gasped.

"This ain't the Cracker Barrel," Ruby quipped.

Both women laughed.

"This way, please." The server led them away from the piano and toward the back of the room. In a corner, behind a potted plant, and right next to the swinging doors of the kitchen sat Maxwell the Photographer. "Your table, if you please." He handed them their menus and disappeared.

Emily stood stock still.

Ruby grinned and took a seat. "Well, look at that. Who would've guessed?"

Max pushed back his chair and stood. "Would you like to sit here? You can see the pianist better."

A slight smile quivered on his full lips. But that couldn't be. Max was confident. Max was gorgeous. Max had nothing to be nervous about.

Emily waved off the offer. "I don't want to put you out."

"Oh take it, Em. He's being nice. Let him be nice." Ruby's face was hidden behind her menu, already plotting her appetizers by the look of it.

Nice. Right. It was niceness. Max couldn't help but be nice. Just like when he let her borrow his jacket.

Emily took the offered chair. "Oh, darn. I should've brought your jacket."

Max pushed in her chair. "How could you have known we'd share a table?"

Oh, wondrous chivalry. Emily's insides nearly melted at the gesture. But it was probably more niceness. Yes, that's what it was. Nice men doing nice things.

"Where's your date?" Ruby asked. "The maître d' told us it was a table for four with two available seats. Wouldn't she want the view of the pianist?"

A darkness came across Max's perfect, masculine features and somehow made him even more appealing. "I don't have a date."

"Oh." Ruby shrugged and returned to her menu. "Okay, I'm getting the Shrimp Cocktail first, and then the Spinach Artichoke Dip with Naan Bites."

Should Emily ask more about his lack of date? Would that be the appropriate thing to do? Her insides squirmed at the opportunity to find out more about what kind of woman—Penelope somebody-or-other if she remembered correctly—would skip out on a tropical cruise with the most perfect male specimen on the planet. Okay, maybe that was an exaggeration. But surely he was close to one of the top ten male specimens on the planet.

She found herself handling her salad fork imagining at any moment she'd need to stab someone in the arm who might disagree.

Before she could speak, Max hailed a server. "Could I get another?" He held up an empty wine glass.

"Of course, sir." The server nodded. "Were you drinking white or red?"

"Red." Max swirled the dregs of his wine in the bottom of his goblet glass and drew his brows together.

With a snap of his fingers, the server drew the attention of the sommelier who poured for a large table of six near the landing of the stairs. "While you are waiting, are you ready to order?" He smiled widely at the trio.

Emily, who'd been so focused on her dream man, had no idea what was on the menu. For once in her life, she couldn't care less about what to eat. "I'll have whatever she's having." She pointed at her friend who probably had already created a mental list of everything she wanted to try and in what order.

The topic was slipping away from her. They were about to be buried in Q&A about each item on the menu—because sometimes that's what Ruby did—and requests for suggestions, then changing her mind, then going with the suggestions, ad infinitum.

"I'd like to try—" Ruby began.

"Did your date stand you up?" The words came out of Emily's mouth in a rush. She'd built up the question in her mind for too long. Oh, God, that was tacky. Oh, God, he would hate her for being so crude. Oh, God, why didn't she just stick her nose in the menu and pick something instead of insert herself into this man's probably horrible heartbreak?

"I'll have the French Onion Soup." Max gave her a sidelong glance while facing the server.

Emily's stomach dropped into her shoes, no, possibly past her shoes through the floor and into the deck below.

"I'm sorry," she mumbled. "That was so ridiculously rude and awful and terrible." Her weapon of choice, the fork, she gripped as if her life depended on it. The heavy silver plate dug into her hand, and her knuckles turned white.

Ruby casually pried apart Emily's death grip until she dropped the fork. Without missing a beat, she said to the server, "I'll have the Spinach Artichoke Dip, please. My wife will have the Shrimp Cocktail. Isn't that right, darling?"

Right. They were supposed to be a loving, newly married couple. Lord, take her now. The rest of her life might as well end right here while the pianist played *How Do You Solve a Problem Like Emily*—ahem—*Like Maria*.

"Absolutely, Love." Emily kissed her best friend on the cheek. "My dream. My Forever."

Was that too much?

Ruby smiled a weird smile. "She's the emotional one. You know how that goes." She looked across the table at Max.

"Right." He jerked down the cuffs of his blue dress shirt.

"Your wine, sir?" The sommelier had reached their table at the perfect time.

Emily nudged her glass toward Max's. "Please?" she asked. She grabbed the fourth wine glass on the table and had the man fill it as well.

"Good idea." Max dumped a half-full water glass into the

potted plant next to their table. "Fill 'er up." He sat it next to Emily's second wine glass.

A metaphorical fork stabbed her in the heart. Max was heartbroken over Penelope What's-her-face. He'd been stood up. Maxwell Keeling. A man who should never be stood up ever.

She clinked her glass with his. "Here's to staying positive and testing negative." *Oh, God.* Did she just say that? Her stupid brother's single guy toast?

Chapter 5
Emily Overshares

Max stopped with his glass in mid-air. The newly poured wine sparkled under the crystal chandelier that hung above them. Then he burst out laughing.

"Good point," he said with a smirk. "Can't say I'm surprised she didn't come. I should've broken up with her weeks ago. I guess I didn't want to admit she was sleeping around on me."

What woman in her right mind would reject this serious hunk of man for any other less hunky hunk? Emily leaned back in her chair. She opened her mouth with so many questions forming, and one of them would surely pop out at any moment.

Ruby eyed her friend, knew it was going to be ugly, and rushed in. "Not everyone is ready for commitment, I guess. I'm sorry that happened to you."

Emily knew the minute the words came out of Ruby's mouth that she'd been thinking about her own situation. How Tyler had disappeared before he could commit to her. "I agree."

She took a deep gulp of wine, hoping to strengthen her resolve to stay true to her role as lesbian newlywed and reject any fantasies she had about Max. "Women can be real bitches."

Ruby took hold of the extra wine glass Emily had filled and sipped. Looked as if all three of them needed a bit of red wine therapy.

Max scratched his neck. "I met her at a photoshoot. Thought she'd make a great model. Hard to find a good one and get all the paperwork signed."

Emily noticed Max taking in Ruby's profile. She bit her lip. She needed to shut up and take it. So what if he found Ruby attractive and equal to his ex in terms of photography worthiness? It wasn't anything new.

"Do you work cruise ships a lot?" Ruby asked.

"I've never done this kind of thing before. Couldn't you tell downstairs?" He looked at both of them.

Ruby shook her head.

He sucked in a quick breath. "Really? Thank God. I thought it was obvious. Those ridiculous lights. The poses. I was winging it."

God, his lack of self-assurance was so damned endearing. Could he be any more adorable?

"You were? But you said you were a photographer and that Penelope—" Oh, would he notice he'd never mentioned her name and that Emily had been listening in when he checked in down at the pier earlier? "That she was a model for you."

"I am a photographer, but I don't do portraits." He pulled out his phone. "I had a gallery showing a few months ago." After a few seconds of scrolling through his photo album, he handed it to Emily. "I like to shoot people, but interesting people doing the daily activities of life. Not this honeymoon nonsense." His eyes opened wide. "I don't mean that those kinds of photos aren't important, only that it's not my thing."

Ruby reassured him, "Don't worry. You didn't offend us. The photo package was part of the cruise deal, or we probably would've skipped it. Right, babe?" She hit Emily in the thigh with her knee.

Emily had been scrolling through gorgeous black-and-white images of people. Old people, young people, couples, families, individuals. "These are amazing." She handed the phone to Ruby. *Wow, what a talent.* "Why did you take the cruise job then? I don't get it. You're a true artist."

Not only was Max amazingly handsome, he was incredibly talented as well. Who in their right mind would debase their skillset to take photos of newlyweds on a cruise?

"These are incredible." Ruby handed the phone back to Max. "I can see why you had a gallery showing."

A flush crept across his cheeks.

The man blushed, people. Red alert! Red alert!

"Thanks." He set the phone on the table. "It was at a small gallery owned by a friend of a friend."

"Still, not every photographer gets that opportunity," Emily said. Oh, the poor gorgeous man with his amazing photos. How could no one see his creative genius?

"Wish I'd sold a few. Then maybe I wouldn't have ended up here." He gestured with his wine glass at the cruise opulence around them. "I'd like to say I'm filling in for a friend, but truth be told the guy did me a favor."

The red wine must be working its magic for Max to reveal so much about himself to two strangers. Or maybe he trusted them. Maybe he liked them a teeny tiny bit. Maybe they would sit at this table with Max every evening for dinner and chat and gab about their lives and their troubles and their dating fiascos and their loneliness at eight o'clock on a Saturday night when everyone else had a date, and Emily merely sat at home with a pint of ice cream calling her name in the freezer.

No.

That would be weird.

Without thinking, Emily reached out and touched him on the arm. "Aw, I'm sure it's not that bad." A sympathetic touch for a starving artist with incredible talents. Oh, and a very muscular forearm. Unexpected that.

He looked down at her hand and then across the table at Ruby, who had focused her attention on the arrival of several trays of food. In a flash he pulled his arm away and put it in his lap. He pushed away his wine glass.

"Oh, look at that would you?" Ruby gasped as the appetizers were set on the table.

"Yes," Emily said, her gaze darting to Max. "Would you look at that?"

* * *

"Oh, my God, Em, you've got to try this." Ruby had scooped up hot artichoke dip on a mini naan and held it out as if she were going to feed a baby. "It's so good." She opened her own coral lipsticked mouth as if doing so would encourage Emily to do the same.

Emily grabbed one of the small hors d'oeuvres plates the server had brought with the food and held it up under the morsel.

Ruby ignored the idea and shoved the food closer to her friend's face. "Take a bite. Come on."

Too much wine had seriously affected the former bride. Maybe Emily should tell the server to cut her off. Did they do that on a cruise? Nobody was driving anywhere. The worst a cruiser could do was maybe stumble into the pool. Or fall over the railing into the vast ocean that surrounded them on all sides.

Yikes.

Emily caught the attention of the sommelier who roamed the main dining area refilling the dozens of wine glasses of celebrating newlyweds. He smiled at her, nodded, and headed to their cozy corner.

As she opened her mouth to explain that their table shouldn't receive any more wine, Ruby shoved in the naan, dip and all. Emily's request came out in a hail of crumbs.

Max, who'd been deeply focusing on his trio of sliders – barbecued pork, beef, and salmon—held back a laugh.

The sommelier stood holding a bottle of red in one hand and a bottle of white in the other. "More, ladies?"

"Yes, please." Ruby held up her glass and pointed at the white wine.

Not exactly the plan Emily had had in mind. But, oh, Ruby had been right. The dip with naan was delightful. Creamy. Rich. Like a night after a good roll in the hay. Oh, so satisfying.

"Well, now that you know all about me, tell me about you two." Max picked up slider number two. "How'd you meet?"

Crap.

Why hadn't they discussed this earlier? Why hadn't the two of them talked about the possible questions people on a cruise would ask two newlyweds? What was the perfect story that would be easy for both of them to remember without messing it up?

"School," Ruby said, casually sipping her wine. "We met at school. Friends since kindergarten."

Max nodded and shifted his gaze from Ruby to Emily and then back again to Ruby. "Friends that developed into something more. Nice."

For some reason, even though Max totally bought that story one-hundred percent without any more questions or a request for more details, Emily felt the need to, well, add more details. "Yes, Mrs. Jackson's class. Southside Elementary. Roanoke. We both wore the same outfit. It was destiny."

"Or the fact both our moms shopped at Target," quipped Ruby. She set aside the empty dip plate and moved onto the massive shrimp cocktail. Half a dozen juicy pink shrimp covered the edge of a wide-rimmed dish that sat in a bowl of crushed ice.

"In middle school, the great tragedy occurred." That mid-August day came back to Emily in a flash.

Ruby's parents had decided to send their only child to a fancy all-girls' Catholic school on the other side of town. They had better sports programs, apparently, and Ruby's mother decided her daughter was going to be a star volleyball player. They'd played in the summer league, and the Catholic school was scouting for new talent. For middle school. At the YMCA gym. Emily didn't even know that was a thing. But Ruby was tall and lean and perfect for their junior varsity team.

Stouter and more solid Emily? Also in the same summer league? Who had a power serve that had given one girl a broken nose? Not interested. Catholic school reject. At least that's what her brother, Hunter, had told her when he heard the news.

"The great tragedy?" Max finished off his final slider.

"Oh, she means when my parents put me in Catholic

school." Ruby shrugged. "It wasn't that big of a deal. We still hung out all the time."

Wasn't a big deal?

Emily had cried for two weeks. She'd had to navigate the horrible world of middle school without her closest friend in the whole wide world. It had sucked.

"It took me forever to get over it." Emily's shoulders slumped. Even years later, the memories dragged her down into a sad place. She had been twelve for God's sake. Why did this bother her so much? To Ruby it seemed to be a blip. A nothing. A temporary setback. To Emily at the time, it had been life shattering and the beginning of 'the change.'

"Well, glad to see that you two made it and ended up together. That's what matters." He raised his almost empty wine glass. "How about a toast to the bride and...bride?" His forehead wrinkled.

Ruby raised her glass. "How about to the brides?" She giggled.

Max was going to figure them out sooner or later, wasn't he? Unless tonight was their only dinner with him. It had been a fluke of sorts. A surprise arrangement due to a mix up with the reservations. Tomorrow? Tomorrow they might end up with some lovey-dovey perfectly happy honeymooners, maybe a whole tableful of them. Not fair. No. No. No. If they had to pretend to be married, at the very least she should be rewarded with the beautiful Max across from her at the table.

"No!" Emily pushed back from her chair and stood.

The pianist stopped playing *Waterfalls* by TLC. The diners stopped eating. The servers stopped serving.

Crap.

An attentive server with a smile plastered on his face glided toward them from the embarrassingly quiet dining room. Even the pianist, paused with her fingers six inches above the keys, appeared scared to continue her playing.

Everyone thought she was a lunatic.

Max thought she was a lunatic

Her heart didn't just sink, it continued to drift downward from her stomach to her yoga-pant covered thighs to her feet. Maybe even beneath her all the way to the ocean below.

"Miss?" the server asked. He had worry lines around his eyes, and his eyebrows raised to his hairline. "May I be of service?"

Ruby sat rigidly in her chair.

Her best and oldest friend didn't even know how to handle such a bizarre outburst.

Max stood.

Emily hyperventilated and stared down at her hors d'oeuvres plate. How to answer him? How to make the diners forget about her and return to their meals?

Their table companion approached the server and, in a low voice, said something that only sounded like a murmur over the ringing in Emily's ears.

The server nodded.

Max slipped him a wad of cash.

The server's eyes lit up, he faced the pianist across the room, and clapped his hands. "We have a request! Table fifty-five would like to hear *Let It Go.*"

The pianist's shoulders dropped. She hesitated for a second, smiled, and then launched into a lilting version of the Disney classic.

One of the tables closest to the pianist joined in singing the well-worn lyrics.

Crisis over.

Embarrassment forgotten.

Was that Max's hand on her shoulder?

Emily turned her head. The warmth of his palm seared through the blouse she wore.

"Weddings can be stressful," he said. "We've all probably had a little bit too much to drink."

Then his hand was gone, and he returned to his seat.

The heat of his hand lingered. Goose bumps rose on her skin.

"Right" Ruby said.

Max picked up the menu. "Have you figured out what entrée you want? I'm thinking Steak Diane with Garlic Smashed Red Potatoes."

Ruby's brows squished together, and she mouthed at Emily '*Are you ok?*'

Emily nodded and let out a controlled breath. "What else do they have?"

Her Max fantasies needed to end. This was not possible. Since she'd seen him at boarding, she'd let her mind get the best of her. Now she'd looked the fool. The cruise was about Ruby healing from her no-good, jerk of a fiancé who hadn't even bothered texting her since the day of the wedding. Was she really so love-lorn that she needed to create impossible fantasies in her head? The last thing she wanted to be was a burden on poor Ruby. Emily was supposed to be the strong one.

Suck it up, Buttercup, and be the best friend that Ruby deserved.

"Salmon, a chicken dish I've never heard of, lasagna, and some vegetarian thing with chickpeas," Max read off the menu.

After they ordered their entrées, Max poured them all a glass of ice water. No more wine, which was a very good idea. One outburst per meal was probably best.

"What do you ladies do for work?" His steak took up two-thirds of his plate, and he seemed eager to dig in and spend most of his time eating rather than talking.

"I'm a pharmaceutical rep," Ruby answered.

He paused mid bite, looked up, and nodded. "Makes sense."

"What do you mean?" Emily asked.

"One of my friends is a doctor. He's maybe mentioned once or twice how good looking the drug reps are." He took a drink of water. "I don't mean anything by it. I'm sure you're very good at what you do—"

"She is." Emily crossed her arms.

He held up his hands in a defensive gesture. "I didn't mean anything negative, just that your wife is a very pretty woman."

He thought Ruby was pretty. Of course he did. Did she really think he wouldn't find Ruby to be attractive? But yet it still bothered her, even though she expected men to see Ruby and not see Emily at all. She was supposed to set this aside. She was supposed to let it lie. Yes, it had to end.

Emily grabbed her best friend's hand and kissed the back of it. "She is the most beautiful woman in the world."

Ruby pressed her lips together. Holding back a laugh?

"Tell him about your business, babe." Ruby freed her hand so she could take another bite of her mystery chicken dish.

Emily blushed. "Oh, you'll think it's ridiculous."

"Ridiculous?" Max set down his fork. "Why would I think it's ridiculous?"

Max glanced from one woman to the next. "Wait, you

aren't one of those people who grooms poodles to look like dinosaurs?" He made a scissoring motion with his fingers.

Emily laughed at his guess. "No."

"Or maybe you're an underwater sex therapist for the elderly?" He winked.

Both Ruby and Emily chortled. A real, true chortle with definite snorts. Text book chortling.

Emily wiped her eyes and prayed her mascara hadn't run. Once she caught her breath, she answered, "I own a gourmet picnic company."

"Gourmet picnics?" He tilted his head to one side. "Explain."

"Well, I used to work as an event planner at one of the big hotels in Roanoke, but the schedule was draining. My social life was a zero." Little did he know her social life had been barely above zero for most of her adult life. "I love to cook, but wanted something less stressful, more fun, and straight catering seemed too, well, boring, to be honest. Weddings, bar mitzvahs, graduations, baby showers. All the same stuff over and over. Chicken or beef? Cake pops or sheet cake? Ugh."

"But picnics?" Max gave a slight shake of his head. He stabbed another bite of steak and continued his meal.

Exactly the same reaction her parents had given her when she told them the news. Her brother had feigned shock, even though she'd bounced the idea off of him weeks earlier. So much for sibling support. Her mother had suggested she see a therapist. Her father had walked out of the room and headed to his man cave in the basement with a worried expression.

"I guess I've loved picnics since I was a kid. My parents would take my brother and me up into the Blue Ridge Mountains for the day. We'd hike and climb and play in the woods and on the rocks until noon, and then my mother would have this huge lunch spread for us." The memory warmed her inside. So many wonderful memories from that stage of her life. "And not PB and J and a bag of chips. No, she'd make Hummingbird Cake, pigs-in-a-blanket, fried chicken, and the best potato salad you'll ever have."

"Oh, yeah, that's true," Ruby said. "I could hardly wait for the Smalls' Fourth of July barbecue. Delicious. Plus, her lemon bars were to die for."

"Picnics seemed more like me." Emily shrugged and ate her lasagna. If she had a little pinch of fresh basil, that would be just the thing to bring her meal to the next level.

Max considered her explanation. "So who is scheduling gourmet picnics exactly?"

"Oh, you'd be surprised." Her muscles relaxed as she explained more about her business. Her baby. The thing besides her friendship with Ruby that gave her the most joy. "Lots of engagements."

He nodded. "Okay, that makes sense."

"Church events on the lawn, family barbecues at the park, book clubs." Emily ticked off her list on her fingers. "You'd be surprised how many people were dying for a gourmet picnic. There's something fun about it. The baskets, the blankets, the whole set up."

"She goes all out, too." Ruby's eyes lit up. "No paper plates or plasticware...all nice stuff. Champagne flutes. Cloth napkins. Decorations. The works. All themed for the customer."

"I suppose I never thought about it." He gave Emily a direct gaze. "That's a pretty unique idea."

Her cheeks heated at his praise. "Thanks." She thought back to when she'd left the hotel and her last serious boyfriend who worked at the front desk. He'd been the least supportive person in her circle of family and friends. Kyle had undermined her confidence so much that she'd almost abandoned the idea. "My boyfriend back then thought I was crazy."

Ruby gasped.

Max's eyes widened. "Boyfriend? I thought—?"

Oh. Holy. Crap.

What did she just do?

Chapter 6
Trivia Night

Emily gagged on a bite of lasagna.

Ruby gasped mid-grimace.

Salvage this screw up, Em. Oh, crap fix it now.

Max sat as if he were a deer on the highway at midnight, and Emily had just driven up over the rise in her pickup truck with the brights on.

"I'm bi." What else could her answer be? "Yep, totally bisexual. I swing both ways. Some days it's lipstick and skirts I'm after, the next it's loafers and aftershave." Her attempt at swallowing her lasagna turned into a duel between her esophagus and her gag reflex.

"I see." Max pushed his plate away, then he scanned the dining room as if to find some escape from the nutjob couple he'd found himself saddled with for the next half hour.

Ruby sighed. "It's okay, Em. You can tell him." She patted her best friend on the arm.

"Really?" Emily's shoulders slumped. How could she have failed at her one mission on this cruise in a single day?

Worst. Friend. Ever.

"Really." The former bride gave her a wan smile.

Did Ruby know she'd fail so quickly? Did Ruby expect eventually she'd have to own up to her situation?

"Tell me what?" Max asked.

A server had arrived at the table most likely summoned by the panicked look on Max's face. That 'get me out of here please' kind of look that some men only use in the worst circumstances: like when his mother talks about childbirth in detail at the family reunion or his girlfriend asks him to retrieve tampons from the next aisle over.

"Sir? Would you like to order your dessert?" The server stood at the ready with an iPad in his hand and a selection stylus perfectly positioned to record whether or not Max wanted bread pudding, peach pie, or the triple brownie sundae.

If he didn't choose the triple brownie sundae, he must be a serial killer because triple brownie sundae was the only right answer. The only one.

Ruby must've realized that Emily's chunk of lasagna had not yet decided if it was coming back up or going down and stepped up to the plate. "We aren't lesbians."

Max swallowed.

Was that a good swallow or a bad swallow? Was goodness or badness even an adjective to modify a swallow? Did Emily even care? No. No, she did not.

"Sir?" The server leaned over the table. "Your order?"

"Hold on," Max addressed him. "Give us a minute."

The server frowned and took a step back from the table.

Max tilted his head and slid his gaze from Ruby to Emily, examining them thoroughly. "You mean to tell me you two booked a honeymoon cruise, and you aren't even married?"

"Yes, that would seem rather strange, wouldn't it?" Emily's lasagna had decided to go down, so she was able to speak once more. "Two single, *straight*—" she emphasized the word 'straight' as if her life depended upon it, "—best friends who wanted to take a cheap cruise to Mexico. Yep, you got it, here for the bargain. Two cheapos trying to have a nice vacay together." Emily did not miss a beat, turned to the server and said, "I'll have the triple brownie sundae, please."

"Me, too," Max said in a bit of a daze. He shook his head several times.

"I'll have the peach pie," Ruby said.

Outrageous. Emily would have to let her friend know she gave off a serious serial killer-y vibe for sure by choosing the pie. Who chose pie when chocolate was available?

"Anyway," continued Emily in a crazy rush of words. "I'd like to propose, since we are likely the only three single people on this cruise—"

The server cleared his throat.

"With the exception of the cruise employees, of course." Emily made a flourish with her hand and a nod of her head in some royal fashion that she thought was appropriate for the occasion. "That the three of us should continue to be dining partners for the rest of the cruise."

Another of the serving staff appeared to clear away their plates and reset the table for dessert with a tiny fork and a massive spoon apparently made only for the eating of ice cream.

Max sat silently for a moment, staring straight at Emily and making her a little too warm under his gaze. "I will agree to that if you promise me one thing."

"Fine, yes, we promise," Emily said. But she would promise gorgeous Max almost anything.

Her best friend, however, seemed to think that was a little cuckoo. "Hold on, what are we promising? Let me remind you,

Max, Emily promised me she wouldn't tell anyone we weren't newlyweds, so I'm not sure how reliable she is in the promise department." Ruby glared at Emily.

Their server delivered two massive sundaes and a piece of peach pie the size of the moon in its first quarter phase.

Max crossed his arms and leaned back in his chair. "All I want is—"

Emily found her mind most inappropriately filling in the blanks:

All I want is someone to slather sunscreen on my naked chest...

All I want is a night of incredible sex with the lights on...

All I want is you...

"—to forget about my life for a few days," he finished. "So no more personal questions. Everything we talk about at this table must be about the cruise, about the here and now."

Somehow instead of having to own up to Ruby's ruined wedding and broken heart, they'd gotten away with the thinnest of excuses and a table companion willing to go along with it.

"Promise accepted." Ruby stretched her hand across the table and cemented the deal with a handshake.

Okay. That could be good. That could be very, very good.

Not only did Ruby end up not having to explain her runaway groom, Emily didn't have to share the usual stories of failed relationships, heartaches, embarrassing moments, and all the other stuff that made up her conversational arsenal. Self-deprecating was her go-to chat mode. She didn't want to be that way, but it came naturally to her after a lifetime of not living up to expectations—her own and the expectations others put upon her.

"Em?" Ruby nudged her.

"Oh, yes, I promise." The opportunity to shake Max's hand had disappeared, as he'd begun eating his dessert. One sexy bite at a time.

Emily licked her lips without thinking.

Max looked up at her at that exact moment. He stared at her mouth, and his gaze warmed to a low burn.

At least, Emily *wanted* to believe it was a low burn. He lingered for a few seconds on her mouth. She froze with the tip of her tongue touching her upper lip.

A lush roll of heat swept from her head to her stomach and maybe even a little lower.

Whoa, Nellie.

He cleared his throat, shifted in his seat, and directed a question at Ruby, ending the moment abruptly, "What are your plans for tonight? After dinner, I mean."

A server appeared to pour them each a cup of coffee and answered, "There's karaoke in the Sunset Lounge, a trivia contest in the casino bar, and then Honeymoon Under the Stars on the pool deck."

"Honeymoon Under the Stars?" Emily found herself asking without thinking. "What's that?" Oof, why did she ask such a dumb question? Any activity with 'honeymoon' in the title would be off limits for sure.

"Romantic music, umbrella drinks the size of a basketball, and they turn off the lights so everyone can see the stars." The server finished pouring coffee and nodded before he headed to the next table.

Yeah, off limits. But it might be nice to do some star gazing...

"Trivia contest," Max and Ruby announced simultaneously.

"I suck at trivia." Emily scooped up another bite of brownie and ice cream and sighed. Last time she'd participated in a trivia contest, she'd mistaken Paul Simon for Phil Collins, and her team—made up of Ruby, Tyler and Kyle, her ex—had laughed and laughed at her error. Emily had accepted no invites for trivia after that. Didn't Ruby remember?

"Maybe we win a prize." Ruby draped her napkin across her half-eaten peach pie, unfolded the schedule of the day's events, and read the description aloud, "Join us for trivia in the casino at 10 p.m. Win a spin on the prize wheel."

"Prize wheel?" Emily asked. Like the *Wheel of Fortune?* Trips, cash, cars? Ok, taking a shot at winning didn't seem so terrible an idea. What if the trivia happened to be in her wheelhouse? Like gourmet cooking or meteorology? She'd earned a minor in meteorology in college. If they had a question about lenticular clouds, she was golden.

Max checked his watch. "It's almost ten. Where's the casino?" He pushed back from the table. "Come on, girls, let's see who is the Trivia King!" The smile on his face was infectious.

"Queen," corrected Ruby. "Trivia Queen."

"Trivia Master," Emily said.

As the pianist swept into a surprisingly rousing version of Ed Sheeran's *Perfect*, the trio headed toward the stairs. Ruby first, Max second, and Emily third.

It was hard not to notice how Ruby and Max complemented each other: ruggedly handsome and dark Max next to willowy and auburn-haired Ruby. Even the diners around them noticed.

But that was silliness. Yesterday Ruby had been broken-hearted at the altar...well, maybe not the literal altar, but very broken-hearted in the choir room at the First Presbyterian Church. Two people looking good together didn't mean anything. That was only a thing people said, right?

Probably nobody had ever said that about her and any of the men she'd dated. In fact, her mother had called Kyle 'sloppy and immature,' which hadn't been that far from the truth. Once, her grandmother had noted the sturdiness of her college boyfriend, Nate. But that was about it. And 'sturdy' didn't exactly equal 'handsome.' That was closer to saying he wouldn't blow over in a windstorm. Solid. Dependable. The kind of man everyone expected her to end up with.

Then solid and dependable Nate dumped her right before graduation for a freshman she'd tutored for a semester in Meteorology 101.

Maybe promising not to talk about their lives off ship would be the best promise she'd ever made. She could be whoever she wanted to be. A mystery woman with a mystery past. Hmm...it grew more tempting by the minute.

"So where's this casino?" Emily asked, tripping up the stairs.

* * *

"Welcome to Trivia Night at the Double Aces Casino," announced Sylvia.

Sylvia seemed to get around. But as the ship's cruise director (which Emily had discovered on the ship's news channel on the in-cabin tv when changing for dinner), she probably was in charge of making sure all the events ran smoothly.

Ruby, Emily, and Max found a small table near a slot machine on the outskirts of the trivia contest area. Max had to grab a stool from one of the blackjack tables so he had somewhere to sit. All the seating had been arranged for couples of two to four players.

Although he sat raised above their table by about eight

inches, he didn't seem to mind looming over the two best friends. He rested his beer on a pony wall that separated the gambling zone from the bar.

A server in black pants and a bright blue polo shirt with 'Double Aces Casino' stamped on the breast pocket handed out small sheets of paper in a variety of colors and tiny little pencils —like the ones they hand out in mini golf.

"Tonight's trivia game is our version of *The Newlywed Game.*" Sylvia smiled broadly, spread out her arms, and made it seem as if the whole casino thought this was the greatest idea ever for trivia.

Emily gulped.

What was Newlywed Game trivia? Didn't sound good.

"Each question will be about your partner. Answer as honestly as you can. At the end of the game, we will compare answers, and the couple with the most correct answers to the same question wins a spin on the prize wheel!"

The server who handed out the paper and pencils rolled in the prize wheel—a bright red wheel on a stand that had at least sixteen prizes possible. Most were silly things like a free drink or a turn on the zip line suspended above the pool area. But then Emily saw a thousand dollars in cash and a free couple's choice excursion. Now things were getting interesting.

"To make this fair, we can't have you sitting next to your partner, can we?" Sylvia wagged her finger. "No, no, no!"

Ruby looked at Emily. Emily looked at Ruby. Max drank his beer and doodled on his yellow piece of paper.

"If you have a pink piece of paper, you will need to sit at the tables marked one, two, three, and four. If you have a blue piece of paper, you will need to sit at the tables marked five, six, seven, and eight."

Ruby held a blue piece of paper. Emily held a pink piece.

Max shook his yellow piece of paper in the air, "What about yellow?"

"Yellow will need to sit at the tables marked nine, ten, eleven, and twelve," Sylvia announced. Her mouth formed a straight line when she saw who'd asked the question.

Maybe Max had been told not to participate in the passenger activities?

"Green will need to sit at the tables marked thirteen, fourteen, fifteen, and sixteen." Sylvia wove her way through the tables to reach Max at the very back. "Please find a table, and we'll begin once everyone is seated. This is going to be fun!"

Max finished off his beer and rose to seek out the correct tables.

Before he had a chance to move, Sylvia reached him and switched off her mic. "Sit down."

"Why?"

"This game is for passengers only." Sylvia crossed her arms. "You aren't a passenger."

"Yes, I am." Max punched the air with his mini pencil.

"No, you are not." Sylvia gestured at the crowd of guests. "Look around. Everyone else has a partner. A wife. A husband. You don't have anyone. This game is for couples. You need to leave."

"I'm a passenger. It says so in my contract." Max raised his voice above the clanging and sirens as a slot machine paid out its winnings. "I exchanged my services on this cruise for a free trip, I'm staying in a passenger's cabin, and I eat in the dining room with the rest of the guests."

"He has a point," Emily said.

Sylvia tapped her foot. "This is a game for couples. You can't play."

Max stood solid as a tree trunk. His eyes shifted back and

forth. He opened his mouth. No sound came out. What kind of defense could he throw out? Where else could he take this?

"Fine." He held up his hands. "Fine. I don't want to play your trivia game anyway." He squinted at the prize wheel. "I mean, who wants to win a turn at the zip line?"

"I do," Ruby said.

Emily shushed her.

"Thank you, Maxwell." Sylvia snapped her mic on. "Has everyone found their new tables?"

"It's Max," Emily shouted. "His name is Max."

A middle-aged woman and her middle-aged husband gave Emily a weird look from their twin slot machines.

"Chop chop!" Sylvia clapped her hands. "Let's go, people! I've got a lot of fun questions for you lovebirds."

Ruby and Emily exchanged glances.

"Do you think we can do this?" Ruby stared at her little blue paper. "I mean, we're not, you know, married." She whispered the last word.

Emily imagined what some of the questions might include. Could be tricky, but they were best friends after all. They knew a lot about each other. A lot.

"Let's give it a try. Why not?" Emily stood and waved her pink paper in the air. "What do we have to lose?"

Max leaned toward them. "If you win a spin on the prize wheel, and you don't like the prize, can I have it?"

"We'll consider it," Emily answered before scouting out for the correct tables based on her pink paper: one, two, three, or four.

"No, we won't," Ruby countered. "We're the couple, and we get the prize."

Max read prizes off the wheel. "What if it's the Captain's Tour of the ship's bowels?"

"It doesn't say 'bowels,' does it?" Ruby squinted at the wheel.

Emily pulled on her friend's arm. "Come on. They might not let us play if we aren't at the correct table in time."

"You won't give Max our prize if we win, will you?" Ruby found table number six and sat with two men who seemed more interested in their oversized cocktail drinks, rather than the stunning tablemate who'd joined them.

"I really am not interested in ship bowels, are you?" Emily found table number four and grabbed the last open seat, sitting next to a man in his sixties and two younger brunette women who seemed to know each other.

"If it's something other than bowels, Em, I think we need to discuss it."

The two husbands at Ruby's table eyed her with curiosity and maybe a bit of disgust. A woman saying the word 'bowels' was apparently a massive turn-off.

Sylvia interrupted the prize debate, "Wonderful, it seems as if everyone has found a seat. Are you ready for some fun questions?" She snatched a paper from the bar and shook it. When she smiled, her high cheekbones created divots in her face. "I want everyone to number their paper from one to fifteen." She leaned in closer to her mic and repeated more slowly. "One. To. Fifteen."

Emily wondered who couldn't understand her the first time. Maybe some of the older brides and grooms. She glanced at a yellow paper table. An elderly woman with a walker standing next to her waved at someone across the room. At a green paper table, an equally aged man with oxygen cannulas in his nose waved back.

True love could happen at any age. Emily hoped she didn't have to wait that long to find it, though.

"All right," Sylvia snapped. Apparently trivia had a very important timeline that must be followed. "Now that we're done numbering our papers—"

Emily scrambled to finish her numbering. Why was she always so easily distracted? Ruby made it clear she wanted to win the game, so Emily had to do her best to answer the questions correctly.

"Question one." Sylvia held up her paper. "Ah, this should be an easy one. Although I have a feeling the brides might do better than the grooms."

A groom raised his hand. "Excuse me, Sylvia."

The cruise director squinted and searched the trivia tables. "Is there a problem?"

The man, with a carefully groomed and styled mop of curls, stood so he could be seen. "What if you are two grooms?"

"Two grooms?" Sylvia's penciled brows drew together.

"Yes, two grooms." As he came forward to emphasize his point, he bumped the table. People's drinks splashed. One bride had her yellow paper ruined. "Not every couple here is straight."

"I need a new paper." The bride held up her drink-doused sheet. "I can't play until I get a new one."

Sylvia snapped her fingers, and a server quickly took the woman's wet paper and replaced it with a fresh one.

The action gave the cruise director a moment to realize her mistake. "Ah, yes, same sex couples. I'm so sorry I did not take that into account." She fumbled with her paper, and scratched at her neck.

"Maybe we could call ourselves Spouse One and Spouse Two?" offered Ruby. "I'll be Spouse One, Em!"

"Yes, that works," mumbled Sylvia. "Spouse One and Spouse Two. Can someone give me a pencil?" She shielded her eyes when the flashing lights of a gambler's slot machine went off. "Javier?"

The server who'd handed out a fresh yellow paper swiftly came to Sylvia's aid and handed her a golf pencil.

"Thank you." Sylvia leaned over her paper and began to write on it. "Let me make a few adjustments to the questions. Mark told me the game was ready to go, but clearly he made a mistake."

Poor Mark—whoever he was—Sylvia was likely to cook his goose later.

The delay allowed Emily enough time to finish numbering her paper.

"Question one: Where did you go on your first date?" Sylvia strolled around the trivia players and repeated the question more slowly, "Where. Did. You. Go. On. Your. First. Date?" She ended up right next to the older groom with the oxygen and rested a hand on his shoulder.

First date? God, already Emily was going to bomb this. She was hoping the questions would be favorite color or least favorite food. Not things related to, well, relationships. Dating. And maybe even—*gulp*—sex.

Max had remained on his stool and ordered another beer. He caught Emily's eye and raised his bottle in the air, toasting her.

Chapter 7
Spin of the Wheel

Emily scribbled the first ideas that popped into her head. Any answer to a trivia question she could base on reality, she wrote down. Several times she shot a look at Ruby from across the room, hoping to teleport her answers into her best friend's mind.

First date?

Why not Ruby's first date with Tyler? Would that work? A bungee jump at Wintergreen Resort in the Blue Ridge Mountains and dinner at one of the nearby wineries. She'd raved about it for weeks afterward.

First kiss?

Well, the two friends had kissed 'by accident' when they were eleven. Neither one wanted to go into middle school without having kissed someone. Too lame. Everyone in seventh grade had probably kissed someone but the two of them. Ruby, before 'the change,' had been a gangly girl with braces and huge feet. Emily had been—well—Emily.

Emily wheeled her mother into letting her stay the night

at Ruby's over Fourth of July weekend, even though it was the big family picnic at the Small house, the one with her mother's world famous—well maybe Virginia state famous—potato salad. But she'd given in. All Emily had to do was promise to be back home in time for the picnic at one o'clock on Saturday.

Done.

That Friday night, she and Ruby locked the door to Ruby's bedroom, sat across from one another, closed their eyes tight, and leaned in. Emily had thought about Brett Howser, the cutest boy in her class. Every girl thought he was perfect. She imagined his eyes, his lips, his face.

But because neither girl could see, they'd bumped noses. Hard. And it had hurt. She and Ruby decided it had been 'close enough' to a real kiss and vowed never to talk of the incident again.

Emily scratched out 'Ruby's Room'—as that would be weird, right?—and wrote down 'beach' and hoped for the best.

"Okay," announced Sylvia. "Glad we're all adults here because now we're getting to the good stuff. You ready?"

"Ready!" shouted several of the drunkest brides and grooms in the room.

One man even burst out with, "Huzzah!"

"Question eleven." Sylvia took a breath.

God, they had five more questions?

"What is the strangest place you've ever made love?" Sylvia read it as if she were trying out for the Glenn Close role in *Fatal Attraction*. Her voice dipped from high to low, and she raised her eyebrows to her hairline, as if making love anywhere but in a bed in your master bedroom would be scandalous, and Sylvia would not stand for it, not one bit.

Poor Sylvia.

Emily was at a complete loss for an answer, as she didn't remember sharing with Ruby any weird places she'd had sex. Had she ever had sex anywhere weird? Did the back of a pickup in the middle of a hay field count? Was that weird? Or was that some normal country thing that farm boys did with their girlfriends? Her college boyfriend had grown up in a small town with horses and cows and chickens and things. He had made it seem like the most normal thing two people could do in a hay field.

Her pencil hesitated over her paper.

Was Ruby having this much trouble?

When she glanced at her friend, Ruby diligently scribbled something on her baby blue paper. Then she looked over at Max. Their gazes met, and he gave her two thumbs up and a big smile, as if that might help her answers be more correct.

"Question twelve."

Dammit.

Emily wrote down 'truck' and moved on.

"What is Spouse One's most irritating habit in the bedroom?" Sylvia asked in the same high-low freaky voice.

Spouse One? She was Spouse One. She'd written it at the top of her pink paper so she wouldn't forget. Oh, God, Ruby wouldn't...she couldn't...she'd never...

Emily distinctly remembered a conversation with Ruby several years ago when she'd shared intimate details of a most embarrassing thing. A bedroom thing. Never thinking, never expecting that such a question would be asked.

But Ruby needed a win. Ruby wanted a spin at the wheel. And if Emily could give that to her, she would—no matter what.

Reluctantly, Emily scribbled the words on her paper and grimaced.

* * *

Emily had been focusing so hard on writing the most difficult confession she could possibly make that she missed the last question. One-hundred percent did not hear it. Did not even notice Sylvia's bright orange lips moving. Did not see two dozen brides and grooms scribbling until it was too late.

What was number fifteen? Oh, God, what did she say?

"All right," Sylvia snapped. "That ends our trivia questions." She placed a hand on her chest and took a deep breath.

Maybe Trivia Night had put her one step away from a breakdown.

The attractive woman ran a hand over her smooth, glistening hair, which had been pulled into a tight bun. "Pencils down." Her voice mellowed. "The servers will collect your papers. Make sure your first and last names are at the top of them, so we can match you up with your spouse."

Emily quickly wrote something in the last question box. She'd glanced at another person's paper at her table, and it had said, 'his intelligence.' So maybe the question was about her partner's best quality. Emily wrote 'her beauty' as her last answer.

Two servers gathered up the papers and carried them to Sylvia at the front of the room.

"Order another drink and relax," the cruise director said. "I'll be narrowing down the answers to the top three couples, and then we'll read through them in order and find out the winner!"

Someone in the casino turned up the music, and the husbands and wives navigated toward their partners. Some laughed, hugged, and kissed. Others immediately headed for the bar to order more drinks.

Max approached Emily and Ruby who had met back up at a blue paper table. "Guess it wasn't quite the kind of trivia we had in mind." He rubbed his hands together. "But this is gonna be good." He waggled his eyebrows.

"I couldn't think of anything for question twelve. What about you?" Emily asked Ruby. Her nerves ratcheted up to the highest, craziest level possible. *God, please, let her say she didn't have an answer either.*

"What was question twelve?" Ruby sipped a massive Bloody Mary that was more celery sticks than drink. "Was that the one about our first fight? 'Cause I put fourth grade when we fought over the last pizza pocket at lunch. Remember that? Hot pizza sauce and cheese all over my new dress? My mom was livid for weeks. Did you know she didn't want me to be friends with you after that?"

"Question twelve, the one about the most irritating habit in the bedroom—" Emily's ears hadn't caught up to Ruby's words. "Wait, I thought your mom loved me?"

Max grabbed an empty chair and sat down, "Fourth grade drama? I'm in!"

"Weren't we supposed to stop talking about our lives off the ship? No more personal stories?" Emily crossed her arms. "I thought we'd made a promise to each other?"

"But this is trivia," Max announced. "Newlywed Game Trivia. A cruise event. I can't help it if the answers reveal embarrassing secrets from your past." A knowing smile took over his gorgeous face.

Not good. No, not good at all. The dinner promise had been no more real talk. Only fun vacation cruise talk. Crappity-crap. Max might find out—*things.*

"Em's right," Ruby said. "No more personal stuff."

"We aren't going to make it to the finals," Emily said.

Max would never find out any of these things because Emily and Ruby would not make it into the top three couples. How could they? They weren't really married. They had never really dated. They were friends, but they couldn't possibly know enough of the answers to the questions asked to score high.

"Oh, damn." Max frowned. "I was looking forward to all the dirt."

"Sorry!" Ruby sing-songed.

Sylvia barked into the mic, "I need the following couples to come to the front: Brian and Sandra Murray, Jayne and Dustin Brightman-White, and Ruby Evers and Emily Small."

"Shit." Emily's stomach dropped.

* * *

Ruby and Emily made their way to the front.

Emily's knees knocked together. Why did she answer the questions so truthfully? If she didn't think they'd win, why did she bother trying? How was it possible she and Ruby had the same answers to the questions? Some of these newlyweds must not have dated that long.

Ruby grabbed her hand and squeezed it. "Maybe we'll win the zip line prize."

"Maybe," Emily mumbled.

If that is what Ruby wanted, she had to be supportive. This was, after all, her revenge cruise. Emily raced through her answers. Some were innocent enough, but some of the others? *Oh my.*

She sneaked a glance at Max, his wavy hair shining under

the colored casino lights, his perfect white teeth sparkling as he smiled, his hard body rippling under his shirt. Well, maybe she was only imagining that bit.

"This is how we will determine the winner. All three couples had ten out of fifteen questions correct."

Brian and Sandra, a middle-aged couple who wore matching bright green T-shirts, raised their fists in the air and whooped it up. Jayne and Dustin, a couple in their mid-30s and impeccably dressed in linen and silk, smiled stiffly and stood as far away from the Murrays as possible. Emily and Ruby took a spot between the two and clapped along with the rest of the audience.

"The final winner comes down to the last five questions. We will be asking the audience to judge the best match to each question, as some were not identical, but we determined they were 'close enough.' Ready?" Sylvia's eyes lit up. She could probably see her shift ending in thirty minutes and some 'me' time waiting down in the crew area. Her second wind must've kicked in.

"Ready!" the audience shouted.

Max joined in.

Emily cringed.

"Let's start with Ruby and Emily."

Of course.

Emily's body flashed hot and cold. She locked eyes with Max and attempted to communicate using a series of rapid blinks that she hoped came across as an SOS message. Was a free zip line experience worth it?

"Ruby, can we just go?" she whispered to her best friend while the room chanted their names.

Ruby leaned in. "What? I can't hear you." The roar of the

audience demanding that Ruby and Emily have all their secrets revealed live on stage to a roomful of strangers drowned out any communication.

Emily took a breath. *Stop it. Stop spoiling this for Ruby.* She wanted to be up here and was excited they were in the running for a spin of the prize wheel. "Nothing."

"All right," began Sylvia. "We need the audience to decide these five questions. Thumbs up for 'yes, we accept the answer' and thumbs down for 'no, we don't accept the answer.' The majority will decide. Question seven: When did you have your first fight and what was it about? Ruby answered: fourth grade —wow, your romance goes way back—and pizza pocket. That must've been some pizza to have a fight over it."

The crowd laughed.

"Emily answered: grade school and cafeteria food. What do you think audience? Is that close enough? Who says thumbs up?"

The audience voted in the affirmative, and Sylvia moved on to the other questions that were close, but not quite close enough. The crowd voted each time for the two women and gave them three more answers.

"The final question that we need a vote on is—"

Emily prayed it wouldn't be the question she feared. The most horrifically embarrassing thing she could ever think read aloud in a public place about her personal life. Her muscles locked up.

"—question eleven."

Oh, holy hell.

"What is Spouse One's most irritating habit in the bedroom?"

Why had Emily even put an answer down for this question? And why had she written an honest answer? She'd done it for Ruby. She'd done it for the stupid spin of the prize wheel. Ruby deserved to win. No matter how horridly embarrassing this final answer would be. No matter what Max thought of her afterwards.

Crap.

"Ruby answered: lots of screaming."

Ruby giggled next to her.

Crap times one hundred.

"Emily answered: loud sex noises."

A hush fell over the room. The couples participating in the contest didn't know how to react. Even though everyone secretly hoped for an answer like this, nobody knew what was an appropriate response. One older husband wearing a bad toupee elbowed his new middle-aged wife who turned red as a beet.

Sylvia rushed past the awkwardness. "Okay, who wants to give a thumbs up to this one?"

Max stood, held up his hand, made an exaggerated thumbs up, and laughed.

* * *

"All right, everyone. Looks like we have our winner." Sylvia waved at Javier, who rolled the prize wheel from its spot next to the bar and placed it front and center. "The couple who will win their shot at the prize wheel is—"

Max drummed his index fingers on the table. Several other audience members did the same, creating a loud drum roll.

Emily, who had yet to recover from the humiliation of everyone in the room knowing she was loud in bed, stared at the floor and crossed her fingers behind her back. She and

Ruby deserved the wheel spin based on personal reveal alone.

Ruby quaked with excitement.

Who knew her bestie would be so thrilled for a go at the prize wheel?

Sylvia took a deep breath, made eye contact with everyone in the room, and shouted into the mic, "Ruby and Emily!"

The trivia player couples burst into applause. Max jumped up and whooped. Ruby clapped her hands together with glee.

Emily shoved the lump of embarrassment in her throat as far down as possible with multiple swallows, deep breaths, and a self-affirming internal mantra that everything would be okay.

Because it would be. Everyone in the room probably had already forgotten the answer to question eleven. The visual of Emily in the throes of loud passion probably disappeared from their cruise-relaxed brains the minute the glorious, colorful, prize-filled wheel rolled center stage with its fake gold accents glinting under the lights. Prizes of every size and value whirring by with the flick of a wrist surely supplanted sex fantasies about lesbians in bed, right? Or maybe only zaftig Emily in bed. Naked. And...well...and...

She maybe hyperventilated a wee bit at that moment.

"Let's hope Emily can keep her—uh—excitement to herself, right audience?" Sylvia gave a big exaggerated wink and then smiled broadly as the two women stepped forward to claim their spin.

The audience guffawed.

Emily cringed and wished she had a paper bag to slow her breathing. What if she went down right here in the casino? Did they have gurneys on cruise ships? Doctors? How did they handle a woman who had a panic attack because of her answer to a trivia question?

Ruby yanked her friend toward the wheel.

If only Emily could run away and hide in their balcony cabin on the starboard side, grab the box of exotic chocolates that had come as part of their Honeymoon Package, and watch Sylvia the Cruise Director ramble on about the features of the cruise ship on their in-room tv screen. Instead, she had to give a wan smile in response to Sylvia's joke at her expense and pretend it didn't mortify her. She had to slow her breathing to stop the dizziness that crept up on her. She had to stop being so damned self-conscious about her sex life. Why did it bother her so much? Some women might love for the world to know they're a screamer—a hypersonic, minutes-long screamer, heard through the walls of apartments and townhouses alike.

"Who wants to spin?" Sylvia hovered over the two women and widened her eyes to saucer-like size.

"Go ahead, Rubes." Emily nudged the former bride toward the wheel.

Her beautiful bestie approached the wheel as if she'd finally made it to the top of Everest after weeks of effort and the help of accommodating Sherpas. "Oh, can I?"

"It's all yours." Emily's heart swelled with sisterly sympathy for her friend. If she could give Ruby these kinds of moments on the cruise, it was all worth it. Who cared about personal embarrassments? Really, didn't Ruby experience the worst embarrassment of her life being left at the altar? A beautiful, sweet, kind hottie like Ruby did not deserve that. She deserved repeated spins on the prize wheel.

Ruby reached up as high as she could and spun it like they'd seen the contestants do on *The Price is Right* over summer breaks when they were girls.

The crowd cheered.

Max smiled broadly and clapped louder than anyone else.

"What will it land on?" Sylvia speculated. "We have so many good prizes on there."

The wheel clicked and clicked and clicked.

After a minute of spinning, it finally began to slow.

Click. Pause. Click. Pause. Click.

"Ruby and Emily, you have won—"

The audience gasped as one voice.

Chapter 8
Hallway Encounter

"**A** Free Boudoir Photo Session!" Sylvia clapped her hands. "Congratulations, ladies. You can collect your prize at the Guest Services counter on Deck Three. Just hand them this card." The cruise director produced a bright orange business card with 'Prize' printed on one side and 'Sexy Boudoir Photos' on the back.

Emily gave Max a stunned look. Was he aware his services were part of the prize wheel? What kind of photos had Max taken that would equal boudoir? Was he really the artistic photographer with a gallery showing or was that made up to impress them?

Max blinked rapidly and ran a hand through that glorious, thick, wavy hair.

Like a camera flash, her mind lit up at the possibilities: Emily, scantily clad in some kind of lacy ruffly confection, draped over a red velvet chaise lounge making goo-goo eyes at Max while he got up close and personal with her cleavage. Pose. Pose. Pose. Flash. Flash. Flash.

Her body ran hot and then cold at the thought of it.

Sexy.

Private.

Intimate.

Oh my.

"Thank you!" Emily snatched the card so quickly out of Sylvia's hands, it was as if the card were the last morsel of food offered to a starving woman.

"What a terrible prize," Ruby said, all the fun and excitement sucked out of her. "Who would want to take photos like that on a Honeymoon Cruise?"

Emily looked at the card in her hand. Guilt stabbed her greedy little heart. Supportive maid-of-honor got tossed out the window and horny single gal had stepped right into her place.

Sylvia's plastered-on smile wavered. Ruby's words had been loud enough for all the players to hear. "Let's give the newlyweds a round of applause."

Tepid clapping filled the space. A few couples left the casino and headed for the higher decks.

"Maybe we can trade it in for another prize," suggested Emily. Whatever it took to remove the sad expression from Ruby's face and encourage a smile, she'd do it. "Something of equal value. How much could a photo shoot be worth anyway?"

"Join us tomorrow night for another round of trivia!" Sylvia's audience depleted rapidly. Although she tried to keep up the same chipper tone she'd had since the beginning of the event, her tiredness came through. "Same time, same place, more prizes." Her voice trailed off.

The space emptied in a matter of seconds.

Sylvia snapped off the mic and muttered to herself, "Last time I'm subbing for Mark. What a nightmare."

Maybe now was not the time to confront Sylvia about

trading their prize for something else on the wheel. The woman appeared as if she needed a long hot bath and maybe a bottle of wine to take the edge off. Better not rock the boat.

As Sylvia ordered Javier to pack up the pencils and paper, Max joined them by the prize wheel. "I swear, I did not know that prize was even on the wheel." Spots of color appeared on his cheeks.

How could a man as hot as this one be so timid about a boudoir photo shoot? Something about his reaction made her even more attracted to him. Was he not aware how absolutely gorgeous he was?

"I really wanted to try out the zip line." Ruby let out a sigh.

"Maybe I need to remind you about all of the gift cash you wanted to spend?" Emily almost bit off her own tongue. She'd gotten close to spilling the beans about the wedding, the reception, the money tree, and Tyler. Oh, boy, Tyler. Max had no idea her friend was dealing with the sharpest of pains, the worst hurt a woman could experience.

"Gift cash?" Max narrowed his eyes.

The two women looked at each other. Ruby attempted to signal something to Emily with rapid blinking and a lip twitch. Or was she panicking?

Emily ran her mouth to fill in the strange silence, "Uh, yeah, from a birthday. Rich grandma. Ruby's so lucky. Got a lot of cash. Very generous."

Max nodded his head.

For some reason he believed it, even though she'd sounded insane.

"Anyway, Ruby, you can do as many zip line runs as you want." To placate her down-in-the-dumps friend, Emily spoke without thinking. "In fact, since we have a day-at-sea tomorrow, why don't we spend it on the pool deck? Sun, fun, and some rum?"

"That sounds awesome," Max said. "I don't have to work until the afternoon. More honeymoon shoots. I'll meet you there at, let's say noon-ish?"

Oh, no.

Emily was reminded she did not have a bathing suit in her minimally packed, wedding weekend only luggage.

Oh, yes.

Emily would be hanging out on the pool deck with Max in swim trunks and no shirt.

"Absolutely." Emily touched his arm.

Ruby smiled at the chance to try out the zip line multiple times using cash handed to her by Mr. Jameson Hardy, father to horrible, bride-dumping Tyler Hardy.

They must sell bathing suits on this ship somewhere, and Emily would find one that suited her overly lush body, right? Perfect in all ways and only showing the parts of her that she liked the best. Like her arms. Or maybe her knees. Her knees weren't too bad. Surely a bathing suit like that would exist on a cruise ship, which was setting sail to a tropical paradise where ninety-nine percent of the people would be wearing bathing suits all day long for dancing, lounging, eating, parasailing, snorkeling. Everything. Bathing suits should be the only things in the ship's stores.

"Before I open up for more honeymoon shoots, I could do the boudoir thing, if you wanted."

Emily bit her tongue for real this time.

* * *

BLAT BLAT BLAT.

Emily's alarm on her phone went off.

Annoying, but effective.

Seven a.m. on the dot. Two hours before the stores opened. Five hours before they'd agreed to meet Max on the pool deck for some drinks and relaxation.

Next to her, Ruby rolled over with a moan. "Shut that stupid thing off, Em." She grabbed her pillow and covered her head.

"Sorry." Emily searched for her phone in the semi-dark and switched off the alarm.

Ruby said something unintelligible.

Emily dug through her suitcase and plucked out clean underwear—her last pair—a T-shirt, and a pair of shorts. Would the ship's stores also carry a decent selection of women's underwear? She crossed her fingers and headed into the cramped bathroom for a shower.

Last night, they'd parted ways with Max and returned to their cabin without too much trouble. Ruby had ordered more drinks than Emily had realized, so it had been necessary to help her friend into bed. No way did Rubes avoid a hangover this morning.

As she washed her hair, bumping her elbows into the walls of the micro-shower, her stomach growled. Even though dinner had been amazing, her stomach had always been on a schedule. Breakfast by seven-thirty, lunch by noon, snack at three, dinner by seven.

Put on repeat.

In fact, wasn't that the reason her purse contained a number of protein bars and baggies of trail mix at all times?

Stepping out of the teeny shower, she toweled dry, slipped into her clothes, and dried her hair. The humidity gave her pretty waves that normally only appeared after a long day at the beach. A touch of mascara, a little bit of lipstick, a dash of pressed powder on her nose, and she was ready to face the breakfast buffet line.

Would they let her bring a plate to the cabin for Ruby?

She slipped on her sandals next to her suitcase and plotted how to sneak something out of the dining room. From the vanity next to the micro-closet, she snatched a couple of tissues and stuffed them into her purse. A bagel. Maybe a few sausages. Rubes didn't eat all that much.

"See you in a little bit," she whispered.

Ruby answered with a single snort, then rolled from her back to her side and pulled the sheets over her head.

Out in the hall, Emily joined an older couple dressed in workout gear and wearing sun visors. The wife strode a few feet ahead of her husband with arms at a ninety degree angle from her body.

"Faster, Stu," the woman urged. "We have to get in at least five thousand steps this morning."

Stu puffed and panted behind his wife, slipping past Emily as she exited her cabin. His face reddened with exertion, he looked her up and down and said, "Morning walk?"

She shook her head.

"Lucky you." Stu picked up the pace and caught up to his wife. "How many more steps, baby?"

Emily smiled to herself. All types on the Honeymoon Cruise. In her head, she had imagined only a bunch of young Just Marrieds. Having a variety of age groups and personalities had been a pleasant surprise, the last thing she wanted was to compare herself to other women her age and wonder why she wasn't married yet. Or at least seriously dating someone.

But looking at Stu and 'baby,' it seemed as if love could happen at any age.

A cabin door opened three doors down.

Max!

A ripple of excitement rolled through her.

"Is this really your cabin?" Emily asked as the luscious photographer turned at her words. "I can't believe we didn't figure it out last night."

How was she going to sleep tonight, knowing she was separated from Max by only a few walls?

His dark hair, still damp from the shower, glistened under the hallway lighting. "Emily, good morning." He flashed his perfect teeth and pointed down the hall. "Since my room is closer to that stairwell, I came from that direction last night."

Emily pointed in the opposite direction. "We came from that way. That's hilarious."

"Where's Ruby?" His brows knit together.

Of course he'd ask about her lovely friend.

"She's sleeping in."

"Guess those umbrella drinks caught up to her."

Emily nodded. "Yeah, she was celebrating a little too much."

Max held out an elbow, "Join me for breakfast?"

Butterflies filled her stomach. "Definitely." She linked arms with him and sashayed down the hall to the stairwell on Cloud Nine.

She could pretend she was Mrs. Max Keeling for an hour, couldn't she?

"And then we could talk about that boudoir photo shoot. Seemed as if Ruby wasn't interested...?"

Emily's knees grew weak. Her heart pounded. Every nerve fiber in her body sang like a church choir on Easter morning. With the usual awkwardness that Emily Small could not escape she asked, "Do I need to bring my own, you know, sexy outfits?"

"Oh, you were serious?" Max's face reddened, and he slowed his steps. "Because I...well, how do I say this?"

Emily swallowed and grimaced.

No surprise. Why would Max the Marvelous want to see mini-rhino, Emily, decked out in some godawful silk confection that emphasized her worst features? Chunky thighs. Massive cleavage. Maybe a back or side roll.

Yes, who would want to see that sprawled across a couch or bed?

She laughed it off. "You thought I wanted to do it? Really?" Would he notice the fake quality of her ha-ha-ha? It sounded wooden and forced to her own ears. "Boudoir, schmoudoir. What dumb-dumb would want to do something so...sleazy?"

"Sexy," Max filled in at the same time.

Wait, what? Sexy?

Did he say 'sexy'?

"You think boudoir photos are sleazy?" His Adam's apple bobbed up and down. "I mean, I think some women find them empowering. But I see what you mean. Sort of like soft porn, or whatever. Male fantasy crap." He pulled at the collar of his T-shirt.

Was there a sheen of sweat on his brow? Was handsome should-be-more-confident-than-Harry-Styles nervous? What to make of this?

She patted his arm with her free hand. "I only meant, sometimes it can be so revealing, and I don't want you to be embarrassed. We hardly know each other." Okay, she saved it, right? They were strangers. Even if she had a crazy idea in her mind that somehow Max would be so overcome with passion for her, the photo shoot would turn into something more, she wasn't his type. No way. Not in a million years. Cuckoo thinking.

As they reached the buffet restaurant, he let out a massive sigh. "Exactly. I wouldn't want you to be...uncomfortable."

In front of them, a stream of cruisers entered the massive buffet area on the main deck of the ship. After breakfast, Emily could head straight to the shops in the 'mall' on the same deck and find that bathing suit. Oh, and the underwear. Better than washing out the few pairs she had in the micro sink in their cabin.

"So, breakfast," she said, hoping to redirect the conversation to something safer. "Maybe we can find a table by a window." Scanning the room, she saw one of the staff clearing a table for four right next to a floor-to-ceiling window that faced the glistening sea. "Look!"

"Why don't I hold the table, while you grab some food," Max offered.

What a gentleman.

As the boudoir photo shoot in her mind played on repeat, she sighed at what could've been. A heated touch on her thigh to set the silk just so. A command to jut out a hip or shake out her hair. An uncontrollable desire would grab hold, and he would scoop her up in his arms and carry her to his cabin, slamming the door open, and...

"Is that okay?" he asked, his brows raised and a questioning look in his eyes.

Emily snapped back to reality. "Oh, sorry. I must need coffee. I'll be back in a jiffy."

"Great." Max took a seat at the empty table.

Heading toward a tower of baked goods, Emily sidestepped couple after couple, love birds all, with heads together whispering couples-only secrets and pointing to the foods they wanted to try. The fact she was single hit her hard at that moment. Would she always be alone? Was she too unserious or too unattractive or too something else that made men run in the other direction?

In the beginning, her last boyfriend, Kyle, made her feel attractive and worthy. He'd been complimentary and generous, taking her out to the movies, restaurants, different events. But after they'd slept together, the interest had worn off. As if he'd only been pursuing her for the sex. Once he'd had a taste of what Emily could offer, he'd decided she was of no interest any longer.

But he kept it going for a while, until one day he broke it off without any real explanation. They were waiting in line for a Virginia Tech football game when he said it was over. He blamed it on her new business saying she didn't have time for him anymore, which confused her.

The following weekend when she was deep into baking 'break up' batches of chocolate chip cookies, she ran into Kyle at the grocery store on a resupply run, and he was with another woman. A petite little thing with dark hair and heavy eye makeup and a frown when she heard who Emily was.

Kyle had only stayed with her until he'd found someone better, someone smaller, someone cuter. The memory stung.

As Emily headed toward the short order cook slinging out omelets and bacon, she glanced toward their table. She'd rather have a fantasy about Max than the real thing. The real thing hurt. The real thing was often made up of manipulation and lies. Look at what happened to Ruby. She'd thought Tyler was the 'real thing,' and he'd dumped her an hour before their wedding.

Then she caught sight of Sylvia, the cruise director, who approached Max with a broad smile.

What was she doing here? And why did she look so interested in Max?

Chapter 9
Sylvia's Claws Come Out

Emily confidently headed to their table, set down her food, and said to the attractive cruise director, "Excuse me, please."

Sylvia blocked the chair next to Max where Emily had placed her tray. "I didn't know you had company, Maxwell."

"He does," Emily said. "And it's Max."

Sylvia stepped back.

Emily yanked out her chair and sat. "Thank you," she said in a clipped tone. "Your turn, Max. If you want waffles, you'll have a long wait."

"Sylvia was wondering if we had room at our table." He smiled in that friendly way he had. "I told her that was fine, right?"

Dammit.

"Yes, I suppose that's all right. If you don't have anywhere else to sit—" Emily turned her head for a clearer view of the dining room. Surely there would be an open table, far away in a dark corner behind a plant?

Why did this woman have to ruin her one little moment alone with Max? It wasn't fair.

"Great. Thanks." Sylvia sat in the chair opposite Emily's attractive breakfast date. "I only have a few minutes before I have to make the morning announcements and then there's the first performance at noon in the theater. It's faster eating up here than down in the employee galley, and I might not get another break until the afternoon."

"Why don't I grab a few things for you, then?" Max offered. Super-duper nice Max who didn't owe Sylvia a dang thing was going to pick out her breakfast? "Sounds as if you're going to be busy."

Sylvia lifted a dozen tiny braids from her shoulder and swept them to her back. "That would be so considerate of you, Max." She gave Emily a pointed look and then threw a white, wide smile at him.

"What would you like? Pancakes? Eggs?" He rose from the table.

Sylvia inspected her glitter nail polish and then looked up at him from beneath her possibly fake eyelashes. "Whatever you think I'd like."

Ugh. Gross.

Max wouldn't go for a woman like that. Would he?

He rubbed his jaw. "Um, okay."

After the handsomest man in the room left, Sylvia asked her, "Where's your 'wife'?"

"Asleep. Why?" Emily picked at her lukewarm hash browns.

"Just wondering."

A server appeared with a pitcher of ice water and a pitcher of orange juice. "What would you like?"

Sylvia flipped over one of the glasses on the table. "Water, please."

"No, thank you." Emily drank her coffee with cream and sugar.

The minute the server moved on to other guests, Sylvia leaned across the table and hissed, "Max will never go for a girl like you, you know."

Emily's fork, loaded with scrambled eggs, stopped halfway to her mouth. "Excuse me?"

"Just look at you." Sylvia's gaze roved over the basic shorts and T-shirt Emily wore. "Plain Jane."

The words cut through her and bad memories from middle school when her best friend had enrolled in the Catholic school and left her alone with the public school wolves replayed in her head.

Laardvark.

Carbzilla.

Chunkster.

When she looked back at photos of herself, she hadn't looked much larger than anyone else. Really, it had been her attempt to hide her oversized chest that made her appear larger than she was—loose sweaters, oversized T-shirts, anything to mask the fact she was a thirteen-year-old girl with the rack of a suburban mom in her thirties.

Nevertheless, Sylvia's snark burned.

"I'm here on a cruise with my best friend." Emily used all her willpower to keep her voice from trembling. "And you work for the cruise line. Do you think it's appropriate to interact with a customer like this?"

Emily's appetite fled. She set down her fork.

Sylvia gave a cruel smile that twisted her orange lipsticked mouth. "Right, I wouldn't want to be 'inappropriate' with a paying customer." She sipped her water and stared at Emily over the edge of the glass. "Maybe you'd like me to make some recommendations about how to make the most of your cruise? I know your friend generously let you accompany her after getting dumped by her fiancé. So really, isn't *she* the paying customer?"

Emily looked away. Her cheeks burned. This woman knew everything about Ruby's pain. What was she supposed to do?

Before she could think how to respond, Max reappeared with a tray laden with breakfast foods. "To be safe, I got a little bit of everything: pancakes, muffins, sausage, eggs, danishes, fruit, bacon. The works."

He set a plate in front of Sylvia and smiled.

The cruise director clapped her hands together. "Oh, fabulous. You are really too kind, Max. Too kind. I love it all."

When Max was distracted by his own plate of breakfast goodies, Sylvia glanced across the table at Emily, shrugged her shoulders, and smirked.

* * *

Thirty uncomfortable minutes later, the table of three wrapped up their breakfast.

"Thank you so much for letting me join you," Sylvia said with the fakest smile on her face.

Seriously, anyone could tell it was as fake as the braided weave Sylvia wore on her head.

"Better than dining alone, right Emily?" Max asked. He stretched his lean body and smiled.

Why did he have to be so polite and kind and beautiful?

"Yes, you're so right," Emily agreed, trying not to grit her teeth.

Why couldn't she be as pleasant as Max? Why couldn't she pour on the charm and make Sylvia believe she had no problems whatsoever with a third wheel sharing their breakfast 'date' that wasn't really a date, but was merely a coincidence of fate? A coincidence that led Emily to believe Max could possibly be more than a fantasy. More than a friend. More than a cruise acquaintance who would promptly forget all about her the minute the ship entered port on their last day.

Le sigh.

Sylvia beamed. "You're in a bit of a strange position, Maxwell—I mean, Max. Sorry."

"That's okay." He waved his hand in protest. "I know Emily thinks it bugs me, but it happens all the time."

It didn't bug him? Was it weird that Emily had been correcting people? Or was Max sorta kinda liking this dark-skinned, attractive, intruding cruise director?

Heat flooded her cheeks.

Sylvia's gaze flipped to Emily and then back to Max. "What I meant to say, rather inelegantly, is that you are more than welcome to hang out with us crew when you're free." She reached across the table and touched his arm. "I know it's a bit awkward to be on deck with all of these honeymooning couples when you're single."

Sylvia touched his arm.

Alarm bells sounded in her head.

But what could Emily do? She was as much a stranger to Max as Sylvia. Why wouldn't he accept such a nice invitation from a pretty-ish single woman flirting with him over empty orange juice glasses, French toast crusts, and cold ham?

Time to stick her neck out.

Emergency situation!

"Yes, Ruby and I have been chatting with Max about that

very thing...the awkwardness. As single, available women"—
Emily emphasized the word 'available' a little too strongly—
"surrounded by married couples, we offered to band together.
The three of us. To make the cruise a little more enjoyable."
Then she smiled the sweetest, kindest smile she knew how to
smile. "It would really be wonderful, Sylvia, if you could give
us your professional opinion—as an employee of the cruise ship
—what the best excursions are for a threesome. Or maybe even
entertainment on the ship?"

"Oh?" Sylvia put a hand to her chest. "You need recommendations? I thought you did just fine at the trivia contest
last night." She directed her next words at Max. "Weren't
their answers hilarious? I mean, my God, I don't know if I
would've been so brave as to reveal some of the personal stuff
they did."

Emily's breath hitched in her throat.

Don't you dare say it. Don't you dare.

"The noises? In the bedroom?" Sylvia waved a hand back
and forth in front of her face as if her temperature had risen
several degrees.

Max fidgeted in his chair and cleared his throat. "Right.
Pretty revealing."

He wouldn't look at Emily. In fact, he seemed to be going
out of his way to look at anything but her. Up, down, left, right.

A thin, tall server appeared at their table. "Madame, may I
take your plate?"

Thank God.

"Yes, please." Emily glanced at her watch, pretending to
read the time. "Oh, dear, looks like I need to be going." Whatever it took to escape from the conversation. Even if it meant
leaving the company of Max. "Ruby will be awake any
minute."

"Oh, then do scamper off." Sylvia made a shooing motion with her hands. "I'll make sure Max is entertained."

Dammit.

This whole breakfast thing was not working out as she'd planned.

Max scooted back his chair. "Let me go with you, Em, and I can pick up my jacket."

Em? Did he call her Em?

She almost fainted.

Only Emily noticed the dejected look that marred Sylvia's pretty face. The cruise director only let that slip for a few moments before pasting on her usual wide smile.

"I suppose I need to go to work anyway." Sylvia shrugged and wiped her mouth with a folded napkin. "I'm sure we'll see each other again. It's not a very big ship."

As Max and Emily headed for the exit, he leaned in close and whispered, "Thanks for saving me back there."

Emily had the strong awareness of her own heartbeat. *Boom. Boom. Boom.* "Save you?" If he came any closer, her heart might burst.

They rounded the corner and headed for the stairs.

"She was coming on to me pretty strong. Didn't you notice?" Max cleared his throat. "Or does that sound as if I'm stuck on myself? Did I misread her?" He looked over his shoulder. "I did, didn't I? Penny used to tell me it was all in my head."

Since when did a supremely handsome man come up with the idea that he was unattractive? Not possible.

"What was all in your head?" To hear his insecurities was truly fascinating.

"My assumptions about women."

She shook her head. "I don't think it was a wrong assumption."

"You don't?" As they reached the stairwell, he slowed his steps. "Okay. Because I have been doubting my abilities to read women lately."

Considering he had yet to notice Emily's blushes, word stumbles, and simplistic flirtations, maybe he was onto something.

"Women can be subtle sometimes." Her chest tightened as she said the words.

Why not just confess?

You are super-hot and I am on fire for you, but you haven't even noticed.

Yikes. No. That would not be good. Focus, Emily, focus.

"But her?" She thumbed toward the buffet entrance. "Yeah, she was full-on flirt level five thousand."

"Five thousand?" His gaze followed the direction of her thumb just in time to see tall, svelte Sylvia glide toward the elevator. "I don't know. She scares me."

"She does?" Emily choked on the question. Max being scared of any woman seemed ludicrous. He could have any woman he wanted.

"She's the type of person who is hot and cold." As he spoke, he kept his eyes on the cruise director as if expecting her to turn around and bite his head off. "I don't know what to make of her. Where is the real Sylvia under all that?"

"She wasn't very nice to you when we were checking in."

"How did you know—?" His brow furrowed. "Were you and Ruby next in line behind me?"

"I'm surprised you didn't remember Ruby." She wanted to say: no man ever forgets Ruby.

"My mind was all over the place. I didn't know what I was doing, and I was in a bit of a panic because Penelope flaked on me." He scraped a hand through his hair. "Not as if I was surprised she flaked, but it was a free vacation. I thought she wouldn't pass it up. Then she didn't show." He sighed. "I've never been on a cruise, and I was freaking out about being stuck on a ship for ten days. Alone. My God, it was horrifying to think about."

"Yeah, well, you kinda knocked me over, so maybe it's better you don't remember." Emily gave a half-hearted laugh.

"I did? Are you serious?" He pinched the bridge of his nose and closed his eyes. "I thought I'd run into a garbage can."

Yep. He said it. She was the size, weight, and shape of a garbage can. Great. How does a woman come back from that?

"Nope." Again with the laugh. Could she fade into the ocean-themed wallpaper and turn invisible? "It was me."

"God, I'm sorry." As he searched her face, his soft green eyes made her melt. "What a jerk you must've thought I was."

"Eh, I'm used to it." She waved it off.

"Used to it? What do you mean?"

"Not being noticed." Couldn't he see how incredibly boring and plain she was in comparison to other women her age?

"Why wouldn't people notice a cute girl like you?"

Did he call her cute?

She wanted to clutch her chest and cry out for the Lord to take her home. Life could not be any better than this moment.

"You'd be surprised how many people don't notice me."

"I don't believe that." He poked her playfully in the arm. "I'll bet back home the guys are falling all over you. In fact, I'll bet if this were a singles cruise, you wouldn't even be giving me the time of day."

"Ha, ha." Beyond the elevators, she noticed the ship stores

opening for business. Her need for underwear shoved itself ahead of 'flirt more with Max' in her mind. "Oh shoot, I have to do some shopping before Ruby wakes up. But we're still on for poolside, right?"

"Oh." A bitter smile crossed his lips.

"Your jacket." She turned toward the stairs. "We can still go get it."

"No, no, that's okay." His fingertips brushed her elbow. "It really was my excuse for getting out of there."

"I can bring it to the pool."

"Sure. That'd be fine." He lingered for a moment, his gaze meeting hers.

Emily's heart thudded. That look had her reconsidering the boudoir photo shoot. Was it too late to revisit the topic?

Chapter 10
Max the Photographer

Max flashed a smile that could melt a thousand icebergs and leave the whole of the world's penguin population floundering at sea. "Noon. Pool Deck." He fired off finger pistols. "See you there." He looked down at his hands. "Did I just fire finger bullets at you? That's embarrassing." In a flash, he tucked them into the pockets of his well-fitting khaki shorts.

Emily mimicked being shot in the chest. "You got me." She stumbled backward and ran into a honeymooning couple who didn't find her antics amusing.

Max grimaced and mouthed *'I'm sorry.'*

"Uh, oh, excuse me." She regained her footing, shook out her hair, and apologized to the newlyweds. "I was fake shot." She smiled and pointed at Max.

The woman, with hair piled high on her head and supported by a neck so thin it could possibly snap, curled her lip. "Maybe skip the mimosa next time."

Her husband grabbed her by the elbow and steered her around the weirdo that was Emily. "Let's go, dear."

Emily brushed her hands together. "Zero sense of humor." She winked at Max.

He held back a laugh until the couple rounded a corner and disappeared from view.

In her pocket, her phone vibrated.

Uh-oh.

That could only mean one thing: a text from Ruby in the cruise line's app.

She plucked it out and read the message. "Ruby's awake. Sorry, Max, I have to run. Gotta grab a few things and then make sure she doesn't need some Pepto or something."

What poor timing. They were on a roll doing stupid stuff, which made her nerves melt away and turned Max into the most approachable hot guy she'd ever fantasized about.

"Got it." Max backed toward the stairs. "See you at noon. Drinks, music, sun. What could be better?"

She waved then booked it for the little mall in the main atrium where she'd seen a few boutiques with clothing in the window. With Ruby awake, she wouldn't have much time to be choosy. Grab some undies, pick out a decent one-piece—because curvy Emily only felt comfortable in a one-piece—and head for the cabin. Maybe she could grab a Bloody Mary for Ruby on the way back? Hair of the dog and all.

She entered the atrium and gaped at the height of the ceiling: at least three decks, maybe four decks, high. Chandeliers hung over a glistening, marble-floored space that echoed with conversation and footsteps as a multitude of couples wandered from fore to aft. It was here that a passenger could shop or pick up a cup of coffee and a pastry at the snack bar—a small café open from morning until night serving drinks, pizza, sandwiches, cookies, and pastries of every variety.

Heading straight for a store that had windows filled with

sexy lingerie, she prayed they had sensible undies. Everything in the window appeared to be thong-oriented or made of scratchy-yet-dainty lace.

When she entered, a helpful male clerk with short, bleached blond hair headed her way. He had been unboxing push-up bras in the back, and his eyes lit up at her appearance. "Good morning! How may I help you?" he asked with a lilt in his voice and the flutter of his hands.

"I need some basics." Her face heated at the admission. Why? She'd bought underwear before at lingerie stores. It wasn't as if everything in her unmentionables drawer was purchased at Target or Walmart. Perhaps it was the fact she kept envisioning a boudoir photo shoot with Max—the photo shoot would never happen and would only be in her fantasies. But buying plain, cotton undies made her heart sink. Why couldn't she buy something fun and adventurous?

"Basics. Got it." The clerk set an elbow on his hand, touched his chin for a few seconds, and scanned her figure. "We've got some sensible stuff near the register that would be your size."

Sensible.

It sounded as if she were buying underwear for her eighty-two-year-old grandmother or a nun.

Sensible equaled boring. Sensible equaled forever single. Sensible is the last thing Emily wanted to be.

She followed the clerk, passing by see-through panties and silk thongs and underwear that young, beautiful women wore. "Stop!" She ground to a halt in front of a rainbow display. "I'll take these." She plucked a bright pink thong off the rack. "And these." Zebra striped and shiny. "And these." Lacy barely-there teeny tiny things.

Why not?

Her vacation. Her money to spend. Her fun to have.

"Oh, I see." The clerk stared at the pile. "And the basics?"

"Forget about the basics." She grabbed five more pairs. Enough to carry her through the ten days of her cruise.

"Wonderful." The clerk gathered up her selections and rang them up at the register.

"Do they carry large bust-size bikinis next door?" If she was going to be bold about her underwear choices, why not do the same for swimwear? The last time she'd wanted to wear a bikini, she'd been twelve years old and as flat as a pancake.

He handed her back her credit card. "I think they go all the way up to a G cup. They expanded their offerings in the last year or so. More demand. You should be able to find something that works." With a grin, he handed her a bag with her purchases. "Hope you and your husband have a wonderful cruise."

Her mind flashed to an afternoon poolside with Max and Ruby. "Oh, I'm sure we will."

At the door to their cabin, Emily held up her key card. Two bags weighed her down at the elbow, and in her other hand she held a Bloody Mary. She'd already dribbled some on the carpet and was hoping she could push the handle with her ass to get inside. She hadn't planned this out very well.

Luckily, when the door lock clicked Ruby opened it.

"Where have you been?" Ruby had circles under her eyes, a green pallor to her usually flawless skin, and a tangle of auburn hair on one side of her head. "Is that for me?" She plucked the Bloody Mary out of Emily's hands.

Emily trailed behind her best friend, closed the door, and

set her bags on the vanity space next to their phone chargers. "Breakfast, then shopping. If you recall I didn't pack for a ten-day cruise. I was supposed to be back in Roanoke already."

Besides the underwear and a bikini, she'd grabbed a few T-shirts on sale, an extra pair of shorts, and a halter sundress that looked easy to wear.

"Oh, right, I forgot." Ruby plunked down on the bed and covered her bare thighs with the sheets. The sliding door to their balcony stood wide open. "I needed some fresh air. But I'm sure this will make me feel even better." She took a deep drink of her beverage. "You are a lifesaver."

Emily surveyed her friend. "Are you sure you don't want me to order some dry toast?" She picked up the cabin phone to call room service.

The former bride crunched on a piece of celery. "I'll be all right."

Emily set the receiver down. "Guess we should be glad we're at sea today. Tomorrow is our first port call. Plenty of time for you to recover from last night and rest up."

"Last night. Right." Ruby set down the glass and put a hand to her forehead. "The trivia contest. All those newly-weds with their husbands. If Tyler had been here, we would've aced it." She sniffled. "He knew everything about me. Everything. Things I never shared with anyone before. I can't believe I'll never see him again—" She sucked in a lungful of air.

Uh-oh.

No lingering thoughts about Tyler were allowed. No way. No how. He was a cad. A jerk. The lowest of the low. He deserved no thoughts whatsoever. This cruise was to be fun, enjoyable, a laugh-a-minute. No time for sadness.

"Sweetie," Emily said, joining her friend on the bed and

wrapping an arm around her shoulders. "Tyler doesn't deserve you."

"What am I going to do, Em? I'm a twenty-nine-year-old Old Maid." A single tear rolled down her perfect cheek.

"I don't think Old Maids are a thing anymore." For some reason, her mind flashed to a self-help book she'd read after Kyle broke up with her. "We're strong, independent women who don't need men to be happy in life. We make our own destinies. We create our own fulfillment." There was something else about enlightenment or maybe was it a light recipe that had less than four-hundred calories a serving?

"But I like men," Ruby said in a little voice. She wiped tears off her face.

Emily sighed. "So do I. Guess we're doomed."

Ruby gulped down more of her Bloody Mary. "Yeah, doomed." She giggled.

Emily smiled and patted her friend on the arm. "You are gorgeous and wonderful and kind. There are plenty of men out there who'd die to date you, much less marry you. Forget about Tyler. Let's find you Mr. X."

"Mr. X?"

"Yeah, your perfect man. Time for you to build a list of what you want in a husband."

"I thought I wanted Tyler." Ruby sniffed again.

"No, you are not allowed to bring him up anymore." Emily wagged a finger. "Remember? Our pact?"

Ruby nodded.

"Okay, so let's talk perfect man instead." Emily to the rescue. No more wallowing in self-pity. "If you could pick what you wanted in your next fiancé what would you choose?"

"Tall."

"Wait! Let me make a list." Emily hopped up off the bed

and grabbed a pad of paper and a pen provided by the cruise line. "Tall. Got it. What's next?"

"At least six-foot-two."

"Six-foot-two. Okay."

"Dark. I like a man with a good head of dark hair."

"Dark hair. What about personality traits?"

"A sense of humor. But not that stupid middle school boy kind of humor."

"No fart jokes. Got it."

"A good job. Doesn't have to make a million dollars, but he has to have a job."

"Job. Check."

"Adventurous. I want someone who will jump out of airplanes with me."

As they crafted Ruby's list, Emily couldn't help but let her mind wander to her ideal man. When she'd first laid eyes on Max at the port, everything she'd thought about him had been based on looks alone. To be honest, it was nearly impossible to avoid. The man was perfection on two feet. But with each new encounter she had, the more she realized he was so much more than wavy dark hair, rippling muscles, and sexy green eyes. Behind all of that, Max made her smile and never once made her feel insignificant or unworthy of notice.

"Did you write down that last one?" Ruby sat cross-legged on the bed and drank the dregs of her Bloody Mary. "Bi-lingual. I want someone who can speak French or Spanish or maybe Chinese. I don't know. Wouldn't that be cool?"

Emily shook her head. She'd lost track of the conversation. "Got it. Bi-lingual."

"When we're at the pool later, we should ask Max's opinion," Ruby suggested.

"His opinion?" Emily finished the list, ripped it off the paper pad, and tossed it at her friend.

"Yeah, maybe we should get a man's opinion on my list. He might have some suggestions." Ruby scooped up the list and reviewed it. "You know, a guy's perspective. What else should I be thinking about?"

"Sure, why not?" Emily shrugged.

"Show me what you bought." Ruby trotted over to her shopping bags. "Anything cute?" She dumped out the swimsuit first.

Emily's stomach tightened.

"Oh wow." Ruby held up the shiny green metallic two-piece with gold braiding that weaved in and out of eyelets all around the edges of the top and bottom. "This is stunning."

"I know it's not really me—" She knew her face was probably as red at the remnants of the Bloody Mary in the glass on the nightstand.

"What do you mean?"

"I don't wear bikinis."

"You don't? Since when?" Ruby held up the top, which had a solid underwire and plenty of support.

"Since the seventh grade."

Ruby stared at her. "You're kidding me."

"Um, no I'm not." She snatched the suit away from her friend. "When you've got my boobs—"

"You show them off!"

* * *

The two best friends dumped their tote bags next to three empty deck chairs beside the pool and within easy walking distance of the tiki bar. The overcast skies had kept a crowd away, but the warm tropical air made lounging poolside as inviting as if the sun shone full force. Relaxed reggae music poured from hidden speakers, perhaps as an homage to their first port of call: Jamaica.

"Where's Max?" Ruby scanned the half-empty pool deck. "I don't see him."

Emily wasn't about to confess she'd been scrutinizing every male body within her view and analyzing him for Max characteristics. "I don't either." Did her voice sound whiny only to her own ears?

Ruby shrugged. "Maybe something came up." Without another worry in her pretty little head, she slipped out of her gauzy floral cover up.

Did choirs of angels break out into song? Possibly.

It was as if Emily could hear the gaze of every man in the vicinity turn their way—bald men, short men, old men, young men, men in the pool, men by the bar, men walking by, men reading books. They all looked.

Ruby in a swimsuit had that affect. The suit wasn't even her sexiest one. Just a plain blue bikini top paired with some floral board shorts. But she had legs for days and a toned midsection. Plus, something about Ruby in a pair of high fashion sunglasses with her auburn hair rippling down her back...so chic.

"Get some sun, girlfriend." Ruby pushed at Emily's leg with her foot as she rested against the propped up back of the lounge chair, oblivious to the male stares and female frowns.

Okay, maybe back in their cabin, two-piece swimsuit in hand, Emily had been bold. Had been confident. Had been sure about her choice to buy this riot of a green bikini. Had resolved to wear it in public, in view of her cruise crush, Max.

Now?

Now she wasn't so sure.

Max had been her inspiration. Buoyed by his statement that she was cute, she'd had the distant hope he might find her body appealing in such a thing. But without Max? Confidence bubble burst.

Without a cover-up in her arsenal, she'd hidden her suit under a pair of shorts and a loose white T-shirt with 'Cruise Crazy' screen printed on the front in a rainbow of colors. Her heart thudded at the idea of removing the shirt to reveal the barely-there bikini.

What had she been thinking? Nobody wanted to see her in a suit like this. Especially next to bombshell Ruby. She'd only look as if she was trying to compete with her best friend. Or, to the cruisers, her wife. That would be weird.

She hugged herself and stood there, uncertain.

Ruby slid her sunglasses down her nose. "Take off that shirt. We are here to look amazing by the pool and if we don't come back with a tan, our revenge will not be as sweet. If I run into Tyler at Whole Foods, I want him to be avocado toast green with envy. Both of us must be tan and gorgeous." Her friend tugged at the edge of Emily's shirt. "Take it off."

Emily's stomach rolled like a ship tossed on the waves during a storm. "I need a minute, Rubes." She brushed of her friend's hand. "Maybe I can do this in steps. I mean, this is the first time I've worn a bikini in sixteen years."

Ruby raised a finger as if an idea had struck, swung her legs around, and stood. "This calls for a margarita. That should help."

While Emily rooted herself to the deck, her mind a mess of worries and stray thoughts about her body, Ruby confidently strode to the bar and ordered drinks.

Why couldn't she be more like Ruby? Why did she care so

much about what people thought? Especially here on a honeymoon cruise? These were all married couples. Not a single man here had an interest in her or her lumpy body.

"Here." Ruby handed her a huge margarita that could serve a whole Mexican village. "Drink up. Then let's see how you feel."

Emily accepted the drink and sat on a deck chair. Couldn't hurt to try.

* * *

Meanwhile on the deck above the pool area...

Max crouched next to his camera bag and rifled through it.

Where did that long lens go?

This was bullshit. Nothing in his contract had mentioned photos outside of the studio.

"We only need you out here for a couple of hours, and then you can go." Sylvia stood over him with crossed arms. "Not as if you had anything better to do."

"Right," he said through clenched teeth. What choice did he have? He needed the cash from this gig, so he couldn't upset the cruise line. The cruise director represented his employer. If he wanted another job like this one, guess he had to do as told.

Sylvia pointed at clumps of people dancing on a makeshift dance floor near the pool. "See over there? Capture some of that and maybe by the bar. The pretty people. The smiling people. The hot ones—like her."

Sylvia's pointing finger landed on Ruby Evers.

Max lifted the view finder to his eye and focused in on the

young woman as she lifted a margarita to her lips. He snapped a few photos of his new friend. She looked the part of a fashionable young traveler who'd attract the target audience for the cruise line.

"Remember." She touched his shoulder. "These aren't for sale. They're marketing photos."

He flinched under the unexpected contact. His camera lens dipped, and the focus shifted to the person in the chair next to Ruby's. A woman pulling off a T-shirt to reveal a sexy green metallic bikini top.

He adjusted the lens to bring the mystery woman into focus. Sylvia said 'the hot ones,' and this woman had potential. Two scoops of flesh in a very flattering top. Maybe her face matched her body.

"Looks as if you have a handle on this," Sylvia said. "Let's meet up later in the crew lounge belowdecks, and you can show me the best ones. Then we'll ask the guests to sign release forms."

The T-shirt came off completely.

Emily.

He sucked in a breath.

Wow.

His thumb pressed on the shutter button, and without thinking he took a quick string of photos: Emily, Emily, Emily, Emily, Emily.

Heat crept across his cheeks.

Why did it feel so wrong? He had a job to do, and Sylvia even pointed out people she wanted him to photograph. But taking secret photos of his friends? No. He needed to find other people to target.

Without Sylvia's oppressive presence to hamper his creativity, he swung his camera away from Emily and toward the group of dancers. They were all ages. Some wore shorts and tank tops, and some had on swimwear.

For thirty minutes he took photo after photo. Newlyweds kissing by the bar. Newlyweds splashing in the pool. Newlyweds grooving to Bob Marley. More innocent. More fun-filled. Less sexy.

Although the job as ship's photographer sounded like loser-level photography work when he'd accepted it, the emotions he captured on the pool deck reminded him of why he loved what he did so much. Each shot was a moment in time and could reveal the soul of an individual. A smile, a look, even wrinkles. The whole of the human experience displayed on a face.

How would he think about the work if it were for a gallery opening?

He changed the angle of his shots and used the muted light from the cloudy afternoon to wring what he could out of ordinary photos. The kinds of photos he'd avoided taking to make sure he kept his portfolio professional

What would Penny say? Would Penny think these photos were jejune—her favorite descriptive word—and low brow?

Penny had thought she was dating an artist. She thought his photos were brilliant and groundbreaking. Until his gallery showing had been a bust, and he hadn't sold a thing. Well, he sold one framed piece to his neighbor, who caught him hauling all of his work back home.

Max hadn't even charged the guy full price.

Penny had been embarrassed by the transaction.

He lowered his camera, his mind numb.

"Hey, mister." A middle-aged woman wearing a caftan and glittery high heels waved at him from a clump of deck chairs twenty feet away. "Could you take our picture?" She gestured at a woman standing next to her in the same get-up. "We're twins!"

An emptiness filled him. His work had been reduced to vacation photos and pictures for brochures. Not the dream he had five years ago when he'd left a dead-end corporate job to pursue his passion for photography.

"Sure, ladies." He used all of his mental energy to give as real a smile as he could muster. "I'll be right there."

As he grabbed his camera bag, he caught one more glance of Emily and Ruby relaxing by the pool. If only he could've kept his word and spent the afternoon lazing with them, drinking some crazy beverage, and chatting about meaningless fluff. But why would they want to hang out with a failed photographer? Pathetic.

Chapter 11
That Wasn't the Assignment

As the hour grew later and the gray clouds thinned, it was obvious Max had stood them up.

Emily ran through the last conversation she'd had with the photographer after breakfast. He'd been upbeat, funny, a little bit flirtatious—or so she thought. Maybe his declaration about her being 'cute' had been merely a kindness.

Her heart shrank a few sizes.

She scanned the happily married couples around her. Yeah, that would probably never be her. Even Ruby had been let down by men. Amazing, stunning Ruby. If Ruby couldn't find a man who wanted to marry her, why did Emily think someone would want to settle down with her?

And not even marry, for God's sake. For some reason, she couldn't even find a decent guy who wanted to date her. According to the internet, that supposedly meant she was too confident and too self-reliant, therefore, men feared her.

The internet was bullshit.

The clouds parted, and the sun shone down on the pool deck. What had been comfortable only a few minutes earlier—

bathing suit covered by T-shirt and shorts—quickly became too warm. Emily guzzled the last of her massive margarita, frowned at the sweat forming on her brow, and whipped off her T-shirt.

"That's it, Em! Revenge honeymoon!" Ruby cheered making a toast in the air with her empty margarita glass. Noticing she'd run out of booze, she rose from her deck chair. "I'm gonna go order two more of these. But you go, girl."

Without Max around, who was Emily trying to impress exactly? No man wanted her anyway. She could walk naked across the deck and nobody would bat an eye. Soon enough she'd be a single woman in her 30s with no prospects and probably cellulite and sagging boobs. May as well make the best of what she had while she had it. Whatever 'it' was.

Ruby danced her way across the deck toward the bar, making a few complete spins with a couple of stumbles.

Emily shed her shorts. She hoped she didn't have a wedgie. The bikini bottoms were a little high cut for the size of her rear end. For a brief moment, she had a flash that the whole ship stared at her and laughed behind their hands at the spectacle.

Then the alcohol fuzzed out her worries. Why did she care so much? These were all married men and women around her. On their honeymoons. They had better things to think about than a slightly pudgy woman who could use a few crunches in a too tiny bikini. Honeymoons should be about sex, sex, and more sex. Not some rando on the pool deck with an overinflated view of herself in a swimsuit.

She adjusted the metallic green top that had crept up a little when she shed her T-shirt. Maybe the next size up would've been better?

Whatever.

"What's a 'revenge honeymoon'?" one of the ship's roving

staff, wearing purple-rimmed glasses and a short bob hairstyle, asked as she swept away their empty margarita glasses.

Whoops. Had Ruby said that out loud?

The tequila hit her with a bang.

Whoa.

"My friend's fiancé left her at the altar. So she invited me on the cruise to exact revenge on him." The words tumbled out without hardly a thought. "A honeymoon cruise without a honeymoon."

Oh no.

What did she just say?

"Wow," the young woman said. "What a scumbag." She touched Emily on the arm. "Please let her know how sorry I am."

"Thanks." Emily's throat felt as if it were closing up. What did she and her big drunk mouth just do?

As the woman moved on to the next set of empty glasses, Ruby arrived with two more mega margaritas. "What was that about?"

Emily's gaze followed the server, who knew her best friend's most terrible secret, while she scooped up used napkins and shot glasses around the pool deck. "Um, nothing. Just asking if we needed more towels."

She hid her mouth behind her hand.

This was bad. Very bad. Extremely bad.

The server approached another of the ship's staff, a man in a suit jacket with a more formal appearance. The young woman and he spoke for a few minutes before the server nodded and pointed across the deck at Emily and Ruby. The man raised a brow and took some notes on a clipboard.

Emily had a funny feeling in her stomach.

"A toast to the bride and bride." Ruby plopped on the lounge chair and raised her very full glass to the sky. "Cheers!"

* * *

Max wiped the sweat off his brow as he went belowdecks to look for Sylvia. He'd completed his assignment on the pool deck, spent a good hour sorting through the photos, and selected the best ones to share. He'd saved the photos of Ruby and the accidental photos of Emily in a separate folder on his laptop. It didn't feel right to include his new friends with the other pictures.

Especially the Emily photos.

For a fleeting moment he'd considered deleting them. But for some reason he held onto the photos of the funny, yet cute, Emily.

Because of that bikini?

Damn.

Did she have any idea what her body in that swimsuit did to every man with a pulse on the pool deck?

He shook his head to clear his mind of the dirty ideas he had developing...such wrong dirty ideas. Mostly because he'd just met the woman after a nasty split with Penny.

Did he really need to jump into another relationship? Emily could be a cruise connection and a fun distraction until they arrived back in Tampa. But he liked her too much to wreck their little friendly threesome. The cruise lasted ten days. Couldn't he set aside any sexual thoughts and find a way to enjoy their burgeoning friendship? Was he really incapable of reining in his sexual side?

No, he was not.

A bad break-up didn't absolve him of treating a woman the

way she deserved to be treated: as a person, not a sex object. Emily was worth his time. She was funny and normal and even a little bit awkward, which made her even cuter. Plus, when he put his own foot in his mouth, which he was very capable of doing, he felt a little less stupid.

At the bottom of the stairs he ran into a ship employee he recognized from last night's honeymoon photo shoot. "Debbie?"

The average-looking blonde wearing pink lip gloss and too much mascara gave him the once over. "Do I know you?" Her mouth turned up in a smile.

That smile gave him the confidence to ask even the stupidest questions. Easier to seek out women to find answers than men. Women tended to be happy to help. Men? Not so much, he'd found in recent years.

He scanned the hall in both directions. "I'm looking for the crew lounge?" Maybe they'd have some signs?

"Guests aren't allowed in the crew area." Debbie blocked the way with her body. "Is there someone in particular you wished to speak with?" The happy light in her eyes had extinguished.

"I'm not exactly a guest." Sylvia would probably agree. "I'm the photographer. Didn't you help with the photo shoot last night?" Maybe she didn't remember him he was wearing a pair of swim trunks and a Hawaiian shirt rather than his professional work wear. "I'm Max." He flashed his best smile. Women usually remembered the smile.

Her nose wrinkled, and a flush crept across her pale cheeks. "Oh, Max. I'm sorry. I didn't recognize you."

"That's okay. I'm looking for Sylvia. She wanted to meet in the crew lounge."

She looked away and fiddled with a thin gold necklace

around her neck. "Sylvia?" She swallowed. "Um, yeah, I did see her in there a few minutes ago." She pointed aft. "Down there, on the left, the sign's on the door."

Max sneaked a peek down the hall. "Great. Thanks. I appreciate it."

Debbie stepped aside and let him pass. "You're lucky she's in a good mood."

Max's eyebrows shot up.

The crew lounge was narrow, but brightly lit by overhead can lights and several portholes that were a deck above sea level. Couches lined one wall with bright blue chairs facing them and small round tables between. A large flat screen TV with a soccer match playing hung on the wall. A few crew members enjoyed a game of foosball, while other crew sat at a small bar near the back of the lounge.

When Max entered, a pair of Hispanic women who sat near the door eyed him with interest.

"Max, back here," Sylvia called out from a table near the bar. While taking a drink from a bottle of hard lemonade, she waved a hand beckoning him.

Not a bad space for the crew to relax when off-duty, and it was nice to escape from the lovey-dovey honeymoon couples up top, which only reminded him of his break-up with Penny and how lonely his apartment would be once he returned home. She'd been a handful and a bit of a snob, but at the beginning it had been really good. The thought of starting all over with someone new—the small talk, the awkwardness—tired him.

Sylvia patted the empty space on the couch next to her. "Can't wait to see what you've got. I've been trying to convince the Captain we need to modernize our ads. This could mean a big promotion for me if we play our cards right."

We?

A promotion for her on the back of his photography? Hm. That didn't sound promising. "I'd receive credit for my work, right?" Maybe he should've scrutinized his contract with the cruise line a little bit better. If only he hadn't needed the cash so badly. Did he miss something?

"Slow down, cowboy." She laughed and touched his arm.

Cowboy?

Max looked down at his attire.

"Let's look at what you have first." The cruise director stroked her long, elegant neck with a well-manicured hand.

He grimaced, but hid his expression while removing his laptop from its bag. "I picked out the best of the bunch. I think you'll find something in here that you like."

He fired it up and then navigated to the folder labeled: 'Pool Photos.'

Sylvia grabbed the laptop before he could even click on a single one. "I know what I'm looking for. It'll go a lot faster if I go through them myself."

Max held his hands up.

Wow. Aggressive.

She reminded him a bit of Penelope when they'd first met. A force. He'd noticed her in downtown Miami. She dressed like a fashion model, but had an interesting face. Unusual some would say. A slightly crooked, too-big nose, a mouth that was a few centimeters too wide, and a very high forehead. She wore her hair swept back and in a complicated twist. But to his creative brain, he saw natural beauty that would jump out in photo.

He'd asked if he could photograph her.

After that first photo shoot, she'd leapt into his life with all guns blazing. First, she helped him dress better. Then she introduced him to her stylist at the most fashionable salon in the city, and they transformed his shaggy, too-long hair into something more refined and more flattering to his face.

And he'd welcomed it. What did he care about clothes or hair? He merely wanted to photograph his new muse as much as possible. Beach shots, night shots, silhouettes. Oh, those silhouettes. Her profile, with her large nose, created a superb effect. That had been his first professional piece to win accolades and even an award in a small, but prestigious, local contest.

Penelope pushed him to believe in his work and to experiment with his photography. At first, the successes came easily. He sold photo after photo without much effort. But that last show? The failure? He hadn't been anticipating that one. And it hurt.

Sylvia frowned. "Wait, where's the picture of that redhead? The hot one? I don't see her here."

Dammit.

Ruby.

He was hoping Sylvia had forgotten about her. He didn't feel right about using his friend in such a way.

"They didn't come out very well," he lied. "I told you I picked the best ones."

"Where are they?" She scrolled through the photos for a second time as if they would magically appear. "I'll be the judge of that."

"I deleted them." He rubbed his hands on the legs of his shorts.

"You deleted them?" She cocked her head and raised an eyebrow. "Why?"

Max shrugged.

Would she blow her top?

Sylvia sighed loudly. "That's just great. I guess we'll have to go with some of these." She scrolled through the photos one last time. "Put the ones I selected on a thumb drive, would you? Then I'll need you to have the guests in them fill out waivers. I'll email the form to you."

"Wait." The pitch of his voice rose a notch or two. "You're expecting me to track all of these people down?"

"Yes. That's your job." She pushed his laptop toward him. "You're the photographer."

"But...do you know how long that will take?" His stomach hardened. "There's over three thousand people on this ship."

"You didn't expect me to waste *my* time with it, did you?" Sylvia's back grew rigid, and she lifted her chin slightly.

Was she kidding? If he had known he'd be the one tracking down the dozens of people in the photos she'd selected, he would've asked for copies of the form to be available there on the pool deck. What a joke. The photography part of the cruise wasn't supposed to take up all of his time. Where was the relaxation part? At this rate, he'd be lucky to have time at any of the ports.

"Great. Thanks, Max." She flashed a brilliant smile at him, as if he had agreed to the chore. "Excellent work. I'll be sure to recommend you to the cruise line for another cruise."

She dangled the carrot as if she'd done it many times before. "I'll need that thumb drive tonight after dinner. I have a staff meeting with the captain, and I'd like to be able to present my idea."

Dammit.

Chapter 12
The Devil's Drink

"Do you think I'm sunburned?" Emily touched her stomach with a forefinger, and a pale white mark appeared then flared up into bright red. A stomach that hadn't seen the sun for more than fifteen years? Yikes. What had she been thinking when she laughed off sunscreen? But it had been cloudy earlier. Who thinks about sunscreen on a cloudy day?

Ruby, deep into her second mega margarita, burst into laughter. "Oh yeah, that's bad, Em."

In a bit of a panic, Emily checked the line of skin beneath the waistband of her bikini bottoms. A bright red line separated the white skin hidden under the green fabric. "Crap. This is our first day. We have a bunch of tropical beaches to visit. I can't go out on the beach with a sunburn."

Ruby sobered a bit and checked her own skin. "Oh, man, doesn't look good." She, too, had a splotchy red sunburn on her stomach, chest and thighs. "And I didn't even swim in the pool yet."

Emily sat up looking down at her arms. "This is going to hurt. Did you bring any aloe?"

Ruby donned her swim cover up and threw a towel across her legs. "What?"

"Aloe. For sunburns." Emily picked up her T-shirt and put it on. When she pulled it back down over her head, a few women gave her glares. *What the hell? Why?* Something wrong with a fat sunburned whale taking up space on the pool deck? Red and green. She must look like a Christmas tree.

"I brought some SPF fifteen."

"Why didn't we think to bring it to the pool?"

"I was saving it for the beach."

"Damn, Rubes." Panic filled Emily as she examined more of her skin. "We need to get out of the sun."

"Aw, but it's so nice out here." Ruby wrapped a towel around her neck and chest to cover what was left exposed to the sun.

"You're going to sweat in all of that. Come on, let's go back to the room." Emily stood and assessed her arms for a second time. Maybe they weren't as red as they appeared out here in the sun?

Ruby dropped the two towels she'd been using as a sun shield and drank the last sip of her drink.

"Maybe we can stop at one of the stores to see if they sell aloe or some cream." Emily stepped into her shorts and then slipped her feet into her sandals. "Are you feeling the burn already?"

Ruby held her arms out from her sides. "I think so." It was hard to tell if Ruby's face was red and splotchy from sunburn or because she was two seconds away from crying. "This is the worst revenge honeymoon I can think of."

Emily winced. "It'll be okay, I swear. You head back to the

cabin, and I'll buy out every sunburn remedy available. One of them has to work, right?"

A forty-something woman, wearing massive insect-eye sunglasses and a matronly one-piece with a skirt and conservative neckline, leaned toward them. "Is it true you aren't lesbians?" she whispered.

The woman's new spouse hid his face behind a Louis L'amour novel.

First, who would dare ask such a question in this day and age? Second, how did she know? Should she have gotten more comfortable with the idea of kissing her friend on the lips?

She shuddered at the thought. Maybe someone else could do it. But her? Emily Small? Who almost couldn't let her first sex partner see her naked? Even though the room was pitch dark, and he couldn't hardly see anything at all, and he mistook her upper arm for her thigh? And kissed her ear instead of her mouth?

"Why would you ask such a thing?" Ruby spouted off. But her face revealed the panic. Their story was unraveling.

"Your friend said something to the server." The woman shrugged. "I thought it was weird. Who would want to come on a honeymoon cruise if they weren't on a honeymoon? I mean, that's just a dumb idea."

Emily froze.

Ruby sniffed. "Emily? Did you tell the server we weren't married?" Her beautiful eyes filled with tears.

Oh, God. Oh, God. Oh, God.

No no no no no!

She was the worst best friend. The most awful best friend. And margaritas were the devil's drink. How was she going to fix this?

* * *

Emily and Ruby lay side by side on the king-sized bed in silence. Both of them were dressed only their underwear and coated in white sunburn relief cream. Thirty minutes had passed since the jilted bride had stopped sniffling and finished wiping tears off her Pepto Bismol tinted face.

"Ruby," whispered Emily. "I'm sorry. I messed up." Her limbs felt heavy. She would do anything to make it up to her friend. Anything at all.

Ruby rubbed at her nose with the palm of her hand to avoid the cream. "Why would you tell some random person about my wedding? I don't understand. That was so humiliating."

"I didn't mean to." Emily stared up at the ceiling and counted the minuscule cracks in the white paint. "It was that stupid margarita. I wasn't thinking, and then it popped out and I couldn't take it back."

"Now the whole ship will know." Ruby sniffed. "How can I even show my face out there? And we have eight more days on this ship. Eight. That's forever."

"More like a week," mumbled Emily.

"I wish I'd never come on this cruise." Ruby smacked her palm on the mattress. "Why did you talk me into it?"

Emily's chest tightened. The hurt in Ruby's voice cut her to the quick. "Tyler sucks, and I didn't want you to spend one damn minute thinking about him. He doesn't deserve you, Rubes."

"I loved him, Em."

"I know."

"And he didn't love me back." Ruby sighed. "I guess I was good enough to date, but not good enough to marry."

"He's a fool." Emily picked up one of the many tubes of

sunburn cream she'd bought at the ship's store and spread a thick layer on her stomach to quell the heat.

Ruby held out her hand for Emily to pass the tube. "I'm the fool."

"You could never be a fool." She squirted a dollop of cream onto her best friend's hand. "You're brilliant and smart and successful..."

"Not that successful." Ruby rubbed cream into her arm.

"What do you mean?" Emily screwed the cap back on and set the tube on the nightstand. "You're the top salesperson at work. You are a sell monster."

"I used to be." Ruby carefully rolled on her side to face Emily.

"But you and Tyler...the big wedding, the new house, and the Beamer." Emily blinked. "I thought you bought that with bonus money."

"It's a lease."

"Oh." Emily rolled on her side so that they were facing each other.

"I thought the wedding would fix everything. Two incomes, shared expenses, and he didn't seem to mind all of the travel I had to do."

Emily wiped a clump of cream off her friend's eyebrow. "So wait? I thought you guys looked so perfect. I thought you were in love. I thought—"

"I don't know." The former bride pressed her lips together. "Maybe I don't know what love is supposed to look like. I mean, he stood me up at our wedding. Clearly, I wasn't reading the signals right."

They both rolled onto their backs.

"So work's not going so well?" Emily asked.

Ruby blew air out of her cheeks. "They like young and hot at my work."

"You're young and hot." How could anyone say Ruby was not young and the hottest of hot?

"I'm pushing thirty, Em."

Emily raised her eyebrows. "That's still young." Who knew gorgeous Ruby was considered old and haggard in her job? Ridiculous. They must've lost their minds.

"Not in the pharmaceutical industry it isn't."

"Why didn't you tell me this before, Rubes? I had no idea." Emily had assumed her friend had it made based on looks alone. That she hardly had to try to sell the latest drugs to the doctors she visited every month.

"It was embarrassing," Ruby said in a low voice.

"Oh, hon, nothing you could tell me would make me think any less of you."

"I had a hard time admitting it to myself."

Emily picked up the room service menu from their night-stand. "Hey, remember when we were kids, what we'd do when we had a bad day?"

"Pig Out City!" Ruby cackled.

"Yes! You remember!"

"How could I forget?" Ruby popped up from her prone position and sat cross-legged on the bed. White cream smeared all over the comforter. "Roll the dice, the number on one die determines the food, the number on the other determines the bites."

"Maybe we need to order room service?" And a new comforter. Emily grimaced at the amount of cream that had transferred to it. "Piles of room service. And play some Pig Out City."

Emily sat up and shared the menu with her best friend, so they could examine the choices together.

Ruby's brown eyes softened. "I'm sorry I got mad at you, Em. I don't think it was fair of me to force you to pretend to be a lesbian just to spare my feelings."

"Aw, Rubes, I never ever ever wanted to hurt your feelings." She grasped her bestie's arm, even knowing she end up with a hand full of cream. "I wanted this to be the happiest of adventures. So I'm sorry I took that away from you with my big drunk mouth."

"I still want it to be the happiest adventure."

"Okay. How do we do that?" Emily took a break from reading the menu.

"Forget about the rest of the guests. Who cares if they stare at me? Jamaica: here we come!"

Max polished off the last of his ribeye steak. Even though it had been cooked to perfection, he had a hard time enjoying it. Sitting alone in a dining room full of paired up, happy people hit like a slap to the face.

Who would blame Ruby and Emily for standing him up?

Not him.

From their perspective he'd blown them off at the pool and didn't deserve a second chance.

Even though his cabin was right down the hall from theirs, he couldn't muster up the courage to knock on their door and apologize once he'd returned from his meeting with Sylvia. And why would they care? He was a stranger to them. They were two best friends with a long history and were here on a fun getaway. He was the third wheel who'd been dumped by his girlfriend. Loser material.

They probably met someone more interesting to sit with for dinner.

He scanned the dining room from behind the potted plant, but could only catch a glimpse of a few tables.

They probably shrugged off his absence as no big deal.

His shoulders slumped, and he picked at the mixed vegetable medley on his plate.

Maybe he should've begged off the cruise and turned around at the port. This was the dumbest idea he'd ever had. Except for the money he could make.

His photography friend, Alex, had talked up the cruise as an opportunity to rake in the bucks. Besides the free room and board, the cruise ship paid a per diem. And any photo packages he sold or framed pieces on display that were purchased, he received a decent cut of the sales. Alex had told him, these honeymoon cruises were rich with newlywed husbands ready to please their new wives.

"Sir, would you like some dessert?" A portly server with a mustache interrupted his thoughts and whisked away his not yet empty plate. "We have three delicious choices this evening: Key Lime Pie, Carmel Sundae Explosion, and a Tropical Cheesecake."

Max's stomach rebelled against the idea of more food. "I'll pass, thanks."

The server brushed some crumbs off the tablecloth. "I'm sorry to see your dinner companions didn't show this evening."

His heart raced. "So they aren't seated at a different table?" Max rose half-way out of his seat for a better view of the dining room.

Where were they?

"No, sir," the server said. "The two pretty ladies? I wouldn't forget them." He smiled, and his mustache twitched.

Who could forget adorable Emily and her engaging laugh? And her friend, Ruby, stood out in a crowd as well.

And they didn't come to dinner?

Maybe their absence at the table had nothing to do with him at all.

Would they think it strange if he stopped by their cabin at —he checked his watch—nine o'clock at night? He did have a good excuse: his suit jacket he'd lent to Emily. Then maybe he could explain himself.

He really didn't relish the idea of being stuck on the cruise for another week, alone, with no one to talk to, no one to hang out with.

"Thanks for letting me know." He gave a curt nod.

As Max rose to leave the dining room and head out on his mission to apologize to his new friends, the fifty-something twins on the pool deck who'd asked for a photograph, stopped him.

"Hi. So good to see you again," said one of the twins. "You remember us?" She pointed at her sister. Both dressed identically once again, but this time in matching silk dresses.

Expensive.

If nothing else had been gained from his last relationship, Penny had taught him how to identify designer clothing.

Max scanned each twin's face and scrunched up his eyes. "You're Diana." He pointed at the twin on the left. "And you're Donna?"

One of the twins covered her mouth with her hand and giggled. "I'm Donna. But even our husbands mix us up, so all is forgiven."

"Can I do something for you two?" Although he wanted to

be on the way to Emily and Ruby's cabin and make his apology, he had an in-born need to remain polite. He was, after all, on a working vacation.

"We were hoping we could buy a copy of the photo you took of us at the pool," Diana-possibly-Donna said.

Was he allowed to sell those photos? Sylvia had claimed they were for marketing purposes, but any photos he sold resulted in money made for both the cruise line and himself. It didn't seem like a conflict.

"Certainly. Would you like to meet me down at the studio in the morning, and I could show you some proofs?"

"Couldn't we look at them tonight?" One of the sisters clasped her hands together in prayer formation, her jade bracelets clacking together.

The other smiled as widely as a shark about to devour a baby seal.

His heart sank. Emily and Ruby would have to wait.

Emily's stomach rolled and writhed as if she were Kane in the movie *Alien* with a creature about to burst from it. "I shouldn't have eaten the crème brûlée." Oh, but it had been delicious. Right now she might be regretting her choice, but every bite had been divine.

"What was this stuff again?" Ruby pointed with a sunburn-cream-laden finger to an empty appetizer plate. "I could eat a whole bowl of that sauce."

Emily rolled on her side to view the plate with only a few crumbs and streak of straw-colored sauce left on it. "I don't remember." She surveyed the two trays of dirty dishware and used cloth napkins. "Maybe we can figure it out from the receipt?"

The former bride lay on her back, stared at the ceiling, and burped.

Emily burst out laughing. "Oh, my God, Rubes, are you sure you weren't a construction worker in a previous life?"

Ruby giggled. "It hurts to laugh." She touched her cream-covered cheeks. "How long does it take for a sunburn to heal?"

"Probably longer than our ten-day cruise."

"Really?"

"I don't know, but we better be careful next time we're in the sun." Emily picked up her phone and clicked on the cruise app. "What excursion did you and Tyler sign up for on Jamaica?"

Please don't let it be a day on the beach. Please, please, please.

"I don't know. Tyler picked everything out."

"You didn't even look?"

"We have—had—the same adventurous spirit." Her voice cracked. "I trusted his judgment."

Emily reached out a hand to her sunburned bestie. "I'm sorry I asked. I didn't mean to upset you." Why couldn't she learn to stop blurting out the first thought that popped into her head?

"It's okay. I need to move past this." She sniffed and almost rubbed her nose with the back of her hand before she remembered it was coated with cream. "My life does not revolve around Tyler Hardy."

Ruby was making progress. By the end of the cruise, maybe she will have gotten over the horror of her ruined wedding.

"That's right." Emily scrolled to tomorrow's activities list. "River rafting." Whew. Thank God. "That sounds jungle-y and shady, right?" She clicked on the activity to read a description. "Relax with a refreshing white water rafting ride down the Rio Bueno."

Ruby clapped her hands. "That sounds spectacular." She bolted upright, and her eyes sparkled. "I think I'm going to take a cold shower, wash off this cream, and figure out what I'm going to wear tomorrow."

Emily stomach roiled when the mattress bounced. "I think I'll digest a little bit longer."

"I want oodles of pictures, so I can post them all over my Instagram when we get back."

"For sure." For a fleeting moment, the reminder of photography had her mind jumping to Max. What had happened today? And what would he think when they didn't turn up at dinner? Maybe nothing. Maybe he'd be glad they didn't show, so he could eat a meal in peace. Clearly, the rapport they'd had at breakfast wasn't real. Max must have been too polite to tell her to her face that he wanted some time to himself. Had she come across as clingy? Or weird in some way?

Oh.

She'd pretended to die when he'd hit her with his finger bullets.

Yeah, a bit much. A bit childish. A bit unsophisticated compared to his ex, Penelope.

That must be it.

She blew a strand of hair out of her eyes. It wouldn't move. She tried several more times. Nothing. Annoyed, she took the deepest breath possible and blew with all her might. The strand still blocked her vision.

"Argh."

"Everything okay?" Ruby called from the bathroom. The sound of running water garbled her words.

"It's fine." Emily lifted her hand to pluck the offending strand. It had been glued to her cheek with cream.

Of course.

Without thinking, she used the back of her hand to wipe across her face. Cream smeared on her eyelids and some got into her eyes. And burned. Badly.

"Dammit. Ouch, ouch, ouch." Emily felt around for one of the cloth napkins on the trays.

Knock, knock, knock.

Great. Probably Room Service back to pick up their trays.

"Hold on!" She cracked one eye open. It burned less than the other one, but everything was blurry. "I'm coming." All she had to do was open the door, usher in the server, and then she could fix her painful eyes.

"Emily? Are you okay?"

Oh, God. It was Max.

Chapter 13
Cream Gets in Your Eyes

Emily, covered in sunburn cream wearing only a beach towel and some risqué underwear, stood frozen at the cabin door. Not the way she had imagined her next encounter with Max the Gorgeous. If she hadn't already been sunburned, her cheeks would've flamed as red as a strawberry daiquiri.

She blinked.

Her eyes burned with more intensity.

"My eyes." Blindly, she rushed for the trays on the bed to retrieve a cloth napkin, but instead she tripped over a pair of sandals and tumbled to the floor.

Of course.

"Let me help." A strong hand grasped her upper arm, and Max lifted her to her feet. "Oh," he breathed.

Her towel had slipped.

Oh no.

Oh, holy hell no.

Sightless, practically naked, and in pain, Emily flailed for the bedding behind her. She pulled at the comforter and yanked it over her teeny-tiny underwear-clad body. Unfortunately, the two trays of plates, silverware, and glasses came along with it.

The crash could be heard half way across the Caribbean. Or at least as far as Deck Fourteen.

"Is everything all right?" Ruby asked from the shower.

"No," Emily choked out.

"It's me. Max."

"Hi, Max!" Ruby called out cheerily. "We missed you at the pool today. I'll be out as soon as I can dry my hair."

Emily knew the tears were forming and couldn't do a thing to stop it. "This is so embarrassing." At least the tears soothed her cream-blinded eyes.

Plates clinked around her.

Was Max cleaning up the mess?

"I stopped by to apologize for this afternoon." He tugged the comforter more closely around her body, making sure she was thoroughly covered. "The cruise director wanted me to take some marketing photos. I couldn't say no."

Wait. He didn't break their date because she was a weirdo? "Oh?"

Then, a soft napkin dabbed at her eyelids. "Sit still." Max carefully wiped at the cream that caused her vision impairment. "Looks like you got a little too much sun."

"I should've bought the one-piece," she mumbled.

He breathed in sharply. "Why?"

"Less area to sunburn." Carefully, she opened her eyes.

Max stood a foot away from her, his green eyes dark in the low lighting. If she leaned forward a little bit, she could kiss him.

If she could find the courage. If she really wanted to.

He licked his lips.

Her nerve endings tingled

Oh, she really did want to kiss those perfectly sculpted lips. He swallowed.

An electric-charged silence filled the space between them—at least for Emily it was—and he moved toward her. His mouth hovered inches from hers.

Emily tried not to think about the swath of sunburn cream covering her face and most of her body. Her pulse quickened. She wanted to run a hand through his marvelous wavy hair, but couldn't because of the blasted cream all over her.

"What happened?" Ruby asked.

Max snapped backward.

Emily's mouth gaped open, and she ping-ponged her gaze from Max to her best friend dressed in a robe.

Was he really going to kiss her? Or was that a figment of her imagination? She looked a fright. No, that wouldn't make sense. Covered in cream, wrapped in a comforter, stomach stuffed full of delightfully sinful food. The least sexy moment in her life.

"She fell." Max stood and stepped away from Emily.

Did he blush?

"I got some cream in my eyes and couldn't see." What an idiot. Only Emily Small could end up in such a situation. Another chance to make a good impression on Max, and she screwed it up. Again.

Even straight out of the shower with wet hair and no makeup, Ruby looked amazing.

"Are you okay, Em?" She sashayed forward in the white cruise bathrobe with an ever-so-slightly wrinkled brow marring her sunburned face.

Emily, self-conscious about her cream-covered, crumb-sprinkled self while her cruise crush stood within an arm's length, said, "I'm okay. Did the shower help with the burn?"

It was as if Max only just noticed the condition of their skin. "Ouch. That looks painful."

Ruby winced as she adjusted the belt of her robe. "Be happy you aren't a victim, too."

"I'd rather have spent the afternoon with the two of you, trust me." He leaned against the small dresser near the bed.

They all stood quietly for a moment. A long, weird moment. Ruby in a bathrobe, Emily ensconced in a comforter, and Max nodding and saying nothing.

Awkward.

"Um, so, Max," began Ruby, yanking the edges of her robe a little bit closer together. "Why did you stop by?"

He opened his mouth, glanced at both of them, and spoke. "Right. Why am I here? That is a very good question." His beautiful face tinted pink, and he cleared his throat several times.

Why was it hard to believe such an attractive man could ever be embarrassed? He could quote lines from Star Wars or bring out the finger guns for a second shootout, and he'd still come across as hot, hot, hot.

To Emily anyway.

Ruby had wrinkled up her nose and quirked her lips. Somehow to her, Max was—judging by the look—kind of a weirdo.

Max noticed and stumbled over his words. "I, uh, took some pictures today on the pool deck, like I was telling Emily."

"The cruise director, that Sylvia person, *made* him do it, Rubes." Emily slung the edge of the comforter over one shoulder like a toga and closed the distance between her and her best friend. "That's why he couldn't meet us."

Ruby scanned red-faced Max up and down. "Well, that wasn't nice of her. You're supposed to be a guest some of the time and not her slave."

"Right?" Emily replied.

Max rubbed his palms together. "Yes, right. I didn't feel I had much choice. I admit, I didn't read the contract my friend forwarded me. So it's probably in the details somewhere."

"They always get you in the fine print." Emily punched the air for emphasis. "Bastards."

"Anyway, the reason I stopped by is that I'm hoping you'll sign a model release form." Max pulled out a folded piece of paper from his back pocket.

Ruby?

Ruby.

Of course Ruby.

Hadn't Emily always assumed someday her friend would be recruited to walk the runways of Milan, Paris, or New York? Some model scout tramping through the Valley View Mall, between the JC Penney and the Victoria's Secret, would spy beautiful Ruby in her low-rise jeans and kitty cat tank top and whisk her away on some grand fashion career. It was inevitable. Even at twenty-nine Ruby had something special.

"Model form?" Ruby blinked rapidly. "I don't understand."

"Your picture. I have one of you. On the pool deck."

Emily's face heated.

Wait. Max had spied on them at the pool. Had he seen her in her bikini?

Oh, God.

She glanced over at the shiny green swimsuit balled up on the floor and then back at Max. Their eyes met. He saw the bikini there, too.

A dull ache grew between her thighs. Her breathing sped up.

Oh my.

He focused on her mouth.

Or was that just her imagination?

"Um, so, I have this really fantastic picture of you, Ruby, and someone wants it for the cruise line's ad campaign." He held out the form. "So if you could sign here, I'd really appreciate it. I think they said they'd pay you for it. But they need the release signed first or something."

Ruby's mouth dropped open. "What? What are you talking about? What picture? When? You were taking secret pictures of me?" She glanced at Emily with rounded eyes.

Emily's heart stopped. Ruby thought Max was creepy.

Well, maybe the way he described it was a little creepy.

Crap.

This was not going well.

"Who wants my picture?" Ruby shook her head. "Why would you do this, Max? I mean, when did you think this was a good idea?"

A sheen of sweat appeared on his face, and he rubbed the back of his neck. "I'm sorry. This came out all wrong." He gestured with his hands. "These twins wanted me to take their picture, and it turns out their family owns the cruise line or something and when I showed them your picture—"

"Why would you show these people my picture? Why did you even take my picture?"

"Well, I meant to show them the picture I took of them, but opened the wrong folder and clicked on your photos and then they loved it so much, and I was only thinking about what a great opportunity it was—"

"For you," Ruby said.

"Well, I thought you'd maybe be flattered and—"

"Flattered that you took secret photos of me in my bathing suit?"

"Well, no...but Sylvia was the one who pointed you out."

Ruby crossed her arms. "So now it's Sylvia's fault?"

Max shifted his gaze sideways to Emily.

Oh, God, what a mess. How to fix it? Somehow she'd ended up in the middle of Ruby and Max and some kind of horrible mix-up nightmare.

No, no, no!

Only a few moments ago Max had maybe been about to kiss her and now her best friend thought he was a lecher.

Dammit.

Max held up his hands. "I'm sorry. I'm doing a terrible job of explaining myself. Sylvia told me I had to take marketing photos of guests on the pool deck—"

Ruby pursed her lips, quirked a brow, and gave Emily a look.

Not a good look, but a *what-is-with-this-guy* kind of look.

Uh-oh.

Max paused mid-sentence. He'd seen the glances that passed between them. "Forget it." His shoulders slumped. "I'm sorry I even told these women you'd consider it. That was wrong of me."

He headed toward the door. "I never should've taken photos of you guys."

Wait, he took photos of Ruby *and* her?

Gulp.

Emily eyed her discarded bikini for a second time.

"No, you shouldn't have," Ruby said in an expressionless voice.

As Emily watched Max head out the door and possibly out

of her life, she panicked. "Wait!" Oh, God, where did she put it? Was it in the closet? Under the bed? "Your jacket."

His figure disappeared from view. The door drifted closed.

On the back of the door it hung.

"Oh." Emily lifted a limp hand and touched the sleeve. "He forgot it."

Ruby let out a sigh. "We can leave it at the Guest Services desk." She scooped up damp pool towels, dumped them in a pile in the bathroom, and then carried the tray of empty plates and set it on top of the dresser. "He seemed like such a nice guy, too."

But he was!

It was all a mistake.

He'd been trying to explain, but Ruby wouldn't let him.

The ship jolted sideways. Emily stumbled. Her stomach fluttered uncomfortably. "Whoa."

Ruby steadied herself by grabbing the door frame of the bathroom. "I thought big cruise ships were smoother than this."

The ship rolled to the other side.

"You think I can shower while this is going on?" The cream was starting to itch. Or was it the sunburn? It was easier to think about mundane things rather than reflect on what just happened with Max.

* * *

"Idiot." Max banged his hand against the wall by the elevator buttons. He'd screwed up royally with Ruby—and by extension Emily.

A couple walking hand-in-hand came around the corner, saw Max's hand slam the wall a second time, and then chose the stairs instead.

He'd better watch out or his behavior would get back to Sylvia. The last thing he needed was another surprise assignment from the ambitious cruise director. Next she'd have him photographing diners during dinner service in a monkey suit.

Earlier, he'd noticed another photographer walking the floor while he ate alone. A younger, nerdier version of himself in uniform.

Would he be reduced to that kind of work after he returned to Florida? His failed show was supposed to pay his car payment next month.

Penelope had probably moved on to one of her New York hedge fund friends. He'd been introduced to them a half a dozen times over the last nine months. Men who were wealthier, more confident, and more successful than he could ever be.

The elevator door opened. The ship rolled to one side, and he stumbled inside.

Where was he even going? His cabin was right down the hall from Emily and Ruby.

He pressed Deck One. The lowest accessible deck for the guests. Maybe he belonged in the crew area. Below decks. Clearly, he didn't fit in with the regular guests.

If only he had the words to explain to Ruby. The twins he'd photographed turned out to be the MacPherson twins— members of the family who owned MacPherson Cruises. The photo the twin sisters liked wasn't raunchy or revealing. It was Ruby in her bikini top and board shorts, holding a margarita and smiling. He'd captured a moment of pure joy. Maybe she hadn't even been aware of it at the time. The incredible lighting due to the cloudy sky had made her outfit pop against the white-and-blue background of the pool deck.

The twins, who knew about Sylvia's marketing proposal, had been entranced by the photo and had asked him all about the girl in it. Who was she? Had she modeled before? Was this a candid shot or something he'd arranged? Did he think she'd say yes to their request? Could he convince her to sign a release form?

Maybe they even mentioned something about a longer-term contract.

He couldn't remember.

When he accidentally opened up the wrong folder of photos, he'd been shocked at their reaction. Thank God he'd stopped clicking before he reached the Emily series.

His groin throbbed at the recollection of Emily in that green swimsuit. All that soft skin exposed for him to see.

Back in her cabin, covered in white cream and wrapped in a comforter, she'd been irresistible. The desire to kiss her and taste those perfect lips and to wrap his arms around her body and feel her curves against him had been overwhelming.

The elevator door opened. He let out a breath and shook his head to free himself of the impossible thoughts he had about Emily.

Ahead he saw the hidden door for the stairs down to the crew levels where he belonged.

He opened the door and took the stairs two at a time. He needed a drink. Maybe two.

Chapter 14
Starfish or Dolphin?

The blaring of Ruby's cell phone alarm woke Emily the next morning.

"Five more minutes," she mumbled and rolled over onto her side. "Ouch." The movement caused her sensitive, burned skin to send a zing of pain up her arm.

"You have to come out here, Em."

She opened one eye, which revealed Ruby standing on the balcony. With a moan, she rolled out of bed. "It's seven in the morning."

"We have to meet in the main theater at eight-thirty for our excursion." Ruby finished braiding her thick hair into one perfect CGI cartoon princess braid, which she draped over her shoulder.

Emily stepped onto the balcony. Before her a beautiful, palm-tree lined coast stretched as far as the eye could see. "Okay, Jamaica is amazing." The morning sun broke through a puffy white cloud and bathed the scene in golden light.

Would Jamaica be enough to keep her mind off of yesterday? The fluttery feeling in her stomach when Max leaned in.

The almost-kiss. It must've been a kiss. What other reason would a man have to lean in so close to her face?

"I know, right?" Ruby reached out a hand. "Come on, experience this with me."

The two friends stood side by side and let the beauty of the island scene wash over them.

"Thanks for letting me share this with you." Emily wanted to focus on the fun day ahead of them, not the lost possibility of a kiss from her dream man.

"I'm glad you could drop everything for me, Em." Ruby leaned away to look her friend in the eye. "You have a life, a business. It was a sacrifice for you to come on the cruise."

Emily breathed in the fresh sea air. "If this is a sacrifice, I'd gladly do it again. Besides, I'm still trying to lift my idea off the ground."

Her friend tilted her head. "I thought you'd lined up a few clients already?"

"Oh, I have, but a few clients doesn't make a business." Emily's stomach knotted at the risk she'd taken launching her gourmet picnic idea after the security of her hotel job.

Ruby scrutinized her fingernail polish. "I think you need to pump up your website."

"Oh?" Emily looked out at the shoreline.

"You have a cute design and a good explanation of the services you provide, but I think it needs something else." She shrugged.

"Like what?" With her life savings invested in her business, Emily would take any advice her super successful saleswoman friend could give.

"I can't quite put my finger on it." Ruby tapped a finger on her chin. "The main page is fantastic, and the ordering page where someone can put together their perfect picnic? Love it."

"But?" The discussion brought the budding entrepreneur to full wakefulness.

"But it's missing the 'Emily' factor." She emphasized her point with her hands. "You are so vibrant and creative. I want your website to get that across to people who don't already know you."

"The Emily factor." What did that mean exactly? "Not sure how I tell my website designer to pump up the Emily."

"I wish I could describe it better."

"I certainly want to attract the right sort of clients, so I'll mull it over. I can't do anything about it while we're on the ship, so no rush." She smiled at her friend. "Nothing is worse than trying to satisfy someone who will never be satisfied."

"Like my mom?"

Rhonda Evers. Mrs. Perfection. Mrs. Demanding. "Maybe?" The last thing she wanted to do was insult Ruby's mom. But Ruby had offered her up as an example.

Ruby bumped her shoulder into her best friend's. "I know she can be difficult to please. No worries. I have to admit, though, I sort of liked it when she did most of the wedding planning for me. It was stressful."

Was this the first time Ruby had talked about her failed wedding without tears welling up in her eyes? Progress! "She knew how to wrangle the caterers, that's for sure. And the florist? What a deal she made."

"Yeah, she might have her moments, but sometimes Rhonda is exactly what you need."

"I'll bet she's giving Tyler's parents an earful right about now."

"She should. We spent a lot of money, and then their son was an epic jerk." Ruby crossed her arms. "Who does that to someone? Why didn't he just tell me he didn't want to get married? Did he think I wouldn't let him loose?"

"I don't know, Rubes." She had to head her friend off at the pass. They were headed into some deep emotional waters. "Some men can't commit, I guess."

"It sucks. I wasted a lot of time with him when I could've been dating other people."

"Oh? Is there someone else you were interested in?"

"Maybe."

Interesting. Ruby had her eye on someone else? Who?

"But even if there wasn't," Ruby continued. "When Tyler proposed, I promised myself to him and nobody else."

Emily's thoughts drifted to Max and how easy it would be for her to promise herself to him. Not only because of his looks —though he was the most attractive man on the planet and she'd fight anyone who disagreed—but because he'd proven himself to be a genuinely kind person. But those ridiculous dreams were over now. She'd have to spend the rest of the cruise avoiding him since Ruby found him creepy.

"Let's get ready and grab some breakfast, shall we?"

"Buffet time!"

"You know it, girl."

* * *

A crew member standing on the stage clapped his hands together. "Where are my starfish?"

The theater full of chattering cruisers quieted at the request.

Each activity had been assigned a sea creature to stay organized and move everyone as a cohesive group as they disembarked the ship and climbed into the appropriate bus for their selected Jamaican adventure.

Emily's body twitched.

Was that their group name?

Her mind blanked.

Why was she more concerned about the wedgie the bikini bottom had inflicted upon her ass than the very important information about their river rafting activity? Were they starfish? or sand dollars? or whales?

"We're dolphins, remember." On her phone Ruby scrolled through the cruise ship activities scheduled for tomorrow's day-at-sea. "Hey, there's 90s karaoke in O'Malley's Pub. We totally need to go."

Emily wriggled in her seat, hoping to scoot the bikini back into place hands-free. "Right. Dolphins. We are the dolphins."

"So karaoke?" Ruby's thumb levitated over the 'add to my day' button.

A familiar figure, Sylvia, came down the aisle followed by another familiar yet handsome figure, Max.

Emily halted her squirming. Why was he here? Why was he with Sylvia? Why wasn't he going on his own excursion?

Her gaze followed him with way too much interest.

Ruby thought he was a creeper, and maybe he was.

"Did you believe his explanation about why he took photos of us?" Ruby noticed the handsome photographer, too. As she followed his movements from aisle to stage, she tucked her phone into her water-proof fanny pack.

"I don't have any reason to not believe him at this point."

Max leaned toward Sylvia, and she whispered something in his ear. He smiled and lit up the whole stage with his perfect white teeth.

Her stomach hardened. It killed her to think it, but the two of them looked good together up there on the stage. Tall, beautiful people with athletic bodies. They would have tall, beautiful children, no doubt.

Emily let out a sigh.

Ruby raised a brow. "You're not serious?"

"Huh?" Emily broke her visual contact with the former man of her dreams as he flirted and chatted with Sylvia. Why did it bother her so? She'd only known the man for two days.

"That Max character. You have a crush on him?" Her best friend in the whole wide world crossed her arms. "I know his kind, Em. It's about him all the time. Those pictures? I mean, who does that? He was hoping to use us to advance his career."

"Use *you*," Emily mumbled. There had been no discussion of Emily signing a model release form. The pictures he'd taken of her in that bikini must've been awful. He didn't even mention them except as a throwaway as he'd left their cabin.

Ruby touched her arm. "He took secret photos of both of us in our bathing suits. I know how private a person you are, Em."

Private meaning self-conscious of her body in public. Yes. Ruby hit that nail on the head in a very kind, best-friendy way. But Max's reveal he'd taken pictures of them on the pool deck didn't outrage her like it did Ruby.

Why?

Maybe deep down she'd felt somewhat attractive in her crazy-wild metallic green swimsuit and wanted Max to see her in it. Was that part of the disappointment she'd felt when he didn't show for their pool date? Could it be her interactions with Max over the last couple of days had made her believe a super-hot man could be interested in a not-so-perfect girl like herself?

But Ruby didn't like it, and she was on this cruise to support Ruby. Hot guy or no.

"Right." Even as Emily agreed with her friend, she peeked past the large bun on the woman sitting in front of her to sneak one last glance at Max.

Max and Sylvia descended off the stage and disappeared through a door near the front of the theater labeled 'crew only.'

Emily chewed at her lip. It was time to give up on her Max fixation.

* * *

Max followed Sylvia through the crew door half-hidden behind some drapery near the front of the theater. He rubbed his forehead. "I paid to take the deep sea fishing excursion. That was my own money. You can't stick me on some other excursion."

As soon as the door shut behind them, the cruise director whirled to face him. "You screwed me over, so you owe me." Her hands fluttered over her crown of braids balanced precariously on the top of her head.

"I already told you when you pulled me out of the line: the sisters recognized me in the dining room." The whole pool deck photo shoot grew into a worse situation every minute. First, he'd ticked off Ruby and Emily. Then, the twin sisters when he had to confess to them he couldn't acquire a signature on the model release form. And now Sylvia. "I didn't pursue them. Heck, I didn't even know who they were."

Why didn't he stay in Miami and sulk about his failed art show? Why did he have to try to run away from his failures as usual? It never worked. And now he'd walked right into another mess. Another fucked up situation with no good solution. No matter which choice he made, it ended up a disaster.

"I knew you had a photo of the hot girl, and you held out on me." Sylvia's finger got awfully close to Max's face. "That was going to be my ticket out of here. Don't you get it? You screwed me. If you don't want me to screw with you and make sure you never are hired as a photographer ever again, you'd better fix this fuck up." Her face twisted into a mask of mean—a sneer to her mouth, crow's feet around her eyes, and flared nostrils. "I will ask every one of the crew I manage to log onto Yelp and destroy you. You won't even be hired to take dog portraits at the animal shelter."

Max's breathing sped up. His career flashed before his eyes. Was it worth it to defy Sylvia's demands? Over a deep sea fishing excursion he could probably do back home if he wanted?

"Fine." He tamped down the burn of defeat, and his stomach soured. "What do you want me to do?"

Why bother anymore? He'd lost pretty much everything. Sylvia had the upper hand. It was going to be a long cruise, so he might as well give in.

Sylvia's snarl transformed into a beaming smile. "I want you to go back out there, wait in the seats, and when they call for the dolphin group, you go with them."

"What's the dolphin group doing?"

She waved her hand. "It doesn't matter what they're doing —Diana and Donna MacPherson are on that excursion, and I want you to keep them on the hook."

"But the woman in the photo won't sign the model release form."

"Let me handle that part."

"She won't do it." Sylvia had no idea what Emily and Ruby thought of him—a creep taking secret photos of girls in bathing suits. No way would Sylvia change their minds.

"No worries, Max. She will." She had a strange gleam in her eye. "You keep talking to the MacPhersons, charm them, whatever it is you do to keep them listening. Don't you dare let them know we're having trouble with the release form."

"Fine."

From a cabinet near the door Sylvia pulled out a bright green wrist band. "Here, put this on. That'll get you on the bus. They won't have your name on the list, but you tell them you switched excursions at the last minute. I'll smooth it over with the tour company."

As she wrapped the band around his wrist, the touch of her hand was like ice. Then she opened the door and shoved him out into the theater.

"They're calling your group," she said. "Go on."

He tripped over his own feet.

"All right, dolphins, follow me!" A crew member held up a sign with a cartoon dolphin on it. "Everyone who selected the river rafting trip, follow me."

A leisurely raft trip down a river? Not bad. It could've been worse. The twins could've been expert scuba divers—and he'd never scuba dived in his life.

As he joined the group forming at the front of the theater, his stomach dropped when Emily and Ruby walked down the aisle and headed his way.

Chapter 15
Little White Lies

"He's holding up the dolphin sign," exclaimed Ruby, as if she'd found a twenty dollar bill on the sidewalk. "Come on. It's our turn."

She squeezed Emily's upper arm so hard, she thought she'd permanently lose feeling in it. "Ouch, that hurts."

"Oh." Ruby looked at the damage her hand was doing to Emily's arm and released her grip. White fingerprints dotted Emily's red skin. "Sorry. Since we didn't have a chance yesterday to try swapping our prize for the zip line instead, I'm super excited we're going to float some class three rapids."

"Wait? What?" When did class three rapids come into the conversation? Shouldn't it be a safe, leisurely excursion with a few waves? Emily's stomach knotted into a half dozen anchor hitches. She'd learned all about complicated knots from the book she'd found at the bar yesterday when waiting for the bartender to mix up another cocktail: *Tie Yourself in Knots*. Little good that would do her on the river. She should've been reading up on *Fifty Ways to Survive Class Three Rapids*.

"Didn't you see the detailed description on your cruise

app?" Ruby unzipped her fanny pack and hauled out her cell phone, tapping on the screen to bring it up.

Emily held up a hand. "I believe you. And, no, I didn't read the details. I heard 'river rafting trip' and thought it would be like those lazy rivers at a hotel resort pool."

"Does that sound like something Tyler and I would choose?" Her best friend raised a brow.

No, it did not. Tyler and Ruby chose crazy activities like helicopter tours and cave spelunking and rock climbing. Not lazy rivers and lying like a bump on a log while thinking about nothing. Why didn't she think of this? Why didn't she ask Ruby more about what they'd signed up for?

Crap.

As they made their way into the aisle and Emily saw her life pass before her eyes, she spied gorgeous Max joining the dolphin group. Her stomach cramped up.

Double crap.

"Excuse me," a voice said from behind. "Are you the model?"

Both Emily and Ruby turned at the same time to see a middle-aged woman in tight sporty leggings and a hot pink rash guard smiling widely at them.

"Model?" Ruby asked with a quizzical twist of her lips.

An identical-looking woman in identical athletic wear, only in blue, joined the stranger. "Yes, it's her." She nodded emphatically. "I'd recognize that gorgeous hair anywhere."

Ruby touched a lock of hair and gave Emily a confused look.

"Bob, it's the girl we were telling you about." The woman in pink called to a fit-looking older man with a completely bald head and a goatee. "Isn't she perfect?"

Ruby blushed.

"Perfect for what?" But as Emily asked the question, she knew the answer. The release form. She took a quick glance toward Max, and their gazes met.

His face paled.

He knew. He knew who these women were, and he knew what they were asking.

"For the marketing photos. Didn't the photographer tell you?" The twin in blue, elbowed her sister. "I told you he didn't even ask. There was something odd about that guy."

"There's nothing odd about him." *Crap.* Why was she defending Max? Beautiful Max who turned into Creepy Max who was now walking in their direction?

"Max, darling," Pink Twin said overly loud and with totally faked friendliness when she spied the handsome photographer. "We found your model." She grabbed hold of Ruby's hands before she could react. "And she's perfect. We want her. Whatever we have to pay, isn't that right, Donna?"

Ruby grimaced and yanked back her hands.

"Dolphins follow me! Our buses are waiting." The crew member with the sign headed toward the far right side of the theater, leading his group of about twenty honeymoon cruisers to the exit. "Let's stick together, folks."

"Donna, Diana, nice to see you again." Max smiled a very forced, weird smile.

What was up? Why had he been up on the stage with Sylvia? Maybe what Ruby believed had been true after all? Was Max merely looking out for his best interests? Had he been friendly only because he'd been interested in Ruby as his model?

* * *

Ruby did the only thing that made sense in an awkward situation, she ignored the questions of the Weird Twins, grabbed Emily's arm, and dragged her down the aisle toward the crew member with the dolphin sign.

They passed right by Max whose face was as red as the sunburn on Emily's stomach. A stomach that hadn't seen the light of day since she was eight years old and caught skinny dipping in her neighbor's pool one hot August evening.

"Miss," Pink Twin said in a clipped tone, waving a hand at Ruby. "Oh, miss, we would like to talk to you, please."

"Keep walking," Ruby said in a harsh whisper. The same sort of whisper a mother used when a child made a ruckus during the church service. That whisper meant blind obedience without question. A do-it-or-else sort of tone.

"Right." Emily kept her gaze focused on the cartoon dolphin on the sign. It smiled a goofy smile with a lot of white teeth.

Wait, did dolphins have teeth?

That didn't seem anatomically correct. She'd have to ask the crew member about the accuracy of the sign.

When they'd made it to the bottom of the aisle in front of the stage, Emily sneaked a quick glance back at Max, the twins, and their respective new husbands. There was a lot of pointing at Ruby and hand gesturing. The ladies were displeased. Max touched his temple and closed his eyes.

Oof.

Not good for Max.

Her throat ached.

She wasn't supposed to care about him anymore. He was a creep. A cruise voyeur, if there was such a thing, who liked taking pictures of women in swimwear.

Hm, but didn't photographers take photos of women in swimwear all the time? Was that so wrong?

Wait, he did it secretively. That was it. And secretively Emily sorta kinda was okay with it. Did he take the photos because he was forced to? Because he wanted to? And did she look good in these photos?

A slow smile built on her face.

A young Hispanic woman with her super tall, super Nordic-looking husband sidled up to them, her chocolate eyes ablaze. "Are you the ones everyone is talking about?"

"Excuse me?" Ruby had rushed them toward the dolphin group so quickly, she didn't even notice the newlyweds approach.

"Who's talking about who?" Emily swung her head around. A few other couples were looking in their direction and talking quietly. As if the Weird Twins and their strange fixation on Ruby weren't enough, now they had cruise gossips saying things?

The dark-haired, dark-eyed woman clutched her hands together. "The runaway bride and her bridesmaid taking our honeymoon cruise. Is the groom after you?"

"Runaway bride?" Ruby scoffed, but her face paled. "Emily?"

This was her moment. Emily had the perfect opportunity to salvage her friend's reputation and smooth it all over before it blew up into something bigger. Sure, she'd blabbed on the pool deck about Ruby's failed wedding after she had a few too many margaritas, but this lovely woman had given them the perfect response that would garner eight days' worth of sympathy.

"Yes, she's a runaway bride," Emily said in a rush of words. Oh, did it feel good to pour it on thick. "The groom was a monster, and she had no idea until the day of the wedding. Can you imagine? So the cruise line was kind enough to let me take his place. Wasn't that wonderful?"

Ruby's mouth opened and closed like a fish stranded on the sand.

Was her bestie upset at the slight twist to the truth? Or merely in shock? To Emily it was a better story than the real one. Who wouldn't be sympathetic to a woman who'd barely avoided being married to a bad guy?

"How horrible." The Nordic husband's face darkened. "If you two need anything when we get back to Tampa, I'd be more than happy to help."

"Thank you," Emily said. Ruby was still too shocked to speak. Tyler had been reduced to a cartoon villain in a Lifetime movie. But did it matter? Her friend's reputation had been saved. What was one more little white lie?

"Dolphins," the crewman announced. "Before we get on the buses, let's break up into four smaller groups—one for each raft." He touched Emily's shoulder and gestured to his left. "I need six of you over there, and six more here."

As the group of dolphins split up, the Nordic man and his wife joined Emily and Ruby in their group. The husband had decided to be their protector of sorts—at least for the day.

The Weird Twins, their husbands, and Max ended up in the last raft group, which would mean they'd be on a different bus.

Emily let out a sigh of relief. Only one drama per day. That's all she could handle. The situation with the women who wanted Ruby as their model using Max's secretly taken photo would have to wait for another day.

Max caught her eye across the crowd and mouthed '*I'm sorry.*'

* * *

Pink Twin, Donna, squished into the empty seat next to Max.

This was going to be the longest bus ride of his life. Emily and Ruby already hated him—that was clear in the theater. As he'd made his way up the aisle, Emily had walked right past him, and when he had tried to make an apology from a distance, she all but rolled her eyes.

How did Sylvia expect him to smooth things over and make this photo deal happen? He was a photographer, not a salesman. He knew about light and apertures and focal length. Solid things he could manipulate for effect very easily. But human beings? Penelope had been the one with the ability to win people over to her side with a few words.

He was screwed.

"Max," Donna said, squeezing his forearm with her bony hand. "I know you can make that girl sign the model release form. You're a good looking man. I'm sure you know how to charm a young thing like her." She batted her eyelashes at him.

Diana, in blue, took the seat across from theirs with her new husband. Donna's husband, Bob, sat directly behind Max and Donna and leaned forward literally breathing down Max's neck. Hot, moist, and decidedly uncomfortable.

"She thinks I'm a creep." Max might as well tell her the truth. There was no papering over that fact, and his stomach roiled at the thought. "She's not going to sign."

"Bob, we want that photo." Donna crossed her arms. "She's perfect. Absolutely perfect." She turned in her seat partway to converse with her spouse. "Isn't there another way? Can't we use it without the release form?"

"Darling," Bob said, only his eyes, eyebrows, and bald head visible above the seat. "That would be illegal. She could sue you. There's never been a problem money couldn't solve. Have you thought about offering her more?"

Diana leaned in across the aisle. "You did tell her we would pay twice the going rate, right?"

Max backed up against the window to put some distance between him and the insistent gang that surrounded him. When was the bus going to reach the starting point of their trip? Soon, he hoped. "Um, I told her you'd pay her well."

"*Well?* That we'd pay her well?" Donna scoffed. "We MacPhersons aren't cheap. You need to talk dollars, my dear. Numbers. Don't be shy. We are willing to offer her a fifty thousand dollar contract. Fifty thousand. Did you say those words: 'fifty thousand'?"

Max shook his head. "No, I didn't. I wasn't sure...I thought maybe it was—"

"What? Crude?" Donna touched her carefully styled hair, which would likely be ruined within minutes of riding down the rapids. "There's nothing to be ashamed of when it comes to making deals. Isn't that right, Bob?"

"That's right." Bob's bushy eyebrows rose up.

"People like honesty. People like frankness." Donna plucked a compact mirror from her fanny pack and scrutinized her makeup, wiping at her lipstick with a finger where it bled outside the lip line.

If that was the only way to make these women and Sylvia back off, maybe he should give it one more try. Would Ruby even listen to him? He didn't see how he'd make it off the cruise alive without a signature on the release form. What if Donna was right? What if Ruby changed her mind once she heard about the money involved?

"We could sweeten the pot. Would that help?" Diana blinked rapidly.

"Um, I don't know." Max wiped the sweat from his brow. *Didn't they have air-conditioning on this stupid bus?*

"Of course it would, Di." Donna scooted even closer to Max. "What if we hired you to be the photographer for our new ad campaign? She's a pretty thing that red-head. Maybe you and she...well, maybe there's a possibility the two of you—"

Max opened his mouth, but couldn't speak. There was so much coming at him all at once. He didn't know what to think. Didn't know how to decide what was the best path.

"Well, folks, we've arrived at our destination." The river raft and tour guide announced over the speakers. "Follow the dolphin sign to the entrance where they'll hand out your gear. Group Four, you will be with me for the entire day."

Max let out a sigh of relief. The guide's speech interrupted the twins and Bob pushing him to answer. "I'll think about it."

Donna patted him on the shoulder. "You'll make the right decision, I know it. Our perfect model is as good as secured. I have every faith in you."

As Max made his way down the aisle to exit the bus, his mind jumped back to that moment on the pool deck when he'd agreed to take the twins' photo. That's when everything had gone sideways. How could he possibly make things right again?

* * *

Meanwhile, on the other bus...

On the bus ride up to the launch point of the raft trip, Ruby sat next to Emily in complete silence. That was not like Ruby. Sure, she had experienced the most devastating day of her life only a few days ago, but she'd come out of her funk and had managed to enjoy the cruise as much as anyone in her situation could have.

Would Ruby forgive her for her little white lie about Tyler?

As they wound their way up into the green mountains of Jamaica, their raft guide, Carson, also acted as tour guide, pointing out relics of the island's plantation past, uniformed children walking to school, and explaining much of the vegetation that created a beautiful jungle-like canopy on either side of the road.

Although the ride was entertaining and the facts interesting, Emily's stomach flip-flopped at the thought of a river ride full of rapids on a pitifully small raft. Would she be bounced out into the water? What if she hit her head on some rocks and had to be airlifted to a hospital? Did Ruby buy trip insurance? If she did, would she be covered?

"Will she be all right?" The Hispanic bride sitting across the aisle, whose name was Daniela, eyed her mute friend. "Is she still in shock?"

Ruby stared out the window and leaned her head against the glass.

"She'll be okay." Though Emily wasn't quite sure about that. Yes, she'd felt a bit of guilt making up a lie about Tyler, but it had all been about salvaging Ruby's feelings. And soon her friend would realize that. Wouldn't she?

Daniela patted her arm. "You're such a good friend."

"Thanks." Emily's stomach churned. But she didn't know if that was guilt because of her lie or worry about the fact she was going to die from fear. "Have you done any river rafting before?"

She wished Ruby would talk to her, reassure her that they'd have all kinds of fun. The usual stuff. But this quiet, no-talking

Ruby was new to her. She'd have to find reassurance elsewhere before she panicked.

"Tony's been dozens of times," Daniela explained. "He says this river is not that bad. I mean, they let anyone sign up for it, even if you have no experience."

Tony did not look like a Tony. He looked like a Sven or maybe even a Thor or a Ragnar, if she were honest. Who named a white blond, blue-eyed baby 'Tony'?

"Right. We paid good money for this. They wouldn't sign us up for certain death." Emily smiled.

Daniela furrowed her brow.

Hm, maybe Daniela didn't have the same sense of humor as Ruby.

"If you'd read the description in the cruise app, you'd see we'll mostly encounter class three rapids on this river, which are considered beginner-level," Ruby said in a monotone without even changing the position of her head. "Everybody will be required to wear a life jacket and helmet, and they'll give us a safety briefing before we ever set foot on a raft. They know what they're doing."

Joy exploded through Emily's body like fireworks on the Fourth of July. Ruby was waking up and acting more like herself. "You are so right." She squeezed her friend's arm. "Perfectly, wonderfully right."

Ruby sat up straight and gave Emily a wan smile.

"As we approach the parking area, please follow the dolphin sign to the entrance where you'll pick up your gear," said their guide. "Group One, you will be with me for the entire day. Don't follow anyone else, just Carson." He pointed at his name tag. "Ya, mon?"

"Ya, mon," the entire busload of tourists echoed. They'd been taught at the beginning of their ride that everyone in

Jamaica said 'ya, mon' for everything. And so far he'd been right.

The bus pulled into the parking lot.

Ruby's phone blinged.

"That's weird." The former bride unzipped her fanny pack. "We don't have any service off the ship."

Emily shrugged and scanned the lot for the other buses that carried dolphins. When would they see Max again? or the Weird Twins?

"Oh, my God, Em." Ruby showed her friend her phone screen. "Tyler texted me."

Chapter 16
River of Doom

Emily's heartbeat raced. "What did Tyler say?" She tried to sneak a peek at Ruby's cell phone. "How could you possibly receive a text with zero service?"

Tony spoke up. "It's possible. If a text was in transit before you left Tampa, and you are in an area with service—?"

"He says he's flying to Cozumel." Ruby's hand flew to her chest. "He said he wants to talk it out," she read the text in a squeaky voice.

"Screw him," Daniela said with nostrils flared. "That's your fiancé, right?"

Emily half-turned her body to block Daniela's view of Ruby. The last thing she needed was for Daniela to remind her best friend about the lie she'd told in the theater. "You aren't seriously going to meet up with him are you?" she whispered.

"I don't know." Ruby stared at her phone. "What am I supposed to do, Em?" She looked up at her best friend with big eyes. The cold shoulder she'd given to Emily during the whole ride from the pier disappeared.

What a relief, as Emily couldn't have handled her friend's irritation much longer. She needed her best buddy back.

If Tyler had sent the text the day they left on the cruise, maybe he was having second thoughts about his crappy wedding no-show. But who cared? He'd chickened out when it mattered the most and left beautiful Ruby broken-hearted and embarrassed. There was no coming back from that. Any man with some sense would've skulked away in shame. Only Tyler would think he had a chance.

"You can't seriously be considering meeting up with that monster." Daniela stood to exit the bus and gave her husband a wide-eyed look. "Babe, tell her he won't change. Tell her men like that don't deserve forgiveness."

"Would everyone please exit the bus and gather near the equipment shed." Carson's voice blasted through the speakers.

"Ya mon." The whole bus repeated the mantra. Even Ruby and Emily found themselves saying it.

Daniela and Tony became swept up in the surge of people who flooded the aisle.

The two remaining women huddled over the cell phone and read the text together.

Babe, I booked a flight to Cozumel. See you Wednesday. Let's talk.

"So is he going to be waiting for you with a bouquet of flowers?" Emily stared at the text.

"I don't know, Em. That's all he sent. And I can't text him

back." Ruby leaned her head against the headrest. "What if I see him and—"

The jilted bride didn't finish her sentence.

What could she be thinking? Would she actually take that lout back? No way. Not after everything he'd put Ruby and her family through.

"Are you still in love with him, Rubes?"

"Maybe?" She sniffed, and tears welled up in her eyes. "I don't know. I'm so confused right now."

Emily wrapped an arm around her friend's shoulders. It didn't feel like the right time to bring up her doubts about Tyler. If Ruby didn't see it for herself, would her words carry any weight? "Why don't you put your phone away and think about it later. You don't need to decide anything now. We're about to take this exciting river rafting trip." Hopefully, she'd be alive at the other end. "Let's enjoy the day. Wednesday is so far away."

"Ladies, if you intend to take your trip, you will need to exit the bus and pick up your protective gear." Carson had made his way down the aisle to the middle of the empty bus where Ruby and Emily sat.

"Right." The auburn-haired beauty tucked her phone in her fanny pack. "Let's go, Em."

For a fleeting moment Emily's mind had been so latched onto the Tyler Text Bomb, she could almost pretend she wasn't about to sacrifice herself to the Jamaican rapids of doom. Almost...

"Yes, right, let's go." Emily stood up and swallowed her fear. There was no turning back now.

* * *

Emily knew she looked ridiculous. With less-than-small boobs, a life jacket was not a pretty sight. The orange contraption wouldn't lay flat against her chest, and the gracious guide had to help tighten the straps until she could barely breathe. Her mind was so focused on blending into the background, rather than drawing attention to her embarrassing situation, she'd lost track of the other dolphin bus.

When the guide gave her vest one last tug, she grunted and lifted her eyes to see Max—still as gorgeous as ever—flanked by the Pink/Blue Twins. Apparently, he was now best friends with them. They smiled. He smiled. Bob smiled. The other husband, whatever his name was, didn't smile. Maybe he wasn't the smiling type. But he downright glowered and stomped behind the other four.

Then Emily saw, perhaps, the reason for the man's expression, Blue Twin had her arm linked with Max's.

She pressed her lips together to keep from laughing.

Her gaze met Max's for a split second.

His pale face and slack expression made her think of a hostage in a bank heist. He looked absolutely petrified. What had him so scared?

Max and his twin companions approached the equipment counter to receive their helmets and lifejackets.

"Em, let's take a selfie." Ruby held her phone and stretched out an arm for her friend to join her outside the equipment shed. "The flowers behind us look so beautiful. Come on."

Emily joined her bestie for a photo. With the life jacket reducing her breathing to nothing more than Mount Everest oxygen levels, she moved slowly. Anything faster than a turtle's pace wore her out.

Tucking her helmet under the arm, Emily smiled and

waited for Ruby to take a few photos. Above the equipment shed were a series of warning signs in bright yellow:

Caution Slippery Surface

Steep Drops Open River Banks

Danger Risk of Falling

Danger Deep Water

Wear Helmets at All Times

Life Jackets Required Beyond This Point

Emily bit the inside of her cheek. This excursion was supposed to be fun. The signs made it seem as if she would walk to certain death if she followed their guide to the river.

Ruby scrutinized the photos, oblivious to the terror that built up in Emily's mind. "These look great."

"I'm scared, Rubes." She pointed at the signs.

"What?" Ruby glanced up at them and waved her hand. "You don't have anything to worry about. They have to put those signs there."

"Why would they have to put signs unless there was a real possibility of danger?"

"It'll be like going on a roller coaster. You like roller coasters."

"No, I don't."

"Oh." Ruby grasped her chin. "I thought when we went to Carowinds we did the Intimidator together."

"That wasn't me."

"It wasn't?" The pretty ex-bride tilted her head to one side and pursed her lips.

No, it wasn't.

Emily was reminded how their paths had headed in opposite directions after they'd attended different middle schools. Ruby turned fourteen and went from gangly, athletic, straight-figured girl with braces to leggy and model-like woman. The change' is what Emily called it in her own head. Although Ruby was Ruby, she'd transformed into a beautiful woman almost overnight, which completely altered the group of friends she hung out with.

Sure, she and Ruby saw each other from time to time and went bike riding and to the mall and all that other girly stuff. But it wasn't the same anymore. Grown men, who shouldn't even be looking at fourteen-year-old girls in that way, approached Ruby to ask her out. And Emily? Well, Emily grew boobs the size of the Appalachian Mountains and hid them under loose sweatshirts and jackets.

Ruby was beautiful and perfect, and Emily was a freak.

"It must've been Brianna, then." Ruby nodded her head. "Anyway, you've got nothing to be afraid of. Would I really let you do something dangerous?"

Emily screwed up her face. "Yes."

Ruby laughed. "I would not."

A group of returning rafters, drenched from head to foot, exited a bus that had returned from the rafting end point a few miles downriver. Mixed in with the adults were a few children who smiled broadly after their adventure.

Ruby pointed at them. "Look at those kids. They had a great time, and you will, too."

Emily sighed. Did she have a choice? She was already here and dressed in the right gear. She may as well give in and trust her best friend.

* * *

Carson the guide stood at the shoreline of the river holding a paddle above his head. "Group One, my colleague will begin handing out your paddles."

"Wait," Emily whispered to Ruby, "we're expected to paddle? I thought this was supposed to be a vacation, not work." What kind of two bit operation were they running here? Maybe someone dropped them off at the wrong river rafting place?

"Shh." Ruby bumped her friend in the shoulder.

Emily scanned the six other honeymooners. None of them seemed to have the same concerns as she. What was their problem?

A tall, skinny Jamaican with a bald head handed each rafter a yellow-and-blue paddle.

Emily held hers as if it were contaminated.

"When I tell you to paddle, you paddle." Carson paced back and forth in front of them. "Understand?"

"Ya mon," the entire group responded enthusiastically except for Emily.

She gulped and imagined leaning over the raft and looking down into the churning waters.

What if the water swept away her paddle? Or her?

Gourmet picnic business owners were not known for their upper body strength. Fabulous fried chicken? Yes. Matching cloth napkins and plates? Yes. But paddling abilities? Not high on the list in the world of picnicking.

Shouldn't the cruise app have warned her that paddling was involved in the activity? Seemed like a bait and switch.

Up the bank, Emily caught sight of the next three groups of rafters making their way to the launch point. Max would be mixed in with those cruisers, and so would the twins.

From a distance, Emily saw the familiar perfect wavy dark hair of Max. Butterflies dive bombed her stomach.

Why did she have to find him so horridly attractive? How could he have betrayed them so? Since she didn't want the

Weird Twins to pressure Ruby again, it was time to get the show on the road despite her worries.

"Does everyone have a paddle?" Carson asked.

"Ya mon," Emily yelled with a little too much enthusiasm.

Daniela and Tony gave her strange looks.

"My buddy and I will help you into the raft." Carson took the hand of the nearest newlywed and helped her into the big yellow inflatable raft. "We will need to balance the load, so please have patience while we seat you."

Within moments Emily found herself seated in the middle of the raft with Ruby in front of her. Probably better her best friend, who loved these kinds of adventures, didn't see how panicked she was.

Carson's colleague shoved the raft out into the water and away from the shoreline.

Last chance to fake a heart attack or something.

"Paddle!" Carson called out from his position at the back of the raft. "Both sides. Let's go!"

The water at this point on the river was calm, so Emily didn't mind leaning over the bulbous edge of the raft to dip her paddle in and help their forward movement. In fact, after a few strokes, she liked the sensation of gliding down the river in the quiet beauty of the Jamaican jungle.

"Great job, folks. We'll be coming up on our first rapid just around this bend." Carson doubled up his efforts and navigated them toward the open water between two large boulders on either side of the river. "It starts off with a bang. Class three rapids right around the corner."

Oh, crap.

Why didn't she think about writing out her will before she'd left for Florida? Oh, right, she didn't know she'd be white water rafting. She thought she was attending a safe, both feet on the ground, wedding. Who in their right mind would climb in a raft with a bunch of strangers and float right into death?

They rounded the bend.

White water churned all around.

Emily's adrenaline spiked. "Oh, my God!"

Chapter 17
Max Has It Bad

As they hit the beginning of the class three rapids, the rubber boat dipped, then rose high into the air and crashed down. Emily almost bit her tongue at the impact. A massive wave of water slammed into her body and obscured her vision.

Was this the end? Was she about to drown in a Jamaican river rafting accident?

Emily imagined the headlines:

Honeymoon Cruisers, and Two Fakers, Die in Most Horrific Way Imaginable

Two Women, Masquerading as Lesbians, Drown Like Rats in Jamaica

A Possible Model and her Chubby Friend Kick the Bucket in Paradise

She sputtered and rubbed at her eyes to clear the water. Why, she did not know. Was she really looking forward to seeing every moment of her last days on earth?

"Right side: paddle!" Carson yelled above the crashing water all around them.

Ruby's bubbling laughter could be heard above it all.

Was she insane? Who laughed at such a time? Death everywhere. More rapids ahead. No seatbelt.

But despite her terror Emily found herself paddling with all her might. She'd rather paddle and be focused on that than be reminded of how little time she had left to live.

"Paddle harder!" Carson boomed from the back of the raft. "We don't want to get stuck on that boulder."

Emily looked up and saw a massive rock the size of the Empire State Building in their direct path. While they headed straight for it, she gripped her paddle and prayed.

"Paddle, Emily." Newly minted 'friend,' Daniela, sat across from her on the left side. "Carson told everyone on the right they need to paddle."

As if Emily didn't know this. But she couldn't move. She was stuck. Arms frozen. Eyeballs frozen. Everything fucking frozen.

In slow motion, the raft began drifting toward the right side of the massive boulder.

"Paddle harder! We're almost around it!"

Emily's muscles unfroze for some reason. She leaned toward the water, meaning to dip her paddle in and pull her weight as a passenger on the Ride from Hell. But she rearranged her body a little bit too far to the right. One butt cheek landed on the edge of the raft. The side dipped as the raft pushed up against the rock. The front of the raft rose up in the air. Ruby grabbed onto the rope that ringed around the edge of the raft and leaned forward. Emily did not and plopped into the raging water.

The last thing that ran through Emily's mind before she landed in the river:

Possible Model's Chubby Friend Dies in River Accident

Water filled her mouth, and she sputtered and coughed. Her adrenaline spiked, and she promptly forgot everything she learned from her guide. The raging water ripped her paddle out of her hands.

"Point your feet downstream!" Carson yelled as the raft continued down the river without her. "Then swim for shore!"

Yes. Right. The safety briefing:

Let the life jacket do its job. Don't struggle. Lean back. Nose and toes to the sky. Point feet downstream. When in calmer water, swim for the shoreline or wait for another raft to pick you up.

The crazy waves carried her in a zigzag pattern downstream. Her feet hit a rock hidden under some white water, but other than that, she managed to escape the head injury she had been certain was inevitable. As the river quieted, pure relief was injected into her bloodstream.

She'd survived.

She'd live another day.

And wasn't that the most thrilling thing that had ever happened in her life?

Okay, maybe Ruby was onto something with these adventures.

Group One's raft was still visible downstream, but she knew she would never catch up. Poor Ruby. Hopefully, she was having fun without her.

In calmer water, she was able to roll over on her stomach and swim toward shore. The heat of the day beat down on her. Once she got out of the water, she should be dry in no time.

As her feet hit the sandy bottom, she heard another raft full of cheering and happy cruisers pass through the massive rapid she'd survived.

She turned to wave and catch their attention. They should be able to give her a ride.

"Emily!" a familiar voice called.

Max lifted his paddle in the air and then pointed to the stranded Emily on shore.

* * *

Emily hesitated. She hadn't been expecting Group Four to reach the rapids before Group Two. What had happened? If she knew the raft held Max and the Weird Twins, she would've hidden behind some bamboo. The last thing she wanted was to be stuck in a raft with those people.

But too late now.

The guide for Group Four had already instructed his raft to slow themselves down by paddling backward against the current.

"Swim out to us," the guide said. "We've got you."

Emily hesitated for a moment. They weren't that far from the starting point. Could she walk along the shore and make her way back to the bus parking lot and avoid Max altogether? She eyed the thick bamboo that lined the shore and slapped at a lazy mosquito who had come out of hiding in the heat of the day to find a meal.

Hm, that didn't seem to be ideal. And she wasn't wearing appropriate footwear for a jungle hike.

She swung her head back toward the river and the beautiful but forbidden man who waited in the raft.

Her heart fluttered. Although she'd been frightened of the rafting experience at first, she'd actually had fun falling out of the raft and floating downstream. She didn't want the experience to end that quickly.

But Max...

Dammit!

"I'm coming!" She flung herself into the cool river and swam toward the raft as it neared her location. With the life jacket keeping her so buoyant it was difficult to swim, but kicking seemed to work better than paddling with her arms.

She reached the raft in a few minutes and grabbed hold of the rope.

Max's face appeared in front of her.

Before she could say anything, he leaned over, grabbed her by the vest, and hauled her into the raft. She landed on top of him, nose to nose.

Oh my.

His green eyes really were very, very green. Like shamrock green. Like the green grass on the golf course behind her parent's house. Like amazing green.

Her naked thighs pressed against his naked thighs.

He smiled warmly and kept his arm tight around her.

"She's in!" he called out to the rest of the raft.

The rafters cheered and raised their paddles in the air.

"Nice job, Max," said Bob.

Max stared into her eyes.

Heat rose from her chest, up her neck, and reached her face.

For a split second she didn't want to move, didn't want to remember what he had done, didn't want to do anything but maybe kiss him right there in front of everyone with plenty of tongue. Her heart hurt so much at the idea of it. Couldn't she —? One little kiss? Just to know what it was like?

But no...

She couldn't...

In a quick motion, she rolled off him and scrambled for a

seat in the middle of the raft. Her limbs shuddered. Because she was cold. Right. Just cold. There was no reason for her to be so...so...affected by Max's body flattened against hers. It wasn't as if she was turned on by the contact—nor was he. No way. And that hard ridge she'd felt against her stomach when she landed on top of him? That was nothing. Nothing. Nothing. Nothing.

Crap.

"Now that we've rescued the damsel in distress," said their guide, "let's prepare for the next rapid. This will be a Class Two. Piece of cake, right?"

"Ya mon," the whole raft said in unison.

Emily focused on the river ahead and tried to tune out what had just happened. What else could she do?

Max paddled as he was instructed. It was better to focus on something as mundane as paddling than to focus on the woman sitting forward and to his left. Everything in him wanted to go back in time, to the moment her soft luscious body had landed on top of him. Her figure had molded to his. And even though the water had been very cold, the heat of her body caused a lightning bolt reaction.

For a moment he thought she'd wanted him to kiss her. She had this dreamy look in her eyes, and her lush lips had parted slightly. It was as if the world disappeared, and it was only the two of them—the length of their bodies entwined.

Oh yes.

And her mouth would've tasted so sweet, so delicious. He knew it.

But then she'd rolled off of him as quickly as she could.

Maybe she had noticed his growing erection and that's what freaked her out?

Dammit.

That was middle school fear number one.

Okay, Keeling, get it together. You're a twenty-nine-year-old man, not an eighth grader. Erections were not something to be embarrassed about.

Or were they?

Emily wasn't interested in him. She made that abundantly clear back in her cabin.

She thinks you're a creep who takes secret photos of women. Practically a stalker.

His valiant 'rescue'—that anyone in the boat could've achieved if they'd paid attention to the safety briefing—didn't make up for everything she thought she knew about him. Was there any point in trying to improve his image in her eyes?

Why did he have this deep need to convince her he was a good guy, a nice guy, a guy who hated creeps and stalkers? A guy who wanted to protect her from those kinds of guys? A guy who wanted to laugh with her and find out every little thing about her?

Oh, man.

He had it bad.

After only a few days he'd managed to jettison whatever feelings he had left for Penelope, which hadn't been much to begin with, and find a girl who he couldn't stop thinking about.

What was it about Emily Small?

He glanced at her back. She sat in between Pink Twin, Donna, and her new husband.

As they approached the next rapid, Emily raised her clenched fists above her head and yelled, "Bring it! You don't scare me!"

Max smiled. She didn't care one bit what people thought about her. She dressed how she wanted, acted how she wanted. So care free. She was the complete opposite of uptight, rules-oriented Penelope. He wished he could be so free and easy. He wished he could live a life without caring about what other people thought.

Yes, Emily had something he wanted, and it was more than a physical attraction. If he could ingest whatever it was that made Emily Emily, he would do it. No matter the cost. Because her life seemed so much brighter and happier and more wonderful than his.

There had to be a way to convince her he wasn't the creep she and Ruby thought him to be. With only a few more days remaining on the cruise, he had to act quickly. Once they docked back in Tampa, she would disappear and go home to Roanoke and probably run the most successful gourmet picnic business on the planet. All of that joy and fun she carried around with her would be gone.

The raft dipped into the first line of rapids. Water splashed up in a huge wave and drenched the entire group.

Emily cheered while everyone else sputtered and prepared for the next one.

"Paddle left, paddle left," shouted their guide.

Emily pointed with both hands to the left. "Left, people." She became guide number two.

The raft chanted in unison, "Ya mon."

Max grinned and instead of watching the river rush by, he kept his gaze on Emily. Sexy, beautiful, delightful Emily.

* * *

The raft rounded a final bend and gently bobbed in the calm water. A group of three Jamaican men stood knee-high in the river near the shore and waved.

"Paddle left, folks, paddle left." The Group Four river rafting guide dug in with his paddle to help everyone with the last push.

Emily frowned.

It was over?

Never would she have guessed, based on her level of anxiety earlier in the day as they wove their way deeper into the mountains, that she would enjoy white water rafting so much. Even though she was disappointed to have experienced most of the trip alone, without her best friend, she still felt a sense of accomplishment.

She couldn't wait to tell her family about her adventure. Her brother, Hunter, would never believe she did it. Never in a million years.

Inwardly, she winced at the fact Ruby would've made sure to document the trip with her cell phone camera.

Oh well.

Not much she could do about it now. Hunter would continue to believe his younger sister was nothing more than a fraidy cat without a sense of adventure.

A strong breeze blew through the tall bamboo, knocking their solid trunks together. Without a paddle to help her fellow rafters, she gazed out across the river and took in one last glimpse of the beauty around her.

"Amazing, isn't it?" Pink Twin, who hadn't said a word to her since the rescue, gave her a brief smile.

Emily nodded. "I didn't think I'd like it so much."

"The white water?"

"Yeah. I'm not really into adrenaline sports."

The group neared the shore. The three Jamaicans grabbed hold of the rope that encircled the raft and pulled them out of the water.

"Well, I thought you were marvelous and brave for a first timer." Pink Twin set down her paddle and unclasped her life jacket.

"You did?" Emily copied her and freed her oversized chest from their buoyant orange prison. Her first deep breath felt like heaven.

"Sure, most women who fall out like that would be a weeping mess." One of the men on shore helped Pink Twin to exit the raft. "You know, it ruins their hair, makeup, whatever. But you? You took it like a champ."

"Uh, thanks." Emily touched the tendrils of damp hair that stuck to her face and removed her helmet. Thank goodness Pink Twin was not talking about photo shoots and modeling and release forms.

"Miss?" Another man extended a hand out to her.

Emily accepted and stepped onto the sandy shore.

A bus waited for them at the top of the rise.

Wait. Where was Ruby?

She had expected all of the buses would be waiting at the end of the journey. That she could meet up with her best friend and ride with her all the way back to the ship.

But now?

Did she have to ride back—a thirty minute bus ride on a very cramped, very small bus—with Pink Twin, Blue Twin, *and* Max?

Max appeared next to her. He'd removed his life jacket, and his wet, white T-shirt clung to his well-sculpted and horridly sexy chest. She could see every ab muscle in bas relief.

One. Two. Three. Four. He had something like a dozen ab muscles. Plus very prominent pecs.

She felt faint.

Life was not fair.

He'd been so gallant rescuing her from the river. All strong and hero-like.

Dammit.

Why did he have to take those stupid photos? Why did he have to mess everything up by being, well, less than perfect?

Their gazes met.

He opened his mouth as if to say something, but no words came out.

Oh, all right, she'd do it, then, if he couldn't. "Thanks for helping me out back there."

Great. She'd done it. Thanks given. No more needed to be exchanged.

She'd board the bus in silence, sit in the very back with some stranger, and stare out the window until they arrived at the dock.

He blinked a few times.

The entire raft-full of people were half way up the slope, leaving the two of them alone on shore.

He scanned her face. "Can I take you to dinner?"

Chapter 18
So Many Abs

Emily couldn't speak. She had words in her head, but her mouth wouldn't move. It had to be a dream or a joke or something other than a sincere date request.

She was boring. She was plain. She was, well, Emily.

He scanned her face, gave a shy smile, and pulled his wet T-shirt from his body.

"Yes."

The abs did it. The quick peek at the bare torso beneath the T-shirt. How could she resist? Ruby would understand, wouldn't she?

"Yes?" His voice cracked.

"Yes." She affirmed with a nod. It all came across as weirdly formal, but visions of shirtless Max floated through her head. Only a few days of the cruise remained. Surely, she was allowed some kind of fun. A once-in-a-lifetime date with the hottest man alive. Her heart sped up at the sexy thoughts running through her mind.

"How about tomorrow?" His green eyes gleamed.

What would be a good time to slip away from Ruby? "It

would have to be late. Like nine o'clock?" She'd figure some-thing out.

He lifted a damp curl from her face and tucked it behind her ear. "Sounds perfect."

Her body shivered.

"Emily!" Ruby stood at the top of the hill near the water's edge. "I'm so glad you're okay."

Both she and Max turned their heads, the moment broken between them.

One side of her wanted to slide her hands under his shirt, run them up his muscled body, and make out with him until the ship's horn blasted for the last time. The other side of her wanted to make him pay for the sneaky way he took photos of her and Ruby at the pool.

Could she do both?

She waved at her friend. Before she left the shore, she said, "Don't tell Ruby you asked me out." Because that would gut her friend, and the last thing she needed to do was choose a practical stranger over the jilted bride on the cruise said bride had paid for. Not very best friend-y.

He scratched his cheek and frowned. "Uh, okay."

He had to know Ruby would be upset. This would be a secret date between the two of them, and then maybe she could correct Max's wrong and fix all this bad blood between them once and for all.

The Weird Twins caught sight of Ruby and booked it up the steep slope.

"Can you call off the dogs?" Emily nodded in their direc-tion. "They're making it worse. That's not how you win Ruby over."

He raised an eyebrow. "There's a way to win her over?"

Emily let out a massive sigh. Her plan had better work.

How else would she mend fences between Max and Ruby and be able to continue her cruise-only fling of a lifetime? She knew the minute they docked in Florida, he'd find someone better. That's how it always was. Sure, she was funny and goofy and maybe even a little bit cute (Max had even called her cute, so that part had to be true, right?), but men didn't see her as the long-term type. She was a curiosity—an oddly proportioned curiosity. Something different from the garden variety twenty-somethings who seemed to pop up everywhere like dandelions in a freshly mowed lawn.

But she'd take it. She couldn't resist trying.

"There might be," she intimated before heading up the slope.

The memory of him rescuing her from the river ran through her mind. His solidness beneath her when she'd landed on him—all muscles and radiating heat.

Lord, have mercy.

If he thought that Emily—the floundering, river water spitting, too tight life jacket wearing Emily—was interesting enough for a date, maybe he might find her more than just interesting, which she could use in her favor.

Her knees wobbled. She didn't want to deceive him, she really did want to go on that date, but if she could accomplish something else, too, she would.

"Donna! Diana!" Max waved at the Weird Twins as he passed her on the upslope. "I have some news."

The twins shifted direction and turned toward Max.

Emily finished her climb and joined her friend at the top.

Ruby rushed over and gave her a hug. "I'm so glad you're okay."

"Thanks for waiting for me."

"I'm sorry I made you do this."

Emily smiled, not only thrilled at the idea of having Max all to herself for a couple of hours tomorrow, but excited she'd actually enjoyed the rafting adventure. "Don't apologize. You were right: it was fun."

"Then does that mean you'll do the ATV adventure without me when we get to Cozumel?"

"Without you?" Emily squinted in the bright sun.

"The text? From Tyler, remember?"

Emily had been so caught up in her fear of the trip, the spill into the river, and the subsequent Max encounter, she'd almost forgotten. "Oh, right, Tyler. You mean, you're actually going to meet up with him?"

Ruby squeezed excess water out of her braid. "I've been thinking about it."

"So you'd forgive him after what he did to you?"

Ruby's face turned a slight shade of pink. "I don't know."

"Everyone, please board the bus. It's time for lunch." The guide stood on the bottom step of the bus and waved the crowd forward.

The two friends joined the queue.

"Let's talk more about it tonight," Emily said. Her mind raced with the possibilities. Should she support her friend in this decision? Warn her away? Go with her to make sure Tyler didn't lie and spin to win her back?

"Okay." Ruby took a seat near the very back of the bus. "But you don't need to worry, Em. I'm a grown woman. I can handle it."

Emily wasn't so sure.

* * *

After an exhausting day—who knew river rafting and being asked out on a date by the most attractive man in the world could be so tiring?—Emily and Ruby decided to order room service.

At the thought of Max eating alone at their dinner table, Emily felt a twinge of sadness. But Ruby still thought he was a creep, and until she fixed that image with her possibly super dumb plan, it would be hard convincing her to share a meal with the man.

Ruby lay on the bed and flipped through channels on the TV. The selection of entertainment was limited, so she settled on the channel that explained the details of the shore excursions on Cozumel. "Look! This is what you're going to be doing." She sat up and folded herself into a cross-legged position.

Emily, who'd just taken a shower to remove the stench of the river from her hair, glanced at the television.

A couple rode ATVs through a muddy jungle, dirt chunks flying.

"That looks so fun," Ruby said.

Emily twisted a towel around her damp hair. "*We're* going to have a blast." She wanted to leave no question that the two of them would be on the excursion together. Tyler shouldn't even be an option.

One of the ATVs drove straight through a huge mud puddle.

"The last time I was on an ATV was near Boise when I went to that pharmaceutical conference." Ruby turned up the volume.

Both women watched the video for a few seconds in silence.

"I've never driven one of those things before. Do you think

they're safe?" Emily imagined being coated in mud, unable to see, and driving off the trail into a palm tree. Spending the rest of the cruise in a neck brace wouldn't be ideal.

Ruby rolled her eyes. "Of course they're safe or the cruise wouldn't give you that activity as an option."

Someone knocked on the door. "Room service!"

Before opening the door, Emily tightened the knot on her robe. "Dinner is served." The smell of freshly grilled steak hit her nostrils.

The server from the dining room handed her a tray and then grabbed another off his cart.

"Rubes, can you help?"

"On it!" Ruby leapt from the bed, snagged the tray out of Emily's hand, and plucked the cover off the plate. "I feel like I haven't eaten all day."

"Me too." Emily thanked the server and shut the door. For a split second she wished she'd seen Max in the hall as he headed to dinner, but she'd only seen a newlywed couple making out near the fire extinguisher.

As the two friends dug into their steak dinners, Emily brought up the topic they'd been silent about since the bus trip. "So, Tyler. What do you think his text is all about?"

Ruby sighed. "I don't know, Em. I'm so confused."

"You shouldn't be. He's not worth your time. You're so much better than that, Rubes."

"Better? What do you mean?" Ruby's voice wavered. "Did you have a problem with Tyler?"

Emily slowly chewed on a piece of steak so she could come up with a good answer.

Ruby tapped her fork on the side of her plate. "Well?"

"To be honest? I don't think he liked me very much." Emily stared down at her plate. "But I didn't think anything of it because you loved him. And if that's the man you wanted to marry, well, then I needed to get out of the way. I'm just a friend...and he would be your husband."

"Just a friend?" Ruby shook her head. "Is that what you think you are?"

"Yes."

"You're my best friend, Em. My very best friend." She squeezed Emily's arm. "When I got married I didn't expect you to disappear."

Emily set down her fork. Tears pricked at the corners of her eyes. "When you two started dating, I hardly ever saw you anymore. I assumed that's what happens when someone falls in love. Your life changes. You have different priorities. I don't know, I guess I thought it was part of growing up, settling down, maturing."

She thought about all of last summer, when she'd been at her lowest, when Kyle had broken up with her. Tyler had told her Ruby was growing annoyed with her constant phone calls and texts. Embarrassed, she'd re-examined her behavior and backed off the communication. Ruby hadn't said a word about it, so she thought Tyler had been telling the truth.

"And I thought you'd moved on from me." Ruby cocked her head to one side. "You seemed to be spending a lot of time with your family and less time with me."

"Well, when I decided to make a go of the picnic business, moving back in with my parents seemed like the best strategy to save a few bucks while I got it off the ground." Emily gave a smile. "You think I wanted to spend every weekend with my mom and dad?"

Ruby laughed. "Yeah, I guess that was pretty dumb of me."

"Not dumb. No. But you were in love. And that can take up your whole life at the beginning."

"I suppose you're right." She moved her green beans around her plate. "I did get pretty caught up with Tyler and forgot about you. I'm sorry."

"It's okay." Emily cleared her plate from the bed. "I wasn't honest with you about my feelings toward Tyler. We both need to learn to communicate better. I don't want to ever lose you as a friend, Rubes."

Ruby sniffed. "Me neither."

The two women hugged over Ruby's half-empty plate.

When they broke apart Emily asked, "So what would you say to him if you saw him again?"

"Tyler? If I had the guts, I'd punch him in the face."

Emily giggled imagining the shock on handsome Tyler's face when Ruby's fist slammed into his perfect nose or knocked out one of his super white teeth.

"I think, though, what I really would want to ask is why."

Emily nodded. "He was a coward the way he stood you up."

"Yeah." Ruby set aside her plate—half the food uneaten— and rubbed her hands together. "Get dressed and let's go grab some ice cream!"

"Now you're talking."

* * *

Max sat at his assigned dining table in the back corner near the kitchen. Even after the server had brought him his drink and his appetizer, he still found himself taking glimpses of the dining room hoping to see Emily and Ruby descend the stairs near the piano.

Although Emily had accepted his date invitation, that didn't mean both women believed his explanation for the pool deck photos. Was Emily only being nice by agreeing to the date? She really didn't seem to have a mean bone in her body. That's what made her so appealing. She was the exact opposite of Penny, who had been calculating and manipulative. Nice to the outside world, but ruthless on the inside.

But Emily?

He smiled.

Something about her awkward, self-conscious personality endeared her to him.

But the fact she didn't show up tonight for their seated dinner time had him concerned.

"Oh, Max!" Pink Twin, Donna, waved her fingers at him from the piano and headed his way.

Shit.

He hadn't been able to secure a signature on the model release form, and he didn't know if he ever would. Why couldn't these women understand the word 'no' and why did he have to be the one to suffer if Ruby wouldn't sign it?

To fortify himself for the twin onslaught, he gulped down his wine. Diana flanked her sister, leaving their new spouses in the dust. Their identical gazes were like laser beams that pinned him to his seat.

Time for the Keeling Charm—if there was such a power.

Max produced his broadest, whitest smile. He hoped the can lights above his table bounced off his recently-whitened teeth (a gift from ex-girlfriend, Penelope, who chose the exact shade of white that complimented his skin tone) and blinded the two middle-aged women.

"Ladies, what can I do for you?" Although his words came out confident enough, inside his stomach roiled like a rowboat on the open ocean during a storm.

Diana and Donna sat at his table without invitation, each twin taking a chair on either side of him.

He was trapped.

Diana folded her hands and rested them on top of the table. "Max, we somehow missed each other after the rafting trip."

Yes, he'd made sure to choose a seat near the front of the bus with a twelve-year-old boy from Nebraska who spoke to him the entire time about his collection of beetles. Which meant when they parked near the pier, he'd been the first one off the bus and booked it back to the ship in five minutes flat.

"Oh?" Better to play stupid in this scenario.

Donna picked up one of the empty wine glasses on the table and signaled to the sommelier to fill it. "When will you have the release form signed? We'd really like to lock this down before the cruise ends. We can't let the perfect girl get away."

Max's mind immediately jumped to Emily. Yes, he couldn't let her get away. The fact she'd agreed to his date invitation against all odds had him calculating how he could avoid squandering the opportunity. He needed to lay all his cards on the table.

"Max?" Diana asked.

The sommelier appeared with a bottle of red and poured a glass for Donna. "Would you like me to send the server to your table for your dinner selections?"

"No," Max said.

"Yes," the twins answered in unison.

The sommelier's eyes popped open. "Uh, very good." He finished pouring the wine and disappeared.

"Well?" Diana tapped a long red fingernail on the clean white tablecloth. "When?"

The twins scooted their chairs closer and boxed him in. His

heart pounded. Sylvia's face floated in his mind. She said she'd ruin him if he couldn't do as she asked.

Could she?

Did he really want another cruise ship job? Maybe Sylvia didn't have the power to destroy his fledgling photography career, but these two high-powered women did. Their family owned the cruise line. They were millionaires many times over. If he screwed this up, what hope did he have of salvaging his reputation? His show had been a bomb, the cruise had not been the fun escape he hoped for, and now he was backed into a corner.

"I have a meeting with them tomorrow night." Sure, it was a date not a meeting, and it was with Emily, not Ruby, but maybe he could subtly bring up the topic?

Was it hot in here?

Sweat prickled around his collar.

"Perfect." Donna clapped her hands and then shoved back her chair. "I'm sure you can manage to fix this. We had no doubts, did we, Di?"

Diana drank the last swig of wine in her glass. "No doubts at all. We'll expect the signed contract in Sylvia's hands by five p.m. the day we dock in Cozumel. Good?"

Max closed his eyes briefly. What had he done? "Yes, good."

Chapter 19
The Elevator

Emily took a deep breath. Confession time. It was—
she checked her phone for the time—an hour before
her date with Max. She'd been trying all day on their
second day-at-sea to find the perfect moment to tell Ruby
about her date and her plan. But every time they sat down for a
drink, went to a show, or grabbed a snack, Emily lost her
courage.

"That's like the hundredth time you've checked your
phone. What's going on?" Ruby kicked off her sandals and
plopped down on the bed. "By the way, thanks for suggesting
the buffet for dinner. All those little desserts? Oh, my God,
adorable. And delicious." She laid back against the pillows and
rubbed her flat stomach.

Emily's nerves had plagued her all day. But maybe she
should be nervous more often—she'd hardly eaten a thing. How
did Ruby not notice her usual Hoover vacuum bestie when it
came to buffets could barely finish a scoop of macaroni and
cheese and steamed broccoli? "I have to tell you something,
Rubes."

Emily took a deep breath and planted her feet on the carpet decorated with little anchors.

"Okay, lay it on me." Ruby folded her arms and rested them behind her head.

"I might have accepted a date from Max yesterday." She nibbled on the inside of her cheek.

Ruby's eyebrows shot up. "What? The Peeping Tom creeper?"

"I don't know if I'd call him a Peeping Tom. I mean, we were in a public place and everyone else on the deck saw us in our bathing suits." Why was she trying to rationalize this? Emily held up a hand. "Okay, let me start over. I know how you feel about him, Ruby."

"Thank you." The former bride gave a curt nod.

"I accepted the date because I have a plan to fix this whole thing."

"Fix what?" Ruby rolled on her side and focused her full attention on Emily.

"The secret photos he took of you." She paced in front of the bed as she explained her plan. "If no photos exist, no more pressure to sign the release form, and the whole thing goes away."

"How are you going to make the photos disappear?"

Emily paused. Her muscles twitched. "I'm going to access his laptop and delete them." She held a hand to her mouth and stared at her friend.

"How are you going to—?" She blinked a few times, and then ran a hand through her luxurious auburn hair. "No, Emily, I would never expect you to do that."

"Do what?"

"Well, pretend to like him—"

"It's not really pretend." Yeah, no way were her feelings for

Max pretend. They were very, very real. Like one hundred thousand percent real.

"—so you can find an opportunity to dump the photos." As Emily's response sank in, Ruby gave her an incredulous stare. "Wait. You actually like this guy? Even after what he did?"

Whoops.

She shouldn't have let that slip. This date was all about helping Ruby have the best revenge cruise a woman could have. "Let's forget about what I feel for this guy."

"No, that's a very important part of this conversation." Ruby pulled herself up into a seated position on the mattress. "You like Max. You think he's cute. But you're going to go out on a date with him to help me out?" She touched her hand to her chest. "Wow. That's pretty selfless, Em. I don't know if I could do that."

"You couldn't?"

"Maybe I could." Ruby tapped her chin with a finger. "I don't know. But if you think you can do that for me—? Wow. I'd be really grateful. I just want to be left alone. I already know half the ship probably heard the story about my wedding, and why we're on the cruise. So I suppose me thinking I could blend in with a ship full of newlyweds and heal in private really wasn't possible. Was it?"

"No, probably not." Emily's shoulders slumped.

"But this idea about me being a model for some cruise line? Seems ridiculous." Ruby feigned a Vogue pose and then laughed.

"Mmm."

"So you have my blessing, Em. If you can get rid of those photos, that would be fantastic." She smiled. "But don't do anything stupid, okay?"

"I can do it, and I won't—do anything stupid, I mean." But

in the back of her mind she worried about how she would accomplish it. Max wouldn't show up for dinner with his laptop in tow. It would be in his cabin. And the only way Emily could think of getting inside Max's cabin would be...well.

Her body flushed hot and cold at the thought. Would Max even be interested in taking her back to his cabin? Hard to believe the Most Gorgeous Male Specimen on Earth would be interested in regular old Emily in that way. But he'd asked her out, hadn't he? And when she'd landed on top of him in the raft...

A wild idea smacked her in the face. "Ruby, can I borrow something from you?"

"Name it."

Emily headed to the small closet near the bathroom door, grabbed Ruby's hot pink halter mini-dress with a daringly cut keyhole neckline in a super stretchy fabric, and held it up to her body. "What do you think?"

Emily tugged on the dress she'd borrowed. She never would've picked something so revealing. This was Ruby's wardrobe on an Emily figure. Did it work?

"Wow, you look amazing." Ruby perched on the edge of the bed and eyed Emily as she looked in the mirror and adjusted the pink stretch fabric that molded to her curves like plastic wrap on a bowl of leftovers. "That dress looks totally different on you."

Emily plucked at the keyhole neckline. "Totally different – bad? Or totally different – good?" She'd never worn something so boob-revealing before. Because most of the time she thought her breasts were a distraction and too much for the eyes. Well, her mother had sort of told her that once.

On her first day of high school when she had descended the stairs in a tight tank top and a miniskirt, Emily's flat-chested, built-like-a-marathon-runner mother, who thought God had smote her daughter with the curse of a mega chest, had gawked and said, "You can't wear that to school. It's obscene."

Emily's face must've turned ten shades of red, because her older brother had burst around the corner from the kitchen and laughed at the sight of his sister. "You look ridiculous."

After those two comments, Emily had turned around, headed up the stairs to her room, put on a pair of her favorite jeans and picked out a hoodie to pull on over her tank top. Problem solved. And that birthed her customary high school outfit for the next four years.

Now here she was in a cabin on a cruise ship about to embark on a date with the hottest man in existence, and she wore something her mother would deem 'immoral.' The cleavage displayed was probably more than Dua Lipa would feel comfortable with on the Grammys.

"Different and definitely good." Ruby nodded. "I'm actually jealous. I think you look ten times better in that dress than I do."

Ruby jealous of Emily? Boring, plain, and top-heavy? All boobs and nothing else? That's what Emily saw in the mirror. She turned sideways and then faced the mirror a second time. "Really? I don't know. Isn't it too much?" She tucked in the 'girls' one more time and pursed her lips.

"No. Not too much. Perfect." Ruby stood behind her and reached out to tighten the halter tie on the back of Emily's neck. "That dress was made for someone with a figure like yours."

Emily glanced at her phone, which she'd laid on the vanity in front of the mirror. "Oh, crap, I'm supposed to meet him at *L'Océan* in five minutes." *L'Océan* was the fancy French restaurant on the upper deck that guests had to pay extra for.

"How did he get a reservation there?" Ruby's eyes rounded. "Those spots were booked up months ago."

"They were?" Emily tucked her cell phone into her purse.

"Yes, Tyler and I tried to reserve something back in September, and there weren't any tables left."

"I don't know how he managed it, but I have to go." She grabbed a wrap that Ruby also let her borrow, a frothy thing with sparkles and fluff at both ends, and swathed herself in it to cover the obvious cleavage. She'd have to come to terms with the ka-pow of her dress with her in it at some point, but she wasn't quite ready to go there yet. "Wish me luck, Rubes."

Ruby blew her a kiss. "You look amazing. He won't be able to resist you."

All kinds of hot and steamy things flew through her mind when her bestie said that. Had she ever been irresistible? Her face heated. "Thanks, sweetie."

"You are truly my best friend, Em."

Emily stepped out into the hall and raced for the elevator. They'd agreed to meet outside the restaurant. As she turned the corner, her high heel twisted under her, and she stumbled right into the arms of Max.

* * *

A bundle of pink and fluff fell into Max's arms. Warm, soft, and so Emily.

For a moment, he considered not letting her go, picking her up, and carrying her back to his cabin. What would he do with her there? Well, he had so many ideas. So, so many. The first of which was to remove that nothing of a dress.

Emily pushed against his chest and propped herself back on her heels. "Oh, I'm sorry." A lovely pink flush spread across her cheeks.

"Don't be." His nerve endings tingled, and his voice dropped a few notes.

She enveloped her upper body in a swath of fluff. "I guess it was kind of silly for us to meet at the restaurant. We're only a few doors down from each other."

He wanted to tug away the distracting bit of fabric so he could take in the sight of her magnificent body. Where did she find such a perfect dress? "Yeah, not sure what I was thinking. Let me call the elevator."

"Okay." She stood rigidly and avoided eye contact.

He punched the up button, rolled his shoulders to loosen the tension, and reached out a hand. "I won't bite."

With a shy smile, she accepted it.

They both stared at the floor indicator and watched the elevator descend from the top deck.

"I've never had French food before," Emily said.

"Never? I thought you were a gourmet chef."

She shook her head. "I put together picnics for people with things like fried chicken and banana pudding. Not escargot and ratatouille."

"Rata-what?" His thoughts froze. Would she think him an idiot? Did most men she dated know this stuff?

"Didn't you watch the movie?" she asked.

"About the rat?" He willed his heart to slow down. This was a casual, fun conversation.

"Yeah, it's a traditional French dish. The rat serves it in the movie."

He scanned his memory banks for the last time he watched an animated movie. "I vaguely remember it."

She gasped. "But it was the cutest movie ever."

"I kinda suck at remembering movie plots—unless it's *Indiana Jones* or *Star Wars*."

"Well," she suggested, "then we'll have to watch it together."

Wait? Was she saying there was some kind of down-the-road thinking? Could it be more than a short-term cruise thing?

The elevator door opened. It was empty.

"After you." Max ushered her inside.

Emily gracefully stepped in. The dress molded to her every curve—butt, hips, thighs. Like a Greek goddess.

The door closed behind them. She leaned against the railing and smiled. Somehow the mild curve of her lips drew him to her. He narrowed the distance between then, touched her bare shoulder, and then slid his fingers into her hair.

"Max?" Her eyes were dark and limpid.

"I have to kiss you." He leaned in until he was lost in those eyes. "Is that okay?" At that moment everything in him held back waiting for her answer.

Waiting. Waiting. Waiting.

His breath stirred a wisp of hair across her perfect forehead.

"Oh, yes." Her answer was a whisper.

He touched his lips to hers. Their plush, pillowy softness made him think of white puffy clouds in the sky. The taste of her was minty and sweet, as if she'd sucked on a peppermint candy. A thrum of desire rippled through him and hit at his core.

This woman had captured him like no one else.

His hands roamed down her body from her naked shoulders to her nipped in waist. She was warm and alive beneath him. His tongue dipped into her mouth to taste her more deeply.

When her arms curled around his neck, and she let out a little whimper, he thought he might lose control right there.

The elevator dinged.

His hands stilled on her body, and he softly cursed the man who hadn't built enough floors into their cruise ship.

Emily's chest moved up and down, as if she'd run a hundred-yard dash. When he made a move to break the kiss, she pressed a hand against the back of his neck to keep their mouths together. She tilted her head in the opposite direction. He followed her lead. The kiss grew frantic and hot and messy.

His groin ached.

Where was the down button? Why bother eating dinner?

The door opened.

"Ahem, monsieur?" A voice interrupted their world made for two.

Max couldn't focus. He broke off the most passionate kiss of his life and asked, "What?"

Emily's hands drifted away. She covered her mouth and froze.

"Keeling reservation for two?" The maître d' straightened his glasses and gave a quick smile, as if it was totally normal to see two people making out in the elevator.

Max faced the intruder and cleared his throat. "Uh, yes." Why didn't he tell the guy to scram, hit the 'close door' button, and spend the next hour or two tasting every inch of Emily's body? That would be dinner enough for him.

Emily quietly fixed the collar of his dress shirt that had turned up in the middle of everything. The touch of her fingers on his neck was like molten lava. Did she have any idea what she did to him?

"That's right." Emily stepped forward, her voice steady and sure. Her wrap slipped off her body exposing her décolletage. "Keeling. Nine o'clock."

The maître d's eyes widened, and he cleared his throat. "Yes, mademoiselle. Please follow me."

At that moment, Max fell hard for Emily. Sexy and strong? Funny and smart? Four boxes checked. How many more could there be?

He offered her his arm, she accepted, and they stepped out of the elevator and followed the maître d' into the restaurant.

Chapter 20
Not What She Expected

As the maître d' led them into the restaurant, Emily hoped Max couldn't see she was trembling. Her knees were weak, her head was a mass of disjointed thoughts, and her whole body had come alive.

He had kissed her.

Thoroughly and completely.

Wow.

She waited for her dream to end and to find herself in bed making out with a pillow.

His hard chest pressed up against hers in the elevator? Yes, please.

His firm lips on hers? Yes, please.

His fingers tangled in her hair? Yes, yes, and yes.

And now she was expected to sit at a table and casually eat a meal while everything in her wanted to drag him back to the elevator and ride it up and down all night.

Ride it up and down...

Oh.

Goodness.

A zing exploded in her core and spread throughout her body. The kiss had started a chain reaction she couldn't stop. She wanted to follow it all the way to the end. Her temperature ratcheted up a few degrees.

She didn't have time for this. She had a job to do. That kiss in the elevator had seriously compromised her focus on the goal: deleting Ruby's photo.

"Madame Keeling?" Their server stood next to their table with an expectant look on his face. "Would you care for a drink?"

When had they been seated?

She touched the suede seat cushion beneath her, grounding herself.

Max cleared his throat. "Oh, we're not married." He avoided her gaze.

The server's brow wrinkled, and his eyes darted to the side. "I see."

Why didn't Emily even ponder what a date on a honeymoon cruise might trigger? How to explain?

"I'll have a glass of pinot," she said before more of an explanation was offered. Maybe wine would calm her nerves.

"Very good, mademoiselle." The server looked at Max pointedly. "And the monsieur?"

He handed back the wine list. "Same."

The server gave a nod and disappeared.

"So," Max began and reached for her hand under the table, "I hope that was okay in the elevator. Your dress." His gaze dipped to her neckline and back up again. "And you in it. Did I tell you how beautiful you look?"

The warmth of his fingers interlaced with hers caused goose bumps to rise. "I don't usually wear—it's Ruby's dress." The outfit was doing exactly what she wanted it to do. Better than she thought possible when she'd thrown it on in the cabin. But now that they were here in the restaurant and after what happened in the elevator, a twinge of guilt hit. She had a plan in mind, and he thought she was on the date solely because of her interest in him. "I wasn't sure if it was my style."

"If I didn't know every other man in the room was on his honeymoon, I'd be worried." He stroked her arm.

"Worried?" Why couldn't she seem to breathe properly?

"Worried I might not be the only one who can't keep his eyes off of you."

"Oh."

Max said every word she'd fantasized hearing from him, and yet she couldn't believe it. How could a man like him desire a woman like her? Now her plans to deceive him and use him to access his laptop seemed wrong. She averted her gaze. Her appetite fled. She couldn't focus on anything else but the deceit.

The sommelier sailed over to their table to deliver their wine glasses and pour the wine.

Emily wanted it all. She wanted to be able to delete those photos to make Ruby happy, and she wanted to be able to follow this budding and unexpected romance wherever it might be going. Even if it was only a cruise affair. But how to achieve both goals without hurting him?

Why did he have to kiss her like that in the elevator?

Damn.

He'd been hurt by that Penelope woman who stood him up, and now she was set to do the same.

Max lifted his glass for a toast. "May the most you wish for be the least you get."

Emily touched her glass to his, pondering the meaning. "What are you wishing for, Max?"

He licked his lips, slid his hand toward her shoulder, and leaned in. "You."

* * *

Somehow Emily had managed to eat some of her meal, Confit de Canard, a delicious duck dish in a rich sauce made with red wine. After their meal had arrived, the conversation had flowed away from their mutual attraction and toward the more every day. Their likes and dislikes. Their worst first dates. Their parents.

By the end of the meal, that super-hot kiss in the elevator was a distant memory, and they were chatting about boring non-sexy things like how to clean a blood stain out of a white shirt and how often to water an African violet.

How did that happen?

How could she steer things back to where they were at the beginning of the meal when he was complimenting her outfit and calling her beautiful? Suddenly, she was no longer confident wearing a dress built for Megan Fox. She was a fraud.

The server brought Max the bill, and he added his cabin number and signed his name.

This time, when they entered the elevator, two honey-mooning couples joined them. The intimacy they shared only ninety minutes earlier had worn off. One of the newlywed husbands engaged Max in a conversation about the Miami Dolphins and their likelihood of making it to the playoffs. Emily fixated on her chipping manicure.

How was she going to swing this date back to the topic at the beginning of the night—that kiss? And then work her way into his cabin, hopefully into his bed—even though she was trying not to focus too much on how that part was going to happen—and then get a shot at his laptop?

Now the idea she'd shared with Ruby—her crazy plan—seemed nearly impossible. How was she going to transition from dinner date to secretly deleting photos from his laptop? Did she think she could force her way into his cabin, take off the plastic wrap dress, blow his mind with some kind of Kama Sutra-style position or whatever, and wait for him to fall asleep? Why didn't she think this through a little better?

The elevator opened at Deck Eleven. They stepped out together, but this time they weren't holding hands.

Max walked her silently back to her cabin.

Was he nervous? Did he think she wasn't interested? Had he forgotten how she kissed him back in the elevator?

"Thanks for dinner," she said. Someone had to break the ice. "That was really good."

"Yep." He scraped a hand through that glorious wavy hair.

Why was he just standing there? When was he going to grab her around the waist and kiss her again?

He rubbed the back of his neck and shifted his weight from one foot to the other.

"Well, guess I'd better go to bed." Was this really how it was going to end? She waved her card in front of the key reader, paused, and then faced him. "Unless—" Would he get the hint?

"Good night, then." He brushed the hair away from her eyes.

This was it. He was going to do it.

He leaned in.

She held her breath.

He kissed her on the cheek.

The cheek.

What?

He backed away with a wistful smile on his face. "Good night, Emily."

"Good night," she mumbled.

Her posture slumped. She unlocked the door and slipped inside. That was not how the evening was supposed to go with the sexy dress and the ultimate plan. Instead, he'd been kind and wonderful and respectful. A gentleman.

Ugh.

The dark, empty cabin awaited her like a cat lady's apartment after animal control removed all her furry companions. Ruby had decided to spend the rest of her evening at one of the bars for some stand-up comedy.

Every nerve ending in Emily's body was firing with need. She'd built up an expectation of how the night would play out, and it ended with nothing more than a chaste 'good night' at the door. Only—she counted on her fingers— a handful of days until the cruise was over and they were leaving the ship and going back to their normal lives.

Emily was not going to miss this chance. For once in her life, she was going to throw herself out there. If she was humiliated so be it. She could avoid Max the rest of the cruise. But this might be her one opportunity to tell him how she felt and delete those photos.

She slipped her shoes back on, rearranged the girls in the revealing dress, and stomped down the hall.

* * *

Max floated back to his cabin, his feet lighter than air. He had the perfect date with Emily. The amazing and incredibly sexy kiss in the elevator, a delicious dinner, and conversation that flowed easily. So easily he was shocked. He'd never been on a first date quite like it.

Was that how dates were supposed to be?

Because every other date before tonight paled in comparison.

Emily had been funny, sexy, and real—and completely unaware about any of it. When she'd stumbled over a few words as she drank her second glass of wine, she had blushed the most attractive shade of pink. When she'd dropped a bit of duck in her lap, she'd made a joke about saving a snack for later. Even when he pointed out a little bit of food in her teeth, she'd laughed and thanked him for it. Penny would've given him a dressing down in front of the whole restaurant for saying something like that. Nothing about their date had been awkward or uncomfortable.

As he waved his room key in front of his door, he thought about how difficult it had been to leave her at her cabin. He wanted nothing more than to repeat their kiss in the elevator and follow it through to the end. All of it. Beginning, middle— oh, especially the middle—and the end. An end he couldn't even imagine as the real thing would be infinitely better than any fantasy he could conjure up.

When he leaned toward her for a goodnight kiss, he knew he had to rein himself in or he'd lose control. And she deserved to be treated with care and concern and respect. He'd never desired a woman more, while at the same time wanting to take his time and make sure she felt the same.

But the way she'd looked at him—with half-lidded eyes and kiss-bruised lips—required him to use every ounce of self-control to redirect his mouth to her cheek.

He stepped into his dark cabin and unbuttoned the top buttons of his dress shirt. Was it hot in here? He checked the thermostat—sixty-eight degrees. He took off his shirt and tossed it on the bed. His armpits were sweaty. A shiver ran through him.

Damn, he couldn't turn it off. His sex drive was barely under control. His mind returned to the softness of her body when they'd kissed. Every curve under his hands. Her skin hot beneath the form-fitting dress.

Why was he torturing himself?

Time for a cold shower.

He kicked off his shoes and stripped naked.

After turning on the shower and adjusting the water to arctic cold, he stepped into the icy stream with his erection as stiff as a flagpole and shivered his way through it.

Emily stood outside Max's cabin with her hand frozen in the air. She had intended to knock and throw herself at him the minute he opened the door. But maybe he didn't find her as attractive as she'd surmised early on in the date. Maybe she had to work harder to seduce him. The kiss in the elevator, the boobalicious dress—perhaps it hadn't been enough.

Didn't most men have zero problems with sex delivered to them on a platter? Or wrapped in plastic wrap?

She pulled down the short hem of the tight dress as it had ridden up her thighs.

How did women wear this stuff? Annoying.

She hesitated, stared at the door, and pursed her lips.

What if he laughed at her? What if he thought she was ridiculous and silly? Was that why he gave her the kiss on the cheek?

"Trouble in paradise?" A man in his thirties approached

wearing a Houston Astros baseball cap and a jersey to match. He was alone. Unusual for the honeymoon cruise. Everyone seemed to travel in pairs.

Emily gave him a tight smile and hoped he moved along.

No such luck.

When the man spoke next, the scent of booze filled her nose. He was three sheets to the wind. "Shy bride? He won't care." Before she could tell him to scram, he pounded on Max's door.

"Hey!" She slapped him on the arm.

The man withdrew his hand, backed away, and shrugged. "Sorry, lady, only wanted to help."

Max opened the door. He wore only a pair of shorts, and a towel rested around his shoulders.

Oh my.

Fresh from a shower?

His abs were too perfect. She wished she could touch his muscled torso.

"Emily?" He scratched his perfect chin and frowned.

This was no time to lose her resolve. With the flat of her hand, she pushed him into his cabin.

Chapter 21
The Chapter Everyone Wants

"Hey." Max lost his balance, stumbled backward, grabbed Emily's hand, and pulled her to him.

Her body aligned with his. And, oh, it was better than she could've imagined. He smelled like coconuts and hibiscus.

Before they both landed in a pile on his bed, the top of her head whacked him in his teeth.

"Ouch," Max said in a low timbre.

The hottest ouch on the planet.

His arm slid down her back until it rested just above her ass. Warm, solid—this was the second best accidental fall on top of a hot man ever (the first being her fall in the raft). She needed to be clumsier around him in the future.

But as much as she wanted to lie there in a sexy pile on his bed, she needed answers. She rolled off of his hard glorious body of muscles, painful as that was, to do what she came there to do. "I want to set something straight."

"Um, okay." His eyes narrowed.

When she rolled off him, his hand ended up under her ass, which caused a wave of heat to undulate through her body.

"Do you or do you not find me—ahem—attractive?" She practically fainted when she said the words. Never in her life had she been so bold. Not even when Greg Stansfeld had asked if he could feel her up after the prom, and she forced his hand down her dress. Because, dammit, she was seventeen and by now some guy should've felt her up.

Max propped himself up on one arm, freeing his hand from under her ass, which was a very sad thing, and looked her straight in the eye as she lay before him. "Yes." He worked his jaw as he waited for another question. His green eyes snapped with fire.

With his rock hard body within touching distance, she had a hard time speaking.

"Would you kiss me again?"

Had the room temperature risen five extra degrees?

Her armpits felt damp.

He trailed his fingers down her bare arm.

Emily thought she would hyperventilate.

"Yes." His voice was dark, dirty, gritty. As he said the word for a second time, he leaned in but stopped short of her mouth. "Do you want me to?"

His warm breath caressed her cheek.

"Yes."

His mouth descended on hers.

Soft, yet solid. And he tasted delicious. Like warm chocolate, which made sense because they'd had chocolate lava cake for dessert.

Was this real? Could it be happening?

Her insides were molten fire. She couldn't even imagine what it would be like to go further than a kiss. Could her body handle it or would she burst into flames and turn into a pile of ash at his feet?

Then the kiss went wild. As if every pent up feeling she'd had about Max came out in lips and tongues.

His hand slid up under the hem of her borrowed dress. He gripped her upper thigh, and then he broke their kiss.

Both of them panted.

"Is that okay?" His pupils were dilated like a wild animal's.

"What?" Her mind was reeling. It didn't seem possible. This was all a dream and then, poof, she was going to find herself in bed with her hand between her legs.

"My hand. On your leg." He gave a quick smile.

"Yes, absolutely okay."

"And this?" A finger slipped under the dainty lace waistband of her teeny tiny underwear.

"Oh yes." Never had she been happier she'd purchased totally un-Emily-like panties in the ship's lingerie store. This was much better than a boudoir photo shoot.

He tugged the itsy bitsy underwear off her body and a cool rush of air conditioned air buffeted between her legs.

"Oh."

Yes, so much better.

When was the last time she'd had sex? Her mind skipped to Kyle and how he'd had trouble knowing what to do with her. Too much flesh. Her breasts seemed to get in his way. And he never understood how much time it took to satisfy her. More time than he seemed willing to spend.

Max smoothed his hand across her bare thighs. Her legs relaxed at his scintillating touch, and her knees splayed apart.

"Not yet, Emily." Gently, he pushed her knees back together. "I want to take my time."

Oh, goodness.

Her core burned. The apex of her thighs trembled. How much time? Her nipples tingled at the thought.

He leaned on one elbow and swept her hair off her forehead. "I'm not interested in some cruise fling, Emily."

His hand slid behind her neck and loosened the knot of her halter dress.

"No?" she squeaked out the question.

Max, her fantasy man, was about to see her naked from the waist up. She held her breath as the knot came undone.

"No, beautiful." With a gentle hand, he lowered the straps of her dress and bared her breasts.

Automatically, she laid her arm across her nakedness, embarrassed. This kind of woman was not his type. His kind of woman was sleek and lean and perfect.

"Stop." His heated gaze met hers. "Let me see you. I want to see every gorgeous inch of you."

She let him brush her arm aside and then he kissed from her bare shoulder, down her collarbone, and over the curve of her breast, capturing the nipple in his mouth. His hand kneaded the soft flesh as he suckled, causing sparks of pleasure to run down her body.

Everything she'd ever wanted was about to come true, but in the back of her mind she thought about her deception to come, and it weighed on her.

Max moved his mouth to her other nipple and pushed her dress further down her body. "Beautiful, beautiful, Emily," he muttered.

Emily's mind could only focus on that singular thing. Her secondary goal pushed far, far away.

* * *

Oh. Holy. Hell.

How did she manage to end up in bed with the most gorgeous perfect man she'd ever met? His lips and tongue were working miracles on her body. Like literal miracles. How come Kyle didn't know how to do this stuff? How come any one of her few-and-far-between sex partners didn't either? And where had her dress disappeared to?

She gripped Max's head with both hands. He'd reached her belly button. Pretty soon he'd be...well...down there. Between her chunky thighs. Thighs he didn't seem to mind. In fact, every touch of her flesh had been a caress, as if he were worshipping her body rather than putting up with it. Could it be possible Max had a thing for curvy bodies? Like, really curvy bodies?

Maybe she didn't have to wear the plastic wrap dress after all. Maybe she could've shown up in a paper bag—well, maybe not a literal paper bag—but how about yoga pants and an old T-shirt?

Max pushed her thighs apart.

Her eyes flew open.

"Relax," he whispered. The warm air of his breath teasing her center. "You don't know how long I've dreamed about doing this."

He dreamed about her?

His tongue did ridiculous things to her most sensitive parts, and her mind turned off completely. Like one-hundred percent nothingness. He seemed to know exactly where to lick.

Her chest tightened, her legs tensed, her whole body trembled in anticipation of...well...of...yes, yes, yes, yes, yes.

That.

Oh, and then the scream. The very loud, very embarrassing, very uncontrollable scream. Probably heard as far as the elevators, maybe even all the way at the pool. Security would probably knock down the door thinking she had been attacked.

She threw a hand across her eyes.

Oh, God. What would he think?

He peeled her hand away. "Don't hide from me." With his arms he'd created a cage around her body. "And you were right: you're a screamer." He gave her a sexy slow smile. "And I love it." He swooped down to kiss a path from her neck to her ear.

She shivered. "You do?"

"Absolutely." His voice rumbled in her ear.

His answer gave her an odd confidence she'd never felt in bed with a man. "Can I be on top?"

He stopped kissing her neck and rested his forehead against her cheek. "You're going to kill me, Emily."

Her insides quivered. "I just thought it might be fun—"

Before she could finish the sentence, he'd grabbed hold of her and rolled them both across the bed until she was above him. "How can you possibly be even more gorgeous?"

Her face heated, but her shyness had melted away. He'd been *down there* for heaven's sake. Straddling him totally naked? No problem.

If this was only going to happen once between them, she wanted to wring as much out of it as she could. Enough memories to last her a lifetime. For one night, Max wanted her. Too bad he'd regret it tomorrow after she'd followed through on her plan. He'd probably never want to see her again.

Max slid his hands up the sides of her waist and fondled her breasts.

Emily threw back her head and shoved her negative thoughts to the back of her mind. All she wanted to do was focus on the two of them, making love, and let the rest of the world be damned.

"Can I?" he asked breathlessly.

She brushed her hair from her eyes and nodded.

He thrust up into her, and she moved in a focused rhythm. All of it felt so right. She rested a palm on his perfect abs and stared into his beautiful green eyes as they rocked together.

"Emily?" he whispered.

"Yes?" Her breathing came faster now. The second time in one night she might scream.

Wow. She always thought that was a myth.

"I think I love you."

* * *

Those words—'*I love you*'—bounced around in Emily's head for an hour after Max had fallen asleep with his arm possessively thrown across her naked torso.

The sex had been the best of her life. Half the reason had been the way Max had made her feel comfortable in her own body. Never had a man made her feel that way about her oversized breasts, extra wide hips, and fleshy stomach.

But love? Did he really love her or only love the sex? Hard to believe in a few days someone could declare love. Look what happened to Ruby and Tyler. And that was after months of dating and making plans to get married.

No, Max didn't love her. It was something he said out of obligation, maybe. What a woman expected to hear perhaps. A way for him to feel okay about a one-night stand on a cruise with a woman he would never see again. Yes, that was probably it. The only explanation that made any sense. She'd been an easy mark...easy and eager for such a perfect male specimen to bed her.

Well, she'd built it into her plan, so could she really blame him for taking the bait? Any man probably would've done the same. Commitment-free sex? Sure. A guy's dream, wasn't it?

Slowly, she slid out from under his arm. He rolled over with a grunt, and she froze. But he went back to sleep. Then she picked up a T-shirt he'd laid across the back of a chair, pulled it over her head, and wriggled into her teeny tiny underwear.

His laptop lay on the vanity next to the bed. She sat in front of it and tapped the touchpad with her fingers to bring the screen to life. The bright light blinded her for a second or two.

She glanced at Max's sleeping figure. Dead to the world. He didn't suspect a thing. She would fulfill her promise to her best friend and rescue her from the Weird Twins. If the photos no longer existed, they couldn't really use them in their ad campaign, now could they?

Emily clicked around on the folders on his desktop. Those pictures had to be there somewhere.

Folder after folder she opened. Eventually, she figured out Max's naming system: Date, Location, Subject. Plenty of folders were dated since the cruise began, most full of portrait photos taken that first night. Everyone's free honeymoon photo shoot. Then, she zeroed in on the day after—when they'd made the date to meet on the pool deck. One folder had the subject: Pool. Another folder dated the same day had the subject: Personal.

Personal?

Hm.

She clicked on the folder and opened it. There were two names in the folder: Ruby and Emily.

Gulp.

He'd taken photos of her?

Seven of them.

Why?

Even though he'd worshipped her body in bed only an hour ago, her heartbeat raced at what kind of photos he might have taken. Was he, in fact, the creep Ruby thought he was? Emily had felt less than confident in the bikini—mega boobs stuffed into two triangles of green with her less-than-toned middle exposed to public view. She yanked down Max's T-shirt and fidgeted in her seat.

Before she could slide her index finger across the touchpad to right-click the Ruby photos and delete them, she double-clicked on a photo labeled 'Emily 1.'

Her heart leaped into her throat. She had the churn of pre-embarassment in her stomach. A familiar tell-tale sensation that predicted blunders of all types throughout her life, which she never seemed to learn from. No, she always blasted straight through her gut instincts screaming at her to stop, stop, stop before the regret set in.

She couldn't prevent what was about to happen.

The photo popped up.

"Oh." Emily blinked at what appeared on the screen.

"What are you doing with my laptop?"

Chapter 22
Where Are My Crabs?

C*rap.*
Max.

He'd woken up and caught Emily in the act.

Dammity damn damn.

He sat up in bed to see what she'd been up to. "Shit." He grimaced.

Every caress, every kiss, every word he'd said to her earlier flew out of her head. Yes, she thought it could be possible it had been meaningless, easy sex for Max, but some little part of her had hoped she was wrong.

But this photo?

No way did he think she was sexy or beautiful. No way in hell would a man like Max love a woman like Emily.

She turned the laptop so he could see the photo she'd opened—her pulling a T-shirt over her head. Her boobs looked like saggy white melons, her stomach a roll of flab, the look on her face—distorted and horrible.

"Why would you save this picture of me? Is it so you could laugh later on? Share them with your friends—with your girlfriend—and crack up about some pathetic girl you met on a cruise? And how easy she was to get into bed?"

His face paled, and his mouth parted. No words came out.

So Emily kept going. "I know I'm not gorgeous like Ruby and that I'm probably the last person you think should be wearing a bikini in public, but there is something called the Body Positivity Movement, and you can't shame me. I will wear whatever I want to wear in public. I'm proud of my body—"

But she most certainly was not and knew that half of the ramblings coming out of her mouth were lies.

"You should be proud," he said quietly.

"—and men certainly don't get to make fun of and belittle women for their less-than-perfect figures—"

"I think you're perfect."

Wait.

Wait, wait, wait.

Back up the train and return to the station.

What did he say? What in the goddamn hell did this beautiful man say?

"—and I...and you...and what?" Emily's face heated as if she'd been sitting too close to the high school bonfire on Homecoming Weekend. Like Kiki the Cheerleader who'd shown up for the big game on Saturday night with a red face and a warning from her mother to never sit that close to a bonfire ever again.

Max kept his gaze down. "I was taking pictures of the pool deck like Sylvia asked me to do, and then my lens moved a little too far to the right. I saw a close-up of you in that swimsuit and my finger might've pressed down on the shutter button a little too long, and I took a bunch of pictures all at once. I mean, wow, Emily. What did you expect?" He shifted his gaze to her face. "I've never seen a woman look sexier in a swimsuit."

Emily's mind blanked as an explosion of epic proportions went off in every square inch of her gray matter. Maybe she wasn't just some girl he could screw. Could he possibly have meant what he said earlier?

"God, you hate me, don't you?" He took a deep breath. "It's embarrassing I wanted to keep these photos. What kind of weirdo does that? I should've deleted them because why in the hell would I keep them?"

Emily couldn't put two words together. For the first time in her life she had zero words in her head, zero ideas for how to respond, zero, zero, zero. All she could do was sit and stare.

He shook his head briefly. "I'll delete the photos—the ones of you, the ones of Ruby. It was wrong. I knew it was then, but —" He climbed out of bed, leaned over her, and focused on the screen.

The smell of him was almost too much to bear. "Well, what?" Words had formed and come out of her mouth. Hallelujah, the Lord had healed her. Her nerve endings tingled. She was more aware of her body than ever in her life. The sensation of the T-shirt fabric against her breasts as her chest rose and fell with her breathing. The warmth between her thighs. The closeness of the naked male body next to her.

"There. Gone. They're deleted."

But somehow instead of feeling relief, a pain hit the back of her throat. Her plan had worked better than she'd imagined, yet she couldn't look at him.

"I—I've got to go."

"What?"

She grabbed her dress off the floor and tied it around her lower half like a skirt. "Thanks for last night. It was—" Perfect? The hottest night of her life? "—nice."

"Nice?" Max's brow wrinkled.

All in a rush, she grabbed her purse, opened the door, and dashed out into the hall. It was two in the morning, so not a honeymooning soul was in sight. As she waved her key card in front of her cabin door, hot tears flowed down her cheeks.

She'd made a mess of everything.

* * *

"Wake up, Emily!" Ruby shook her.

After she'd returned to her cabin, Emily had tossed and turned for an hour. Her body remembered everything in fine detail. Every touch, every kiss, every lick. Which made sleeping impossible. She'd had sex—incredible, mind-blowing sex—with Max, and it had all fallen apart in a matter of seconds.

Had she really told him it was 'nice'?

Cringe.

Her eyelids were glued together, probably from the seven layers of mascara she'd piled on before her date last night. "What time is it?" she mumbled. Way too early. Horrifically early. So early only roosters and race walking retirees should be awake.

"It's seven-thirty." The mattress dipped as Ruby sat next to her. "You have to meet at eight for the ATV jungle adventure, so I thought you might like some time to get ready, maybe eat something?"

"Seven-thirty?" Emily sat up in bed and pried her eyes open. "Why did you let me sleep so late?"

"Your alarm went off an hour ago, but you didn't move. I thought maybe you'd gotten home pretty late—" Ruby chewed a Mexican Coral fingernail. "Should I have made you get up? I was thinking about it."

Emily threw back the covers, grabbed a pair of shorts and a

shirt, and rushed into the teeny tiny bathroom to shower. "Give me five minutes." She turned on the shower and took off the T-shirt she'd stolen from Max's cabin. It smelled heavenly. Like man sweat and hisbiscus-scented soap.

But that had been a mistake. The whole night had been a set up, and she'd achieved what she wanted: making the photos disappear.

"Hey, Rubes," she called out from underneath the full blast of the shower head. "The photos have been deleted." Instead of joy rushing through her at the thought of salvaging Ruby's revenge cruise experience and fending off the intrusive Weird Twins, an odd tightness wrapped around her chest and squeezed. She'd used him. She'd led Max on and used him. Did that make her a bad person?

"Your plan worked?"

Emily leaned into the spray and washed away every trace of Max the Gorgeous. The best sex of her life would always have an asterisk next to it in her mind: insecure liar seduces hot man. "Yes, it worked. No more photos."

"You are fab, Em. Thank you so much. I should've guessed no crazy scheme of yours was ever going to fail. Everything you do turns to gold."

"What?" Did she hear Ruby right? She thought Emily had a golden touch? Was she serious? Her messed up, pathetic, ridiculous life where she moved in with her parents to save on rent yet struggled to keep up with the payments for her car insurance? Sounded more like a crap touch to her—everything she touched turned to crap. If she thought about it long enough, she'd probably find a reason to blame herself for Tyler bailing on the wedding. Why not? She'd screwed up everything else.

"I'm hungry. You almost out of there?"

"Almost." She toweled herself off and slipped into her

clothes. "Hey, wait a minute, what about that text from Tyler?" Emily opened the door to see her best friend adding more lipstick to her perfectly made-up face.

Hold on, who puts full on make-up to go ATV riding in the jungle?

Ruby caught her best friend eyeballing her. "What?" The auburn-haired beauty capped the lipstick. "Something wrong with a girl wanting to look her best?"

Emily rubbed her hair as dry as she could with the towel. "For a muddy, sweaty ride through the jungle?" She picked up her phone from the nightstand and read the excursion description in the cruise app. "*Start your engines and prepare for an unforgettable adventure driving your own all-terrain vehicle along well-maintained trails through the interior jungle. Get your adrenaline pumping as you maneuver these easy handling machines on the best trails around. Enjoy the beautiful jungle as the flora and fauna envelop your off-road trail.*" She cocked an eyebrow.

Ruby tightened her thick hair into a high ponytail and avoided eye contact. "Okay, I'll admit it's just in case."

"Just in case what?"

"Just in case Tyler's really there at the pier."

"So you were planning on abandoning me in the dangerous jungles of Mexico to hook up with the man who jilted you?" Emily crossed her arms. Would Ruby really make her drive the ATV all by herself?

This sounded bad. Very very bad.

Ruby patted her nose with pressed powder. "I wanted to hear his reasoning, his excuse. Maybe even see if he was going to apologize. I mean, if he flew all the way down to Cozumel—"

"He hurt you." Emily placed her hands on her friend's shoulders.

Ruby caught her gaze in the mirror and set down her compact.

"He ruined what was supposed to be the happiest day of your life. He doesn't deserve you, Rubes."

The former bride squeezed Emily's hand. "I know. And it means a lot to me that you're so supportive, Em. But if he's there, I have to find out what he has to say. I have to."

Although Emily wished Tyler would be sucked up into space never to be heard from again, that wasn't realistic. Ruby and Tyler shared the same adventurous spirit and would be living in the same town. It was inevitable they'd run into each other again. "If I have to drive an ATV by myself, I can do it." But even as she smiled, she worried about flipping it over and breaking a bone, driving it through a mud puddle so deep that she ended up coated in brown, or crying in frustration when she forgot which was the clutch and which was the brake.

Ruby gave a faint smile. "Thanks. I want to have the option if he's there waiting for me."

Emily tried to squish her fears into a tiny little box inside her chest and, at the same time, squish her mixed feelings about Max and how they left things last night into the same cramped space. "Whatever you want. I'm here for you."

* * *

Emily and Ruby waited in line to exit the ship and join up with their ATV group. They'd arrived late, so had been ushered out of the theater seconds after arrival to make sure they didn't miss the group bus for their excursion.

"Remember, look for the crab flag." Ruby stood on her tiptoes trying to see over the line of people in front of them, past the gangplank, and out to the pier.

"Do you see it?" Emily's view was not only blocked by her much taller friend, but by a portly newlywed husband who struggled to carry two massive tote bags full of beach gear.

"Oh, my God! Look at that." Portly man's wife, wearing a one-piece bathing suit and a see-through rainbow cover-up, pointed at the sky. "Can you read it, Sherman?"

Several cruisers who had reached the gangplank also gawked at something above.

Ruby touched her cruise card to the reader near the exit. "Have a wonderful day, Ms. Evers," the uniformed cruise employee said in a chipper tone, as he read her name off the computer screen in front of him.

"Just call me Ruby, please."

"Your name's Ruby Evers?" The portly man asked, his eyes round. "Maybe the message is for you." He pointed at the sky.

The former bride shielded her eyes with her hand and squinted up into the bright, cloudless blue above them. Her face paled. "Emily." She gripped her friend's arm so tightly the circulation cut off.

After scanning her own card, Emily slipped it into her pocket. "What's wrong?" Besides a delightful sunburn and peeling skin, she'd arrive home with the world's largest bruise on her upper arm.

"It's Tyler." Ruby jerked her chin upward.

Above the cruise ship, the pier, and the crowds of people flew a black-and-yellow biplane flying a banner that read:

Ruby Evers, forgive me. I love you. Meet me in the Plaza Del Sol.

Dammit.

What was Tyler up to, the jerk? Was he going to play around with Ruby's feelings and leave her even worse off than he did less than a week ago?

"You aren't seriously considering meeting him, are you?" She had to give it to the man, though, he knew how to get a girl's attention.

"I'm looking for my crabs. All my crabs." Down on the pier, a woman waving a flag with a cartoon crab holding an umbrella drink called out to the disembarking guests. "I'm missing some of my crabs."

"There's our group, Rubes." Emily turned her gaze away from the ridiculous flying sign and pointed at their ATV excursion group. "We have to go."

Ruby took a step back. She wrinkled her nose.

Oh no.

No, no, no, no.

"You're going to meet up with him, aren't you?" Emily's heart sank. Visions of every ATV accident possible filled her head. Ruby had promised to be the driver. She'd done this before. Emily knew zip about ATVs and off-roading.

Ruby played with the end of her ponytail. "I told you in the room that if Tyler was here in Cozumel, I wanted to hear what he had to say." She gestured at the banner as it flew by for a second time. "I think I have to do this."

Emily's mind flashed back to the panicked look on Ruby's face the day of the wedding. Her disbelief, then horror, then uncontrollable tears. "I don't understand it, but I support you, Ruby. Whatever you want. Don't worry about me. I'll be fine." If Tyler hurt her best friend again, she'd strangle him. Well, maybe not really strangle him, but launch a nonstop barrage of whatever terrible insults she could come up with.

Ruby hugged her hard. "Thanks." Her friend let out a heavy breath. "I'm going to find a taxi and figure out how to get to Plaza Del Sol. I'll see you back here before five. Promise me you'll have fun."

Emily clutched her string bag close to her chest. "I will." Even though she knew she wouldn't. Maybe she could beg off and sit with the bus driver while everyone else rode the trails.

As Ruby headed toward town and away from the clusters of excursion goers, Emily joined the crabs.

"Are you one of my missing crabs?" the woman with the flag asked.

"Yep," said a familiar voice behind her.

Holy Hell. It was Max.

Chapter 23
ATVs Are Death Traps

Every nerve fiber in her body erupted into flames. That voice. The low, rumbly voice. The same one from last night, in bed, when they were naked together.

What to do? What to do?

She froze. The hairs on the back of her neck stood up.

"Are you together?" the crab flag holder asked.

"No," said Emily.

"I don't think so," said Max.

Why did it hurt so much to hear him say that?

"Looks like your friend might've skipped out on you." Max leaned in and pointed at the banner sailing by for a fourth time.

Emily swallowed.

The woman with the crab flag stared up at the sky.

He must hate her guts. She'd told him the sex was 'nice.' Probably the worst insult a woman could give a man. Then, she'd sneaked onto his laptop and fooled around with his files.

"Great. We've got everyone here then." The woman tucked the crab flag under one arm. "Ruby Evers won't be joining us." She crossed her name off the list on a clipboard she carried.

"Excuse me." Emily's voice squeaked. "How long is this excursion?" If she had to be trapped with Max, she wanted to know how many hours she'd have to endure.

"Ninety minutes on the bus each way, thirty minute safety briefing, two hour ride." The woman screwed up her mouth as she thought through the timeline. "Five-and-a-half hours."

Emily's stomach rolled.

She didn't have to do this. She could leave. The group was still on the pier. Nobody could make her ride on an ATV. How would Ruby even know?

She glanced over her shoulder.

"So you're going to chicken out?" Max smirked. "Hope I'm not scaring you away."

She deserved the snark he threw at her, but she wasn't ready for this. Her plan in the middle of the night had been to avoid him for the last few days of the cruise. Then she'd hop in a taxi, ride to the airport in Tampa, and never see him again.

But then the river rafting trip in Jamaica filled her mind. She'd been terrified of that, too, and she'd had a blast. Wasn't it about time she started enjoying life instead of being afraid of it? Besides, she had the courage to leave her full-time job and start her own business from scratch. Should she really be scared of learning how to operate an ATV? It was about time she grabbed life by the *cojones* and stopped waiting for life to come to her. If this was Ruby's revenge honeymoon, maybe this was Emily's revenge on all the people in her past who had made her feel less than—the cool girls in middle school, the immature boys in high school, and the bad boyfriends who'd torn down her self-confidence.

She sneaked a glance at Max. He'd never made her feel

anything but confident about herself. Too bad she'd screwed things up.

Thrusting out her chin, she answered him, "Nope. I'm all in. What about you?"

"Bring it." His voice rumbled, like a tiger on the prowl or a leopard stalking its prey.

A zing of electricity ran down her spine. Is this what it felt like before someone fainted? A hot flush. A lack of air. Spots in front of one's eyes.

The woman with the crab flag clapped her hands. "All right, folks, time to load up on the bus. We have a bit of a drive to reach the trails, so let's get moving."

Emily immediately strode to the front of the crowd. Since it was all newlywed pairs, she wanted to be able to choose her seat and place her bag next to her so that Max didn't have any ideas. Or was she flattering herself? Would Max even want to sit next to her?

Maybe zooming down jungle trails on an ATV was the thing she needed to move past her feelings. Shake it all out. Reset her mind. All she had to do was pretend Max wasn't there.

Easy peasy.

* * *

The safety brief ended. One of the guides, his name had been Miguel or Mateo or maybe even Marco, had run through the operation of the ATV. Although he'd asked for hands of anyone who'd never driven an ATV before, Emily's had been the only one, and she was beginning to wonder if he'd even noticed. He'd mentioned a key, a button, a clutch, a gear shift, and the brakes in rapid accented English. The part she'd focused on the most was about how to apply the brakes.

The review flew by in what seemed like minutes. Minutes for her to grasp the whole concept. Minutes that were a fuzz in her brain now. A very faint fuzz.

"Do you think you got all that?" Max asked.

He'd had the audacity to stand right behind her during the briefing. How was she supposed to concentrate on all the important stuff Miguel/Mateo/Marco was saying with sexy Max vibes invading her mind? He was doing it to bug her. She knew it.

But, oh, did her traitorous mind want to revisit last night. The feathery touch of his lips on her collarbone, his caressing hands on her breasts, and when he kissed his way down to...

No, she wouldn't think about it. It had been a mistake. A passing lustful fancy that had ended and would go nowhere. Why bother even fantasizing about it?

Emily didn't look at him. His presence was bad enough. Her stomach fluttered and rolled and tilted. All the bad things. "Yep," she answered in a clipped tone.

Did he think she wouldn't do it? Did he think she'd wimp out? And why did she care so much what he thought of her? This was supposed to be a fun, exciting honeymoon cruise doing fun, exciting things. And, dammit, she was going to do all of it. Ruby would be so proud of her.

"Good," Max said.

Her nerves began to get the better of her as Miguel/Mateo/Marco handed out helmets. "Everyone at Jungle ATV Adventures must wear a helmet. It must remain on your head at all times. The chin strap must be secured under your chin. Do not remove the helmet when on your ATV."

Then, as honeymooning couples climbed on the backs of

their ATVs, her mouth turned as dry as a batch of cornbread muffins after they'd been left in the oven too long.

Was she really going to do this by herself?

What if she turned around and asked if she could ride on the back of Max's ATV? Even though she'd decided to be the new, confident, life-grabbing Emily only a couple of hours ago, somehow she'd lost that bravery when her fellow cruisers began to zip into the jungle one after the other.

Why was this even legal? No seatbelts? No air bags? ATVs were deathtraps.

"Miss?" M-something said. "Your helmet?"

She, Max, and a young newlywed couple who looked like they'd stepped out of a travel blog were the last ones waiting.

Emily took a deep breath—so deep her lungs hurt.

Exude confidence.

No fear.

You can do this, Emily!

Too late to back out now.

She grabbed a helmet, put it on, cinched the chin strap, and climbed aboard a mud-splattered ATV with a bright green stripe down the side. For a few seconds, she froze. All the instructions flew out of her head. But handy M-something turned the key and pressed the start button for her. Maybe to make sure their group stayed on schedule?

Somehow she remembered to step on the brake and pull the shift lever from P to H. As she pushed the throttle with her thumb, the ATV jumped forward and zoomed into the jungle. She clamped her hands down on the handlebars as if her life depended on it—wait, her life *did* depend on it.

* * *

The wind rushed through Emily's hair, cooling her down. At first, she'd been terrified. The speed of the ATV while bumping over the ruts of the jungle trail had been a little too much at first. But then, after a minute or two, she caught herself taking in the beauty of the scenery and forgetting about being scared. As she learned how to adjust her speed and avoid the worst holes to keep a smooth ride, her confidence grew .

Ruby would be so proud of her!

Ruby.

She'd forgotten all about Ruby.

Lord, Emily hoped her best friend's decision to meet up with Tyler hadn't been a mistake. Would she return to the cruise ship to find Ruby had chosen to fly back to Florida with her ex-fiancé?

Wait, was he still her fiancé if he left her at the altar? How did that work anyway?

Even though she'd come to terms with the idea of them meeting today and had told Ruby she supported her, hours later on her own with lots of time to think had her wondering if she should've gone with her friend. Ruby hadn't offered, so Emily assumed this was a couple's thing. Emily would've been a third wheel.

But she could have tailed Ruby in another taxi to make sure everything went okay. What if Tyler said nasty things to her, and poor Ruby was all alone in Cozumel surrounded by strangers and bawling her eyes out? He'd hurt her once, he could certainly do it again. Right after Ruby had seemed happy and ready to face a life without Tyler. They'd even talked about a possible career change, as her company seemed intent on edging her out of a job and replacing her with a younger saleswoman.

All positive, woman-hear-me-roar kind of stuff.

But seeing that banner in the sky—what was Tyler thinking? Would Ruby fall for it?

She couldn't bear it if Tyler hurt her bestie for a second time. She wasn't sure Ruby could live through that kind of pain again without permanent damage to her psyche.

Her ATV hit a patch of mud.

Water and dirt flew up on either side of her, creating a curtain of brown yuck. Her bare arms and legs were covered in mud.

For a moment, she wanted to cringe, cry out in disgust, slow down, and wipe herself off with the tail of her shirt. But then a rush of adrenaline hit her.

Whoosh!

Okay, that was kind of fun.

Why did she care about a little mud? Who was there to see her? Wasn't part of the adventure accepting the mud and water and sweat that came along with it?

She pressed harder on the throttle.

"Bring it on, Cozumel!" She shook her fist at the sky and gave a feral grunt that came from deep within. Not very lady-like, but who cared?

Up ahead she could see an even deeper and wider puddle. A mini-lake in the middle of the trail. Wonder how high she could make the mud fly this time?

Just as she was about to enter the next puddle, an ATV flew past with two people astride it: Mr. and Mrs. Travel Blog. They whooped and hollered as they passed her. Their ATV spat a deluge of muddy water backward. It poured over Emily, like that girl in *Flashdance*, covering her helmet's visor and obscuring her vision.

"Hey!" she protested, unable to see. She immediately

pulled on the brakes. When her ATV stopped with its front wheels in the puddle, she flipped up her visor.

The bride on the back of the ATV looked back, waved, and said, "Last one to the beach is a loser!"

Her new husband poured on the speed, and they disappeared down the trail.

The joy that had flowed through her body like an electric jolt, evanesced like fog under a strong summer sun. Mud and water flowed down from her face to her shoulders to her legs. She shook out her arms and bits of muck flew in all directions.

Ugh.

Behind her she heard the unmistakable rumble of another ATV. Max's ATV. He had been the last one to receive a helmet after the safety briefing.

Great.

She clenched her teeth and prepared for the mocking that would be sure to ensue.

Max rode down the trail lost in his thoughts. He hadn't expected to see Emily again so soon. It had taken all of his self-control to tamp down his feelings when she'd shown up by the crab flag.

What a complete idiot he'd been last night. What was he thinking when he told Emily he loved her? She must've thought he was a clingy, bizarre weirdo. Her dispassionate response when questioned if they were a couple before they'd boarded the bus told him his suspicions were correct.

Dumb. Dumb. Dumb.

Plus, she'd declared his lovemaking skills 'nice.'

The death blow.

Everything he thought he knew about women and sex went completely out the window when she'd said that.

Guess Penny had been right. It was one of the things she'd dumped on him after the photography show failure. Sort of a last turn of the screw before she'd driven off in her Mercedes SUV. The words echoed in his head: "I've had better lovers, you know."

He'd assumed she was angry and embarrassed for supporting his show and inviting all her rich friends. A few had come, but none had purchased anything. They'd drunk the champagne and scarfed down the fancy hors d'oeuvres she'd paid for, frowned at his work, and left in a hurry.

But Emily made him think perhaps Penny's assessment had been accurate.

His mind went numb.

After one night with her, the differences between the two women had been night and day. Why had he ever been attracted to a spoiled rich girl who never accepted him for who he was? He'd let her change him, shape him, mold him into what she wanted him to be, and then, when she didn't like the results, she dumped him. Without even really telling him it was over. He'd had to guess at the status of their relationship when she didn't show at the ship.

But Emily?

She'd zapped into his life like a static shock on a cold winter's day.

Whammo.

All curves and dimples and goofy jokes. He never thought a woman like her would be into a guy like him. He envied her creative talent. Beauty, brains, and artistic flair? She'd hit on a unique business idea that was sure to skyrocket her to success. He could learn a lot from a woman like her.

Then she'd kissed him back in the elevator. Like, *really* kissed him back.

From that moment, all he could think about was how to keep from screwing it up. And he'd tried, he'd really tried. He'd wanted to prove she was more than a one night fling to him. But when she fell into his arms in his cabin? All soft and luscious?

A hot jolting surge to his body had made him set aside his attempts to slow things down.

But he'd ruined it all by confessing too much too soon. They'd only met a week ago. He should've kept his feelings to himself, until they were on surer footing. He'd been scared of losing her, of her disappearing once they'd returned to Florida. Might've been smarter to ask for her number or even her Instagram handle.

"Dumbass," he mumbled under his breath as he gripped the handlebars.

Bumping down the trail, he took a sharp right and splashed through a small puddle. At least he could have a good time on the ATV. Donna and Diana MacPherson had spied him at breakfast, but only gave him a wave. They must've been too immersed in their plans for Cozumel to corner him again and ask about the photos, which were now deleted.

Sylvia wasn't going to be happy when she found out. She might even ruin him, if her threats could be believed. But in a way he was relieved Emily had found the photos and forced his hand. If they no longer existed, what could Sylvia do?

He kicked up his speed. If he got too far behind his group, he might not have as much time at the beach as he'd hoped for. He'd stuffed his camera in his backpack with a plan to take a few nature shots.

Up ahead he could see a larger, broader puddle that

covered the whole trail. A mud-covered rider appeared stuck only a few feet in.

Could that be Emily?

He slowed to make sure she was okay.

The rider waved him on.

He stopped anyway, flipped up his visor, and asked, "Everything all right?"

If it was Emily, it was hard to tell. Her entire body was covered in mud—from the top of her helmet to her feet.

How had that happened?

She hadn't even made it through the puddle yet.

Keeping her visor down, she nodded her head and then made larger waving motions with both hands.

His shoulders drooped. She really had no interest in talking to him, not even for basic common courtesy to make sure she wasn't in trouble. Time to face up to the truth: he'd screwed up his chances with her.

Slowly, he crept forward into the deeper puddle to avoid showering her with more mud. Once he'd sensed he was far enough away, he increased the gas. Instead of moving forward, the tires dug into the thick mud at the bottom.

Shit.

He gingerly gave it a little bit more gas, hoping instead of sinking deeper, he would move forward and out.

Nope.

In fact, the ATV sank lower.

His face heated. He stared down at his feet, as they submerged under the murky surface. He wanted to be anywhere but here, on the ATV stuck, sinking, and all in front of Emily.

Chapter 24
Confessions in the Jungle

Was he stuck?

Emily had made it as clear as she possibly could Max should drive around her and keep on going. Maybe she'd run into some good luck and a rainstorm would pop up out of nowhere and rinse away all the mud and muck covering her. But one thing she did not want was Max seeing her in such a ridiculous state.

He'd finally taken the hint, crept around her and into the puddle, and after only fifteen feet, he'd stopped. The odd angle of the ATV told her it had sunk unevenly into the mud below.

Now what?

The distant sound of the Travel Blog duo's ATV meant she and Max were alone on the trail. No one else was behind them.

Emily held her breath, her mind whirring.

Max pulled off his helmet and shook out his luxurious wavy locks. It seemed to happen in slow motion, like a model in a cologne ad.

Emily blinked a few times.

He climbed off his ATV and landed knee-deep in the

mucky water. He lifted up one foot, then the other, shaking them off.

Should she say something?

Her heart pounded.

Without acknowledging her presence, he took a few steps back and scanned the ATV from nose to tail. Then he grabbed the handlebars, leaned into the machine, and pushed with all his might. The ATV maybe moved an inch. He pushed again, this time with a grunt and then a strangled cry of frustration.

"Dammit!" He kicked one of the submerged tires causing a splash of muddy water.

Emily's eyebrows shot up. She'd never seen him angry before.

Back at the safety briefing, she'd envisioned this sort of situation happening to her and how horrible it would be, how embarrassing. "That sucks." The words popped out of her mouth before she could stop herself. As if she had zero control, even more flowed out, "Do you need some help?"

"I don't think it's going to move." He covered his mouth with his hand. Then, he let out a huge sigh. "Could you give me a lift?" Before she could respond, he held up a hand. "Just until we find a guide on the trail who can maybe tow this thing out of here."

Emily nodded. Could she really say no? That would be super mean. Besides, if the same thing had happened to her, she was quite positive Max would've provided assistance. In fact, she couldn't imagine him *not* doing that.

Huh.

Her mind flitted through all of the encounters she'd had with Max since she'd stepped foot on the ship. All the gentlemanly moves. No matter how ridiculous the situation, he'd made her feel safe and respected. Even last night in bed.

She'd never given a man permission so many times during sex.

He cleared his throat. "Well?"

"Yes, of course. No problem." She rubbed at her cheek with the back of her forearm, which only smeared more mud across her face. Great. Perfect time to share an ATV with a man—when she looked as if an alligator had drug her through the swamp several times.

"Thanks." Max trudged through the water with helmet in hand. "I'd suggest you ride around the edge."

"Right." As he drew nearer, her whole body froze. Her spine turned as rigid as a Catholic in line for the Confessional after a wild weekend.

His hand gripped her shoulder, and he threw a leg over the back of the ATV.

All the feelings she'd had last night came rushing back in a flood.

"What happened to you, anyway?" His breath tickled the back of her neck.

She let out a measured sigh. Why did he have to be so gorgeous? "Nothing. Let's get going. Don't want to hold you up." When his arm snaked around her middle, she pressed on the gas a little too quickly and shot out into the puddle.

"Whoa, better veer off to the right," Max gestured with his free hand, "Or we're both stuck here together."

Right. Together. In the jungle. Alone.

No, she could not handle that.

Emily pointed the ATV away from the murky middle and skirted around the outside of the massive puddle. Branches caught at her face, but she didn't care. She had to find a guide ASAP. This would not do at all.

When they hit a large dip in the trail, Max's other arm

curled around her. His hard chest pressed up against her back, and his grip around her middle seemed more intimate than necessary for a tagalong on the back of an ATV.

All kinds of things fluttered inside her stomach: butterflies, bumblebees, maybe even hummingbirds.

She closed her eyes briefly. She wanted this. She wanted him. She wanted all of the awkwardness and the stupid things she said and did last night to go away. She wanted the words he'd said—*I think I love you*'—to be real, to be genuine.

"Why did you lie to me, Emily?"

His question gutted her. What *hadn't* she lied about?

"Lie?" she asked, slowing down for a curve in the trail. The beauty of the jungle had become a blur. Her whole being focused on Max's body touching hers and how much she wanted his hands to stray from their solid position on either side of her hips and work their way upward to her breasts.

"About the reason for you and Ruby to be on the cruise." He leaned away from her a fraction and his voice grew fainter. "I saw the banner like everyone else. What's going on?"

The whine of the engine made it difficult for her to hear him. "I'm sorry." She let up on the gas. The ATV came to a slow stop.

"What are you doing?" Max's grip relaxed.

Emily took off her helmet and hung it on the handlebars. She probably looked like the muddy Bride of Frankenstein, but did it matter? He deserved the truth—the entire truth—from her. Her reasons for hiding it from him were no longer valid. "I want you to be able to hear me, and I don't want to make up any more stories. After last night—" If only she could go back and do things differently. "I want to be honest with you."

Maybe he'd hate her once he heard everything, but the guilt she'd been dragging around would finally disappear.

"Okay." Max's voice dropped a few notes. That low grumbly sexy thing he'd done last night. Was he even aware he did that? "Go for it."

As they sat back to front on an ATV in the middle of a Mexican jungle, Emily poured her heart out. "Ruby and I came on this cruise together because I was the maid-of-honor in her wedding. And, well, that wedding didn't happen. Her fiancé left her at the altar. So I suggested we take the honeymoon cruise they'd already paid for to turn it into something positive." The heavy weight that squished her heart a week ago returned. How awful it had been to see the look in Ruby's eyes when she realized Tyler wasn't coming. "I mean, a tropical cruise? With drinks and music and adventures? I thought it would take her mind off her horrible, awful fiancé who'd turned what should've been the most wonderful day of her life into one of the worst. We didn't mean to lie to anyone. Not really. But when we were standing in line to board, Ruby made me swear not to tell anyone what happened. She's my best friend. What could I do? I wanted her to be fixed. I wanted her to be happy again. I'd do almost anything to make that happen."

"Even pretend you were newlyweds."

Did Max chuckle? Was he maybe *not* mad at her deception and lies?

"Yes, even that." Emily smiled to herself. "But that day on the pool deck, I drank too much and blurted out the truth—so the story spread around the ship and turned into something worse than it actually was. I was so worried you'd figure it out, so I kept on with the lies when I should've told you everything. Then the photos happened and all of that."

"Right."

Max climbed off the ATV and loosened the chinstrap on his helmet.

"Hey, wait, no," Emily said following after him.

"I shouldn't have agreed to that—the picture of Ruby." He stuffed his hands into his pockets. "You have no idea how embarrassed and stupid I feel after you found those photos."

"I shouldn't have snooped."

"I shouldn't have kept them." He lowered his gaze, and his face grew splotchy. "But I couldn't help myself. I knew right then I was falling for you. I couldn't get you out of my mind." He pulled off his helmet and kicked some loose gravel near the edge of the trail.

"Oh." She bit her lip. Should she confess? Should she tell him how she'd noticed him that very first day at the pier before they boarded? How she'd fantasized about him? "I'm sorry I said the sex was nice."

He froze.

"It was so much more than nice." She stepped toward him. "It was, well, probably the hottest sex I've ever had in my whole life."

She'd never been so vulnerable. So exposed. Her usual reaction to anything embarrassing would be deflection—humorous deflection. But not this time. It might be her only chance with Max, so she had to try. Even if it ended in failure. He was worth it.

"Oh, Emily." His green eyes lit up, and he reached out to caress her jaw. "I want that to be every day for you. Every single day." He drew her toward him, and his head bent down to hers. "If you want me to," he whispered mere centimeters above her lips.

Could this really be happening? Could she, a mud-covered, sweaty mess in the middle of nowhere, be talking with Mr. Gorgeous about a relationship? Like more than a cruise fling? Something with permanency and a future and all of that?

He kissed away every thought in her head and even the mosquitoes that buzzed around her disappeared.

Emily was in love.

* * *

The rumble of an ATV interrupted their kiss.

Emily didn't know where things would go from here with Max, but she didn't care. All she cared about now was that someone had interrupted them and how much she wished that person would turn around and go back where he came from.

Max was the first to break away. He squeezed her waist and stared into her eyes for a few moments. Emily never realized how much emotion could be exchanged with a mere look. Warmth radiated through her body.

He smiled crookedly and turned to assess the approaching ATV. The driver wore a shirt that read 'GUIDE' in bright yellow lettering. Guess the tour company hadn't planned on abandoning them on the trail. She hadn't needed to give Max a ride after all.

Would she have done it anyway had she known?

She touched her lips still wet from their kiss.

One-hundred percent yes.

The guide braked and flipped up his visor. It was Miguel/Mateo/Marco. "I saw the stuck ATV back there."

Max's face reddened.

"Yours?" The guide looked to Emily.

"Yes," Emily said. Why not take the blame? Did she care? Not really. In fact, she was surprised it hadn't been her stuck in the mud.

Giving a nod, he dug a radio out of his backpack. "You two okay?" He pointed at each of them in turn.

Emily joined Max near the middle of the trail and slid her hand into his. "We are totally, absolutely okay."

Max gazed at her. Another look passed between them. Last night hadn't been a fling. It hadn't been some one night stand. They both knew it. Something deeper had happened in his cabin last night, and they both seemed to wordlessly agree it was worth exploring.

"Yes," Max rumbled in that low, sexy voice she loved.

It took everything inside her not to push him into the jungle, strip him naked, and try a few things they hadn't had time for last night. She would never tire of touching his body, especially the rippling abs she knew existed under his shirt. Maybe she could try kissing each muscle.

Hmmmm.

The guide held a walkie-talkie to his mouth and spoke in rapid Spanish.

While he arranged a pick up for the stuck ATV, Max returned to their earlier conversation. "I don't need to stay in Florida, you know."

Was he suggesting what she thought he was suggesting? "You mean you'd move to Roanoke?"

Gulp.

Was she ready for that? A man she'd only met a few days ago? What if it all went wrong? And there were so many ways it could go wrong. He could decide her family was annoying—especially her brother—because he *was* annoying. Then there was the fact she had a business to build. Would she have time for a relationship with client consults, all the food prep, and the picnic theme shopping? Or maybe he would tire of her. Maybe he'd find someone he liked better. Candace Beckley across the street from her parent's place would definitely throw her hat in the ring, as she was always going after any hot guy she ran into. She'd been that way since high school. No way was Emily going to let that woman get anywhere near her Max.

Her Max.

She'd said it.

He was hers.

"I couldn't imagine docking in Tampa and watching you walk away." He drew her hand to his chest. "I only just found you. I'm not letting you out of my sight."

The steady rhythm of his heartbeat calmed her fears.

"My parents have a guest room in the basement," she blurted out. As if her parents would be okay with Emily's hunky boyfriend living in the same house.

"Wow. Uh, okay." He gazed into the jungle and rubbed at an eyebrow. "Thanks for the offer."

"That was too much, wasn't it?"

He let out a huge breath. "I don't want to be ungrateful—"

"Sometimes I can blurt out dumb things. I mean, why would you want to live in their basement?" Quick, high pitched laughter tumbled out of her mouth. "You don't even know them. You barely know me." She sounded like a lunatic. Had this relationship ended before it had ever begun?

Max placed his hands on her shoulders and gently turned her toward him. "I know you, Emily. You are kind and genuine and loyal to your friends."

"And I have a mouth that never shuts up." She scanned his face.

He smiled. "That means I know everything you're thinking."

"Not everything." Her face heated. If he only knew the things she'd been thinking about him and his body in particular since the first day she saw him.

He tipped her chin up with his finger. "I know everything." His green eyes lit up with an inner fire.

Miguel/Mateo/Marco interrupted them, "Do you want me to escort you to the beach rendezvous point?"

The lovebirds stared into each other's eyes and said simultaneously, "No!"

* * *

Not missing her chance to touch Max's body, Emily chose to ride behind him on her unstuck ATV all the way to the end of the trail. They arrived at a secluded beach sprinkled with some lounge chairs and a few vendors hawking snacks and drinks. Standing in the surf, she'd been able to rinse off most of the mud, even though Max hadn't seemed to mind her body being covered in brown gunk. The rest would have to wait until she could take a shower back on board the ship.

With the air cleared between them, she could somehow turn off her mind (how was that possible?) and focus purely on the pleasure of being close to him. The hardness of his body, the smell of his sweat mixed with sunscreen, the exhilaration of knowing he truly did like her—no, love her—even with all her weird quirks and soft body parts.

When she'd thought up the idea of embarking on Ruby and Tyler's honeymoon cruise, she had no idea by the end of it all she would have found the man of her dreams. And she'd never thought Ruby would ever want to talk to Tyler again.

"Worried about Ruby?" Max handed her a lemonade after returning from one of the food stands.

She accepted the cup and took a sip of the refreshing drink. "How did you know?" He had been right: he knew what she was thinking.

He shrugged, sat in a beach chair next to her, and stared out at the ocean. "For you, this whole cruise has been about taking care of your best friend, which is admirable. But you have to trust she'll do the right thing."

She bit her lip. "I don't want her to be hurt again."

"I know you don't."

"She's the sweetest, kindest person I know and didn't deserve to be treated that way. I wanted to follow her today so I could punch Tyler in the nose and give him a piece of my mind."

"I'm glad you didn't follow through on that."

"Oh?"

"Because then we wouldn't be here." He reached out and squeezed her hand.

He was right. The view was spectacular: blue ocean, vibrant jungle greenery, open sky with a few puffy white clouds. The whole trip she'd been so focused on Ruby, she'd barely paid attention to the gorgeous destinations and the entertainment on board the ship. If she hadn't taken the ATV adventure, would she and Max be together? Her stomach turned rock hard at the thought.

She leaned over to kiss him lightly on the lips. Everything about him was comfortable. Now that she'd gotten past her fears about his feelings for her and her insecurities about herself, the whole world seemed so much brighter and more beautiful.

"I want the same joy for Ruby." Her heart ached. It didn't seem fair. Why should she end up with such a wonderful man while her friend was left with nothing?

"I know you do, sweetness." He lightly stroked her forearm and his brows drew together, as if he were deep in thought.

"Unfortunately, I'm not a mind reader like you." Emily

shifted on her lounge chair so that she rested on one hip. "What are you thinking?"

His forehead relaxed, and he smiled. "Just an idea I have."

"What sort of idea?"

"It's not fully formed yet. But when it is, I'll let you know."

She wanted to push him for more but knew she shouldn't. Plus, she wanted to enjoy these last few minutes with Max in the sun on a beach in Mexico before they had to zip back to the tour bus on the ATV.

Even though she wanted to believe Max and his view that Ruby would do the right thing, Max didn't know Tyler. And Tyler could be a persuasive, charming man. How else did he win over Ruby who had dated men more attractive and more successful than he? Would Ruby fall for whatever excuse he'd come up with for standing her up at their wedding? Maybe he'd even demand to take the rest of the cruise with Ruby and force Emily to find her own way home. After all, the cruise had been purchased for the newlyweds, not for the bride and her best friend.

But Ruby wouldn't do that to her—would she?

"Whatever you're worried about now, let it go." Max's voice brought her back to the beach and his gorgeous face. "No matter what happens, I'll be there for you. We can face it together."

"Even if Ruby kicks me off the cruise ship, and Tyler dumps my suitcase on the dock?"

A low rumble of laughter escaped from Max. "That's what you're worrying about?"

"It's not funny." She crossed her arms. "It could happen."

He swept a curl off her forehead. "And if it did happen— which it won't because Ruby would never do that to you—I'd move you right into my cabin. No worries, okay?"

Emily imagined sharing a cabin with Max. They'd never leave it if she had any say. A flush of heat crept across her body.

"I wouldn't want to leave it either." He leaned in, curved a hand behind her head, and drew her closer to him for a sexy, slow kiss that took her breath away.

Wow. He really could read her mind.

Chapter 25
Meanie-Pants

As Max and Emily returned to the ship, they held hands. The ride back from the beach had been uneventful, except for the fact Emily had her hands all over Max's abs for the entire ride and wondered how much longer it would be until they could be alone—in his cabin, in her cabin, behind the bar, in an empty theater, in an elevator...anywhere would do.

Max must've been thinking similar thoughts as he lifted their joined hands to his mouth and kissed her knuckles. "Dinner tonight?"

"I'll need to take a shower first." Dried mud still coated some of her hair and face.

"Ooh, can I join?" His deep sexy voice almost undid her.

Did he realize how much the rumble affected her? From her head to her toes—goose bumps on her arms and sparkles in her eyes and those crazy hummingbirds inside her.

The vision of a naked Max under a shower head was almost more than she could stand.

But then she was reminded of the postage stamp size of the cabin showers. "I don't think the shower was built for two."

"Let's find out." He waggled his eyebrows.

She laughed and thought seriously about calculating the square footage of the shower and the average size of a human body multiplied by two. Or was it multiplied by pi? She wished she'd paid more attention in her high school algebra class. Why didn't they give students real world problems? If Janie wanted to have sex with Johnny in the shower, how many square feet would they need?

Yes, that would've been helpful math knowledge.

As they approached the gangway, they both pulled out their room cards, which served as their entry passes onto the ship. Max scanned his first. Emily followed.

"There you are, Maxie-poo," a familiar voice said.

Beyond the scanning machine, Sylvia stood with a frown.

Maxie-poo? What sort of ridiculous nickname was that for hot, gorgeous, manly Max? And who would dare call him that?

Emily's irritation rose to level twelve out of twelve possible levels.

"Sylvia," Max said in a voice that sounded like a cross between annoyance and worry.

Emily crept up behind him and touched a hand to his lower back to let him know she was there to support him against meanie-pants Sylvia, who could be customer service perfection one minute and nasty ice queen the next.

"I thought we were going to meet this morning, but I couldn't find you at the breakfast buffet." The cruise director's thin arms were akimbo.

"I didn't think it would be a problem if I postponed until after the excursion."

"You are here to work." She glanced at Emily. "Not to philander with the guests."

Emily sensed a tremor in his body beneath her hand.

"I have a contract," Max said. "I'm not one of your employees. You know that. I know that. I exchanged my photography services for a free vacation. That's exactly how it was sold to me."

"Is that what your friend told you?" Sylvia replied with an ugly twist to her mouth. "The professional photographer who bailed on us at the last minute and left us with an amateur?"

Whoa, whoa, whoa.

Being a meanie was one thing, but insulting Max and his talents? That was a bridge too far.

Emily stepped out in front of her newly minted boyfriend to give the tall, slim woman a piece of her mind.

"Emily," Max soothed. "It's all right."

"Ah, you're going to let your cruise floozy defend you?"

Emily gasped. Max narrowed his eyes.

Sylvia raised a brow. "When am I going to be able to tell the MacPherson sisters you have the model release form secured, and we can move forward with the advertising campaign?"

"There aren't any photos," he said.

"What?"

"I deleted them." Max caught Emily's eye, and he smiled a quick smile.

"Why would you do that?" Her gaze jumped from Max to Emily and back to Max. "Wait, are you trying to ruin my career?" Sylvia clutched at her throat. "I asked you to take those photos. They are the property of the cruise line. We'll sue your ass. When you land in Tampa you're going to be in some serious hot water."

As the argument grew heated, Emily noticed the line of cruisers grew behind them. The three of them were blocking most of the space between the card scanner and the hallway.

The usual cool, calm, and friendly cruise director had morphed into a completely different person before everyone's eyes. Sylvia's face contorted into an ugly mask, and her gestures grew wild and threatening.

Then, it was as if a switch turned on. Sylvia looked around at the audience that had gathered, dropped her hands, smiled broadly, and said in a surprisingly sweet tone, "Welcome back, folks. Hope you had a wonderful day in Cozumel. Tonight's entertainment includes a juggling spectacular in the main theater at eight and a karaoke contest on the pool deck with Mario at nine."

Sylvia stepped back against the bulkhead to allow passengers to board.

What a psycho! How dare she threaten Max. Talented, kind, gorgeous Max. Her boyfriend.

Emily squeezed his hand in reassurance—one, to reassure Max she had his back no matter what nasty two-faced Sylvia dished out and, two, to reassure herself Max was real and not a figment of her imagination after a day of too much sun.

"If I don't have the photo and the signed form in my hands by midnight tonight, we'll be dropping you in Grand Cayman, and you can find your own way home." Sylvia turned on her heel and disappeared.

* * *

"Wow, what's wrong with her?" Ruby asked as Sylvia stomped toward the stairs.

Emily turned her head. "Hey, I was wondering if I'd see

you before dinner." She gave her bestie a warm embrace. At least one bit of good news: Ruby had returned to the ship rather than run off with Tyler. She was dying to ask what happened between Ruby and her ex, but didn't want to be pushy.

"Looks like you had a good day." Ruby touched a lock of Emily's hair still encased in jungle mud.

"We did," Max said. Then he wrapped an arm around Emily's waist.

As she took in the move, Ruby's eyes lit up. "Oh, wow."

Emily's face heated.

Would her best friend be mad at her for breaking her promise to focus on Ruby and her mental wellbeing after the wedding disaster?

"Max and I—" Why was it so hard to force the words out? "Me and Max. He and I, well, we kind of, sort of—" Was she about to faint? Was light-headedness a symptom of best friend betrayal?

"I'm in love with Emily." Max's grip on her side relaxed. "And I think she feels the same."

A gush of warmth filled her body at the words. Even though he'd said it before, it still surprised her like a participant on *Love is Blind* when she sees her fiancé for the first time.

He loved her.

Sexy, gorgeous, smart, funny, amazing Max.

Her heart stopped or maybe skipped a few beats, she wasn't sure which.

Ruby stared at her.

"I love Max." To say the words filled her with giddiness. Bubbly, silly, crazy giddiness. She loved Maxwell *Some Middle Name* Keeling. She'd have to ask him what his middle name was. How could she not know it? When would she meet his parents? What would they think of her? Oh, did he have any siblings? Maybe he had a hot brother Ruby would be interested in. Wait, what about today? What about Tyler?

"Earth to Emily." Ruby waved her hand in front of Emily's eyes.

"She gets like that sometimes," Max said.

"I know, right?" Ruby laughed. "Always thinking too much."

"Totally."

Emily snapped back and ignored their comments. "Hey, what happened with Tyler today?"

Ruby's laughter subsided, and spots of color entered her cheeks. "That jerk? Thank God I didn't marry him."

The parade of cruisers grew thicker as the deadline approached to board the ship before it set sail.

"Maybe we should go get a drink?" Max suggested as they were surrounded by sunburned, tired newlyweds of all shapes and sizes.

Ruby linked arms with Emily. "That sounds perfect."

At a table in the corner of the Sunset Lounge, the threesome downed strawberry daiquiris. Ruby mostly stirred hers as she recounted her meeting with Tyler.

"You were so right, Em, I should've gone ATV riding with you. It wasn't worth the pesos for the taxi ride to see Tyler."

"Did he at least apologize to you?"

She shook her head. "I think he thought I'd be crying, upset, and begging him to come back to me."

"Ruby Evers beg?" Emily couldn't even imagine it. "I don't think so."

"I know, right? I'm no doormat. He ruined our wedding.

He embarrassed me. So I called him out on it. Right there in front of the mariachi band and the lady selling straw handbags. I said no decent man would leave his fiancée at the altar and call her on the phone to tell her it was off. He would've showed up in person and begged for mercy. Would've faced up to my dad who shelled out an arm and a leg for everything. The venue, the food, the flowers—the cruise. Like, what kind of jerk slinks away and leaves the bride to deal with all that crap alone?"

Max grimaced.

Emily boiled inside and wished she could've been next to her friend and slugged Tyler like she had thought about in the jungle.

"Then he told me he wasn't really sure if he wanted to be married in the first place and proposed so I'd get off his back about it."

Emily rapidly blinked. "Didn't he think at some point there'd be a wedding? Were you supposed to be engaged forever?"

"I know, right?" Ruby let out a snort. "I guess when I set a date, it really freaked him out."

"He should've told you right then he wasn't serious."

"That's when he did his little puppy dog face—the face that could get me to agree to almost anything."

Emily nodded. She knew that face.

"You know what, Em? It didn't work anymore. It was as if I'd been freed from a magic spell." She snapped her fingers. "Like that, it was over. Feelings gone. That's when I unloaded on him and laughed in his face about getting back together."

A sense of peace came over Emily. Her guilt about hauling her devastated friend on a honeymoon cruise dissipated. "What did he say?"

"That's when he turned nasty," Ruby said. "Can you believe he had the gall to tell me he never could've married someone 'as old' as me? Old! He called me old!"

Emily took in her friend's beautiful, wrinkle-free face, her perfect pouty lips, her wide eyes and thick luxurious auburn hair. Like a fairytale princess. A million different guys would fall all over themselves to call Ruby their wife.

"What a dog."

Ruby nodded vigorously. "Then the handbag lady smacked him with one of her bags—the big one for the beach—and said something in Spanish that made the trumpet player blush."

"Bravo, Rubes! Bravo, handbag lady!" Emily clapped. "I hope Tyler had to pay through the nose for his plane ticket and that ridiculous message. Did he really think it would be that easy to make it up to you?"

A familiar duo approached their table—Diana and Donna, the Weird Twins. For once they were dressed in different outfits. One wore a freshly pressed linen pantsuit in bright white, the other had donned a slinky gold lamé evening dress.

"Could we speak with you, Max?" one of the twins asked. "We've heard some disturbing news about Sylvia."

Ruby picked up her drink and scooted closer to Emily on the padded bench seat that circled the corner table. "Why don't you join us?"

Emily's body tensed. Didn't Ruby think the Weird Twins were awful and intrusive? Maybe the adrenaline was still flowing after her encounter with Tyler. It was the only plausible explanation.

"Why thank you so much." Gold Twin slid in. White Twin joined her without a word. "She's that model!"

"Yes, that's right." Ruby smiled and then held up a hand.

"Before you chat about Sylvia, though, I wanted to let both of you know I decided to sign the model release form."

Both twins' mouths gaped open.

In Emily's mind a nuclear bomb went off burning away any thoughts she had in one mega blast. Was her best friend crazy? There weren't any photos. There was nothing to sign a release for. Maybe the Tyler confrontation had made her blow a fuse.

She poked at the ex-bride's leg with one finger and whispered, "Ix-nay on the otos-phay."

Ruby shoved her hand away. "What?" she hissed.

Max leaned in, "It's pig Latin."

Ruby made a face and then turned to the two older women with a smile plastered on. "Excuse my friend. She's had a little too much sun today."

"We were actually going to let Max know we'd changed our minds." The Gold Twin smiled at Max across the table. "Sylvia —well, we heard she lost it on some customers during the embarkation process. Very unprofessional behavior. We aren't interested in any deals that woman wanted to make. A real liability for our firm. She's been referred to HR for some counseling. Not MacPherson Cruise material."

The White Twin's eyebrows gathered in. "But the deal wasn't with that Sylvia woman, it was with Max and this lovely lady here." She reached out a hand for Ruby. "You're just what our cruise line needs, dear. Fresh, young, vibrant."

"Beautiful," Emily said.

Max rested his elbows on the table, and his hands formed into a steeple. "I didn't want to say anything until I had a chance to talk to Ruby about it." He'd drained his daiquiri, so maybe he was feeling more confident than usual.

"Max?" Emily gazed up at him. What had he been planning? When had he been planning it? Since he deleted the photos? A twinge of guilt burned inside her at what she'd made him do.

"What's your idea?" Ruby asked.

"A new photo shoot. One you consent to ahead of time." Under the table Max's knee bounced. "Similar to the shot on the pool deck, but maybe with some staging, some lighting. Better than the photos I deleted."

"You deleted the photos?" the twins declared simultaneously.

The Gold Twin blanched and then waved over a server. "Your best whiskey. Neat."

"Make that two." The White Twin was as pale as her jumpsuit. "He deleted the photos," she mumbled to herself.

"I'll do it. The photo shoot." Ruby beamed as if angels from heaven radiated supernatural light from above. "But only if Max is my photographer."

Emily's insides warmed at her friend's kindness.

Max smacked the table. "Hell yes." He faced the twins. "I will guarantee you these photos will be better than the originals. Ruby Evers is about to be the face of MacPherson Cruises." Max stared into the distance and spread out his hands. "I can see it now: Ruby on the pool deck, Ruby in the casino, Ruby in the dining room, Ruby in a parka looking out at the fjords of Norway."

"We don't sail to Norway," the White Twin said.

"Well, Alaska then." Max grinned.

"Does Alaska have fjords?" Emily asked.

"They've got glaciers," Ruby said.

"Yes, glaciers," Max said brightly. "We'll put Ruby on a glacier."

"What does a glacier have to do with cruising?" Ruby whispered to Emily.

Emily shrugged.

The server delivered the whiskey.

Both twins sipped the liquor, looked at each other, gave slight nods, and said together, "You have a deal."

They clinked glasses and then offered the same to the table. Max picked up his empty daiquiri glass, and Ruby and Emily lifted their half-full glasses.

"To Ruby Evers—the new face of MacPherson Cruises." Max's green eyes sparkled.

* * *

Five days later....

Someone knocked on Max's cabin door.

"Hel-lo? Are you in there?"

Ruby's chipper voice at—Emily looked at her phone—six in the morning attacked her ears. She groaned and elbowed the sleeping form next to her. "Bae, it's Ruby."

The hunky photographer rolled over. "What? What time is it?"

Ruby knocked again. This time a lot more loudly.

"Six."

Max covered his head with a pillow.

Emily sat up in bed as if she'd been stung in the back by a jellyfish. Or was it a lionfish she'd stepped on in Grand Cayman? She couldn't remember. But the lingering pain in her little toe reminded her that the ocean held many dangers even when on a tropical vacation with your gorgeous new boyfriend.

"We have to wake up." Emily gently prodded Max.

"Remember our departing group leaves at nine. I want one last shot at the buffet."

"We're up!" he shouted in a muffled voice from under the pillow. "We'll meet you upstairs. Save us a table."

"Check!" Ruby said in a slightly less megaphone-like voice. "Don't forget, luggage out in the hall by seven."

"Okay." Emily grabbed a bathrobe from the floor and put it on. The math actually did work and two people *could* fit into the tiny cabin shower. She flushed at the memory. Thigh to thigh. Boobs to chest. Hot water flowing. And lots of soap involved. That would be one for the data banks.

"Where are you going?" Max tugged at one of the robe's loose ties.

She snatched it out of his hand. "I have to take a shower."

"We took one last night."

He could be such a tease. "A real shower."

"That was a real shower," he said in his masculine rumbly voice.

Damn him and his raw sex appeal. Did he even know how irresistible he was?

Emily pulled a knee up on the mattress to face him. "I don't know how I'm going to get any work done back home with you around all the time."

He lay on two propped up pillows, bare to his waist, which made it nearly impossible to avoid staring at his well-sculpted body. "What are you talking about? We saved time last night. All you have to do is get dressed, and you can meet Ruby for breakfast."

"*We* can meet Ruby for breakfast." She placed a hand on his muscular shoulder and resisted the urge to caress the firm deltoid. "Unlike you, I have to wash my hair and restyle it. Morning hair is not my best look."

He pulled her down to him. "It's your absolute best look." With a gentle hand, he combed his fingers through her messy beach waves.

Their lips met in a hard kiss.

Would she ever tire of him? No way. Her body wanted to stick to him like iron filings to a magnet. Maybe the ship's captain would have to pry them out of bed if they overstayed their cruise welcome. Would they even notice if two passengers stowed away for another voyage? Probably.

Emily groaned and rolled away. "I wish I could stay here in bed with you all day, but we have to disembark and go back to our regular lives." She knotted the robe tightly around her middle. "I hate regular life."

"I should be able to move to Roanoke in about a month. My name was never on the apartment lease, so—"

Penelope. He didn't want to say it, but she knew that was who paid the rent on the condo they'd shared in Miami. Her stomach churned. "I'm going to hop in the shower. Give me five."

As she stood under the hot water spray, her mind drifted to negative places. Penelope had been his muse, his model. How could she compete with that? No matter how much she wanted to set aside her worries about Max comparing her to a rich, pretty, Ruby-like ex, she couldn't stop the negative thoughts about herself.

She had to overcome this weakness or she might ruin everything. Who would want to date someone as insecure as she?

Eventually, it would grow old.

And did she want to be the girlfriend who needed constant reassurances and praise?

No. She did not.

Emily shut off the water. Max had done nothing but gush

over her curves. Never once had he said anything derogatory, or even given her a look that indicated he was anything but smitten. Time to get over herself.

After toweling her body dry and squeezing as much water out of her hair as she could, she opened the bathroom door, took a deep breath, and strutted fully naked into the bedroom.

Max, who had been packing a few final things into his suitcase, stared. His lips parted, and he clenched his hands briefly. "Um, wow. Are you trying to tempt me?"

His gaze scanned her whole figure from top to bottom.

Emily's body flooded with warmth. The pure desire she saw on his face made a shiver run down her back.

As he stepped forward to lock her in an embrace, she knew deep inside no other woman had a hold on him. He kissed down her neck, and Emily vowed she'd never belittle herself again. Not even for a laugh.

He loved her inside and out.

"Max," she whispered in his ear as he worked his way across her collarbone.

"Yes, Sweetness?" he answered in that dark, sexy voice that made her heart flutter.

"I love you."

"I know."

Epilogue

Six months later...

Max stepped behind his camera set up on a tripod in the Smalls' family kitchen and focused his lens on the plate of freshly fried chicken and the accompanying sides of marinated veggie salad, cornbread muffins, and Mrs. Small's famous potato salad.

"Can we hurry this up?" Emily asked. Did he not realize she had three more picnic combos to plate? "The garnish is wilting on the baby back ribs, and I still don't know if I got the look right on the macaroni and cheese. More shredded cheddar?" She held a block of cheese and a grater over the cooling side dish waiting on the granite countertop.

"I want your website to look as professional as possible." He adjusted a chicken thigh by two millimeters, then took another photo. "I know I told you I hadn't done food shots before, but there's this guy on TikTok who gives you the behind the scenes on how they do it for the restaurant chains. Just give me a chance to try a few things and see what turns out best."

Emily smiled weakly. "Okay, Bae." After cooking for most

of the day, the counters were littered with dirty measuring spoons, mixing bowls, frying pans, and even a dozen corn cob holders she thought would look cute until Max said no.

It was really, really nice he wanted to do this for her, and she knew the pictures would all come out fantastic. If she'd learned anything about Max in the last five months since he'd moved to Roanoke, it was that he was a bit of a perfectionist when it came to his photography.

Time to take a breath.

No need to stress.

Everything would be okay.

Emily breathed in through her nose and out through her mouth. She learned that in the yoga class they took the last day-at-sea on the cruise. Ruby had more money to spend from her wedding reception bust, so they'd splurged on a Private Hot Yoga Session with Andre. Max had wanted to join for some reason and ended up giving the instructor the side eye the whole time without really performing any of the yoga moves accurately.

But was the breathing really doing anything to bring down her stress levels? She had two picnics scheduled on Saturday—one client wanted a Low Country Boil, the other a bunch of fancy little sandwiches and cakes as part of her Two for Tea Picnic Package. After all the photos were done, she still had to clean up, shop for her clients, and check out that one-bedroom apartment on the other side of town.

"Okay, I think I got it." Max looked up from his camera. Those green eyes shocked her every time she saw them. So damned sexy. What did it matter if she had to painstakingly follow his instructions for arranging the food just so? Afterwards, they could sneak down to the basement and maybe test out the recliner chair in the corner. How far back did it tilt?

Max cleared his throat. "Earth to Emily."

Heat crept into her cheeks.

"What were you thinking, bad girl?" Maxwell the Serious Professional Photographer disappeared and Max the Super-Hot Boyfriend took his place. "Whatever it is, don't stop thinking it." He swooped in for a kiss.

Emily never tired of those full delicious lips kissing hers. This time he tasted like the lemon bars he'd photographed earlier that day.

Max grabbed an ass cheek.

Emily crawled her hands up under his form-fitting henley.

"Hey, FedEx just delivered something for you." Hunter, Emily's super annoying older brother, sailed into the kitchen and dumped a package next to her. "Oh, you two weren't busy or something, were you?" He grinned, pointed at them both, and backed away.

The kissing couple broke apart.

She picked up the slim envelope and whacked her brother on the head.

"Hey, those are my proofs from the MacPhersons!" Max snatched it out of her hands. "Ruby would kill you if you damaged these. The ads are going live nationwide in a month. I have to make sure they're perfect."

"They will be." Emily narrowed her eyes at her dumb-dumb brother. He was thirty-one and acted as if he were twelve. "Don't you have something better to do than hang around mom and dad's house on a Wednesday afternoon?" She stroked her chin. "Oh, wait a minute, that's right, you don't have a job."

"I'm between careers," he corrected. "At least my girlfriend isn't living in our parent's basement."

Max shot Hunter a scathing look. "Temporarily. We've got that apartment showing...tomorrow, Sweetness?"

She was glad Max finally figured out how annoying Hunter could be. He'd thought she'd been exaggerating until he experienced the full-on douche-baggery himself.

"Wait. Back up." Emily held up a hand. "What girlfriend?" she scoffed.

"Jayde." Hunter stared hard at both of them. "Remember: Jayde?"

Emily looked at Max. "Do you know a Jayde, Bae?"

Max shrugged. "Never heard of her."

She cocked her head. "Is she real, Hunter? Or is this another one of your online 'girlfriends'?"

Hunter frowned. "She's real."

"Then why don't I remember meeting her?"

"Well—"

"Yeah, that's what I thought." She turned her back on her perjuring brother. He wasn't worth her time. "Open the package. Let's see the ad copy. I'll bet it turned out amazing. You were lucky they had record snow up at Snowshoe in February. Perfect setting to help relaunch their Alaskan cruises."

Max looked through the proofs. "Still wish we could've flown to Norway for that."

"The fjords?"

"Yeah."

"Maybe next time, Bae."

They both paused to look at the best photo of the bunch: Ruby in full arctic gear on a pair of skis wearing reflective sunglasses with her auburn hair glinting in the sun with the tagline: *MacPherson? MacFearless. Our Alaskan cruises aren't for the faint of heart.*

"Hey, I'll prove to you she's real." Hunter scrolled frantically through his phone. "Her brother's getting married, see?"

"Uh-huh." Hunter managed to increase his annoy-a-sister score to an eight out of ten.

"No, he is. Really." He scrolled some more.

When did Hunter care so much about her opinion? He seemed overly distraught about proving this Jayde person existed.

Her brother gave a shaky laugh. "Here." He held up his phone and a wedding website appeared. "Jayden Thomas and Iris Bickler. Wedding. Next month."

Emily took the phone and stared at the page. "Jayde and Jayden? You're kidding right? Their parents named them Jayde and Jayden." She slid her gaze to Max and suppressed a grin.

"How does this prove you're dating her?" Max asked the obvious.

Hunter tucked his polo shirt into his jeans. "Okay, well, she invited me to be her date for the wedding." He snatched the phone back, and his finger brushed up on the screen in a violent fashion.

"Since when were you going to a wedding?" She pursed her lips. "Mom would've been all over that—making sure you had the right thing to wear, wanting to know what the colors were for the wedding, asking about this Jayde person. She hasn't said a thing."

Hunter, who never got embarrassed even when he should be, turned bright red. "Well, that's because—"

"Because what?" Emily jacked up a brow.

"Because I wasn't going to go," he said quietly.

She burst out laughing. "So this Jayde person isn't your girlfriend then." She turned back to the plate of ribs and swapped out the wilting parsley for a fresh sprig.

"She is."

"Prove it." Emily crossed her arms, parsley crushed. "Call her up, right now, and tell her you'll happily be her date for the wedding."

Hunter stared at his phone.

"And put it on speaker," Max added.

"Yeah, we want to hear the whole conversation."

"Fine." Her brother pressed his phone to his broad chest. He was six-foot-three and beefy, as her grandma used to say. "But you guys have to promise to be quiet. Like, absolute silence."

Emily and Max exchanged glances. They nodded.

Man, she never realized how much fun it would be with Max around. Besides all the bedroom stuff, and the way he supported her business, he also had turned into her best friend.

Hunter set the phone on the counter. The kitchen filled with multiple rings. Her brother stared at the phone with a look so focused, she wondered if he was mentally willing Jayde to pick up.

"Hello?" a breathy voice on the other end answered.

"Jayde, babe, it's me. Hunter."

"Hunter?"

Max hid a laugh behind his hand.

"Hunter Small." A few drops of sweat appeared on her brother's brow. He scooped up the phone and whispered into it, "We met at Josh's place. I had the ranch dip, you had the potato chips?" He flashed a nervous smile at Max and Emily.

"Oh, right! Big Hunter."

His smile widened. "Right, Big Hunter. Just wanted to confirm that I'm happy to be your date for your brother's wedding."

"What?"

"At Josh's. You said you needed a date."

"Oh, I didn't need a date. But the maid-of-honor does. She's coming in from out-of-town. Maybe from Kentucky or Oklahoma? I can't remember. Anyway, the Best Man wants to sit with his wife, so you can see why she needs a date for the reception."

"Right. Uh-huh." Hunter picked up the phone, took it off speaker, and exited through the French doors onto the backyard patio. "I suppose I could do that. She's never been to Virginia? Uh-huh. Is she tall?" The door closed behind him.

Max and Emily burst out laughing.

"That was perfection." It was rare to catch her brother in a lie so huge. "I'm going to remember this day for the rest of my life." With a satisfied sigh, she finished garnishing the plate.

Max grabbed her by the hand. "Sweetness?"

"Yes?" The sudden seriousness in his voice made her knit her brows.

"Let's take the apartment."

"But we haven't even looked at it yet."

"Not the one-bedroom." He brushed aside a wisp of hair in her eyes. "The two-bedroom, on the north side of town."

"But that place was so expensive."

Max drew out a check from between the ad proofs. "We can afford it."

Her eyes widened at the number of figures on the check. She snatched it out of his hand. "When were you going to tell me about this?"

"I've been negotiating with the Twins for a few weeks now. They were so pleased with how these shots turned out, they want Ruby and me to do a whole other series for their European cruises."

"Amazing."

"No, Sweetness, you are amazing." He caught her by the hips. "You believed in me, in my ideas."

"They were all great ideas." She looked up at his incredibly handsome movie star face. Tingles ran up and down her arms. "Those Weird Twins would've been stupid to pass up on what you offered them."

"Oh, Emily," he rumbled in that low voice she loved. "You are the absolute best thing that ever happened in my life, you know that?"

And they made out in her parents' kitchen until the food grew cold and the tripod was knocked out of alignment.

THE END

Coming Soon
The Genesis Machine

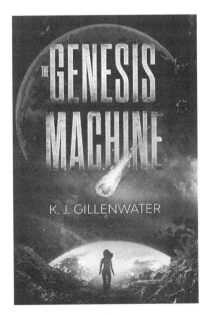

Coming to print in 2023!

An exhilarating sci fi thriller that will keep you guessing all the way to the end.

Coming Soon

Charlie Cutter is a military cryptologist who is recruited to NCIS-A, a secret division of the Navy that investigates alien activity on earth. Her first assignment: studying a strange pod that landed during a storm in North Dakota. As the newest team member, she learns on the fly as she races to figure out where the pod came from and why it landed on earth. The mystery deepens when it's revealed this isn't the first pod to arrive, and someone at NCIS-A may know more than anyone realized.

About the Author

K. J. Gillenwater has a B.A. in English and Spanish from Valparaiso University and an M.A. in Latin American Studies from University of California, Santa Barbara. She worked as a Russian linguist in the U.S. Navy, spending time at the National Security Agency doing secret things. After six years of service, she ended up as a technical writer in the software industry. She has lived all over the U.S. and currently resides in Wyoming with her family where she runs her own business writing government proposals and squeezes in fiction writing when she can. In the winter she likes to ski and snowshoe; in the summer she likes to garden with her husband and take walks with her dog.

Visit K.J.'s website to join her newsletter or for more information about her writing, her books, and what's coming next. www.kjgillenwater.com.

If you enjoyed this book, K. J. Gillenwater is the author of multiple books, which are available in print and in eBook format at multiple vendors.

- Illegal
- Aurora's Gold
- The Little Black Box
- Acapulco Nights
- Blood Moon

Short Stories & Short Story Collections:

- Skyfall
- Nemesis
- The Man in 14C
- Charlie and the Zombie Factory

Made in the USA
Columbia, SC
06 October 2022

68797214R00159